AN OASIS OF HORROR

BOOKS BY BRIAN STABLEFORD

FOR BORGO PRESS / WILDSIDE PRESS:

*Algebraic Fantasies and Realistic Romances: More Masters
    of Science Fiction*
Changelings and Other Metamorphic Tales
A Clash of Symbols: The Triumph of James Blish
The Cure for Love and Other Tales of the Biotech Revolution
The Devil's Party: A Brief History of Satanic Abuse
The Dragon Man: A Novel
Firefly: A Novel of the Far Future
The Gardens of Tantalus and Other Delusions
*Glorious Perversity: The Decline and Fall of Literary
    Decadence*
Gothic Grotesques: Essays on Fantastic Literature
The Haunted Bookshop and Other Apparitions
Heterocosms: Science Fiction in Context and Practice
In the Flesh and Other Tales of the Biotech Revolution
*Jaunting on the Scoriac Tempests and Other Essays on
    Fantastic Literature*
The Moment of Truth: A Novel
News of the Black Feast and Other Random Reviews
An Oasis of Horror: Decadent Tales and Contes Cruels
Opening Minds: Essays on Fantastic Literature
*Outside the Human Aquarium: Masters of Science Fiction,
    Second Edition*
*Slaves of the Death Spiders and Other Essays on Fantastic
    Literature*
The Sociology of Science Fiction
Space, Time, and Infinity: Essays on Fantastic Literature
The Tree of Life and Other Tales of the Biotech Revolution
Yesterday's Bestsellers: A Voyage Through Literary History

AN OASIS OF HORROR

DECADENT TALES & CONTES CRUELS

by

Brian Stableford

The Borgo Press
An Imprint of Wildside Press

MMVII

CONTENTS

INTRODUCTION

The sentiment expressed by the verse from Charles Baudelaire's "Le Voyage" that is used as a head-quote in the title-piece of this collection is translatable into English prose as: "A bitter knowledge it is that draws us to travel; today, yesterday and tomorrow, the monotonous and tiny world always makes us see our own reflection: an oasis of horror in a desert of deadly tedium." To some, this might seem a depressing thought, but it did not seem so to Baudelaire and it does not seem so to me.

Baudelaire thought of horror as a species of exhilaration, whose principal effect on the human imagination was one of refreshment; in so saying he echoed the conviction of Edmund Burke who argued in his *Philosophical Enquiry into the Origin of Our Ideas of the Sublime and Beautiful* (1757) —which extrapolates arguments from Mark Akenside's *The Pleasures of the Imagination* (1744) to the effect that the healthy imagination requires mental exercise just as the healthy body requires physical exercise—that our awareness and perception of the sublime are invariably seasoned with horror.

It was the poems that Baudelaire collected in *Les Fleurs du Mal* [Flowers of Evil]—of which "Le voyage" is one of the key items—that came to embody and exemplify the notion of literary Decadence. The third edition of the collection, during whose preparation Baudelaire died, was published with a preface by Théophile Gautier, who identified the essence of the work as its "Decadent style", which he defined in the following terms:

> Art arrived at that point of extreme maturity that determines civilizations which have grown old; ingenious, complicated, clever, full of delicate hints and refinements, gathering all the delicacies of speech, borrowing from technical vocabularies, taking color from every palette, tones from all musical instruments, contours vague and fleeting, listening to translate subtle confidences, confessions of depraved passions and the odd hallucinations of a fixed idea turning to madness.

Such a style is, according to Gautier, "summoned to express all and to venture to the very extremes". He claims that Baudelaire's work partakes of "language already veined with the greenness of decomposition"—which is, he asserts, entirely appropriate to a civilization "where an artificial life has replaced a natural one and developed in a man who does not know his own needs." Literary decadence is, in essence, calculatedly perverse in its assessments of beauty and morality, providing by its valiant opposition a necessary counterweight to vulgar and unthinking assumption.

Long after he was dead, Baudelaire inspired a Decadent Movement in France, which became definitive of *fin de siècle* sensibility. One of the historical and influential links between Baudelaire and the new Decadents was the Comte de Villiers de l'Isle Adam, who called the first of his own collections of Decadent prose *Contes cruels*, because they spurned conventional means of attaining literary closure by celebrating "the irony of fate"—the capacity that the course of events has for thwarting human ambition in a frankly mocking fashion.

Because it became so firmly linked to the notion of the *fin de siècle*, the Decadent Movement did not survive the end of the nineteenth century in France and Decadent literature became increasingly unfashionable thereafter—but it was, by definition, a literary species guaranteed to thrive on its own unfashionability. The stories collected here have been woefully unappreciated, even when they have succeeded in reaching print—as some have not until now—but I have

8

never been tempted to abandon the production of such items, and am far fonder of them than I am of many works that proved more economically viable. Throughout the early phases of my literary career, such as it has been, I remained acutely aware of the fact that Baudelaire and Oscar Wilde had died, miserable, wretched and almost universally despised, at the age of forty-six, and that poor Edgar Poe had not even got that far. Now that I am fifty-eight I feel that I am way ahead of the game, and I take what meager delight I can in the knowledge that I am highly likely to die beyond my means.

"An Oasis of Horror" was first published on the *Infinity Plus* website on 17 September 2006. "Justice" first appeared in *Far Point* 1 (November/December 1991). "The Copper Cauldron" is previously unpublished. "Nobody Else to Blame" first appeared in *Redsine* 7 (January 2002). "Heartbeat", "The Lamia's Soliloquy" and "The Riddle of the Sphinx" first appeared in *Horrors! 365 Scary Stories* (Barnes & Noble, 1998) edited by Stefan Dziemianowicz, Robert Weinberg & Martin H. Greenberg. "Upon the Gallows-Tree" first appeared in *Narrow Houses* (Little Brown, 1992) edited by Peter Crowther. "The Devil's Men" first appeared in *100 Wicked Little Witch Stories* (Barnes & Noble, 1995) edited by Robert Weinberg, Stefan Dziemianowicz & Martin H. Greenberg. "The Elixir of Youth" first appeared in French translation as "L'Élixir de jouvence" in *Asphodale* 4 (Août 2003); the English version appeared in Weird Tales 341 (August-September 2006). "And the Hunter Home from the Hill" was supposed to feature in an anthology called *Sailing on the Seas of Night* edited by John Pelan, whose publication was indefinitely postponed. "My Mother, the Hag" first appeared in *Chronicles of the Round Table* (Robinson, 1997) edited by Michel Ashley. "The Devil's Comedy" first appeared in *Phantoms of Venice* (Shadow, 2001) edited by David Sutton. "The Power of Prayer" first appeared in *Paradox* 1 (Spring 2003).

AN OASIS OF HORROR

Amer savoir, celui qu'on tire du voyage!
Le monde, monotone et petit, aujourd'hui,
Hier, demain, toujours, nous fait voir image:
Une oasis d'horreur dans un désert d'ennui!
                           —Charles Baudelaire, "Le Voyage"

1. *Spleen de Paris: 30 June 1845*

"Existence," said Charles Baudelaire to his father's ghost, "moves in the midst of a multifarious epidemic in which no one is ever quite content with the disease that has fallen to his lot. The metaphorical consumptive contemplates with peevish frustration those afflicted with St. Anthony's fire; the spiritual leper would prefer the particular ruination of lupus; those whose souls bear the scars of smallpox would rather entertain the demon of cholera...no, it won't do, will it? Too obvious. We're all sick—so what? To yearn to be sick in a different way is as good a definition of futile hope as any, but it can't explain...."

Waiting for a reply from his absent father, present only in feeble spirit, would also have been as good a definition of futile hope as any, but that wasn't why Charles trailed off. He had conceived a new beginning.

"It is unnecessary to envy the dead body its oblivion," he said, "for annihilation is within the grasp of any man, but to envy the dead soul its transcendence of life is another matter. The objective of one who is unhappy with life is not to cease to be, but rather to discover a realm in which being is not so direly bound by discomfiting circumstance—which is to say, a realm in which the pattern of discomfiting circum-

11

stance is not so stifling in its arid monotony. No—it pains me to admit it, but it may be true that there are points at which all communication fails, where silence is preferable to verbal expression because the act speaks for itself, more eloquently than any steel nib...."

Charles set down his pen. He had, in any case, already taken care of the formal necessities; he had written his will and placed it in an envelope, with a covering letter, addressed to his lawyer, Ancelle. He had bequeathed all his possessions to his savior, Jeanne Duval, and had asked the lawyer to watch over her and guide her, just as he would have watched over and guided him, in accordance with the order of guardianship for which his mother had applied to the Tribunal in the previous September. He had asked Ancelle to remember him to Jeanne as a hideous example—a dire warning of the extremes to which a disorderly life might go. That was enough; his dead father needed no suicide note to understand what Charles was doing and why, and nothing could be said that would enlighten Madame Aupick, let alone the general. His mother and stepfather had long grown used to their particular sicknesses, and did not understand the politics of resistance. When his mother had gone to the Tribunal to have Ancelle appointed as his legal guardian, it was in the genuine belief that she was acting in his best interests, in a spirit of valiant palliation.

Charles picked up the dagger in the same hand that had set down the pen, and placed the point to his left breast, feeling for a gap between the ribs.

He did not expect to discover what it felt like to die. He expected to feel a sudden shock of pain, in which his consciousness would sooner or later dissolve—sooner, if his hand were steady and the blade punctured his heart at the first stroke; later if he faltered, and was forced to move the blade from side to side, groping for fatality.

Jeanne had told him that he need have no fear of death, because she had favored him with a special kiss that would deliver him to vampire undeath, but he had not believed it when she said it and he did not believe it now. He did not expect to be clawing his way out of the tomb on the day after his burial. Jeanne Duval was certainly a lamia—a serpent in human form, a temptress asp—but Charles did not believe that her sting was more powerful than that of death.

He took a deep breath, and pressed the dagger home.

His hand was not steady, and he cursed his heart for being so unexpectedly hard to find. Then he found it, and he felt the point strike like a cobra's fang, opening the ventricle to let out the pulsing blood.

He waited to die. And waited. In the end, the pain faded away, but consciousness did not. He never lost his grip on consciousness for a instant, and never would again.

"Has heaven rejected me, then?" he asked his father, eventually. "Or is it simply that my blood is no longer my own, and will not flow to my bidding."

He checked his pulse, and could not find one. He breathed on a mirror, and it did not fog—although his reflection was still there, as dull and sickly as ever, wearing a rictus snarl. His heart had evidently stopped; his lungs no longer sucked in air; he had left life behind—but not for death. Jeanne had told him the truth.

Another man might have picked up his hat and rushed to see his sometime mistress, in order to begin his education in the politics and practices of undeath, but Charles did not. Jeanne was an actress, of sorts, but she was not a poet. She knew how to exist as she existed, but Charles did not think for a moment that she had the slightest idea what possibilities there were in undeath.

"Perhaps there have been undead poets before," he said, no longer to his father but more straightforwardly to himself, "and perhaps there are some still active, in the New World if not in the old—but that does not matter. They could no more teach me what I need to learn than Jeanne could. It is 1845, and wisdom is being rewritten with every day that passes. It is not the ancient alchemy of undeath that I need to discover but the new chemistry: the new atomism. It is not a mentor that I need but a method of investigation; I am the Lavoisier of vampirism, appointed by fate to discover its oxygen. I am the sick man who has finally found the disease that will fulfill me. I cannot ask, and do not want, to be happy, but I have found my sublimity, my astonishment, my horror. Henceforth, I am the poet of undeath—and could never have wished for any other fate, had I ever believed that this one might be achievable."

He did take up his hat, then. Before he closed the door behind him he looked around his room with new eyes, no longer seeing its shabbiness, its unworthiness, its vile mundanity. It was no longer a manger fit for beasts but a cradle fit for a messiah. He no longer had the slightest desire to leave it behind forever.

"I need to look at the world," He said, to his impatient writing-desk, "but I shall return—and in time, I shall know how to vent my spleen!"

2. *Les Métamorphoses du vampire: 1845-1848*

It was not that simple, nor that easy. He never missed the beating of his heart, or the necessity to draw breath, and learned to feign the latter easily enough. He would not have missed the necessity to eat and drink, either, had he been relieved of them, but he was not. The undead, he discovered, hungered and thirsted for more than blood. Indeed, the first of many inherited misconceptions he had to put aside was the notion that the undead were entirely dependent for their sustenance on human blood. Human blood tasted sweet, to be sure, but it was an indulgence—perhaps a fetish—rather than an appetite. To sustain himself, he learned by trial and error, his only absolute requirements were red meat and water—in which, he presumed, all the raw materials of blood were conserved.

What he did miss, however, was sleep. His sleep, as a living man, had long been so overfull of dreams as never to give him a moment's respite, but he had never grasped the significance of that fact until sleep was denied to him. He could feign sleep as easily as he could feign breathing, but he could not actually lose consciousness. He could dream, but he could no longer cage his dreams, carefully placing them beyond the bounds of conscious life. His dreams were free now, and would have to be tamed—if he did intend to tame them, and if it were possible to tame them—in a different manner.

That, he knew, would take time.

14

For a while, he considered the possibility of becoming an apostle of undeath, openly acknowledging his condition and advertising its merits. From time to time he planned essays on the subject, but never took the risk of writing one down, let alone attempting to publish one.

"The transition to undeath is not pleasant," he told his imagined audience, "but nor is it surprising. It is more like waking up than going to sleep; the sensation seems familiar. That may seem odd to you, but one sometimes requires a spur to bring out the fullness of what one has always known. Perhaps, when you leave life behind, you will find death more familiar than you had anticipated. You might think of death as a moment that cannot be experienced twice, but it is entirely possible that you will one day realize—cursing yourself for not having realized it before—that death is always with us, an inevitable companion of life. We begin to die before we are born, and even as we are conceived we carry forward a legacy of death that extends throughout the history of creation. Death is original sin, and we live with it constantly. The embryo in the womb is sculpted by death, as an artist chips a statue free from inchoate stone. The elements of the growing body are ceaselessly replaced; every aspect of our form has been remade a dozen times before we achieve maturity. We know death intimately, but it is the dullest sickness of all, the ultimate uniformity. It is a rare victim who learns the desire to be rid of it, and a rarer one who finds the means, but it can be done. Only follow me, and I shall show you the way. I am the resurrection and the undeath, the way to salvation."

He could not do it, not because he would have been staked through the heart, burned at the stake, beheaded or crucified merely for making the suggestion, but because it was essentially blasphemous. He was, after all, an incorrigible Catholic.

In that respect, if not in any other, Charles learned to do as other vampires did; he feigned humility as he feigned life; he pretended to be a man. He took care to appear to breathe as a man breathed, and he took care to appear to write as a man wrote. As Jeanne Duval was an actress, whether she was on stage at the Théâtre de la Porte-Saint-Antoine or in his bed, so Charles became an actor, not merely in the *salons* he frequented and the Café Brasserie, but in the privacy of his room and his writing-desk. He was undead, but he played the part of a living man addressing other living men.

He stuck to his resolution of never seeking help from Jeanne—although she understood the change in his condition from the first moment she saw him undead—but he did begin to understand her a little better than he had before. He came to understand the peculiarity of her whoredom—why she did not like to accept the gifts that pleased other whores, including money; why she was reluctant to accept food or wine in restaurants; and why she was so proud of her seemingly meager needs. He never tried to discover her real name, age or place of origin, not so much because he was not curious or because he suspected that she had long since forgotten all those details, but because he preferred to exercise his imagination on such questions. He wanted to think of her as a representative of some primal African race, ancestral to all humankind: an infertile Eve, who lived in civilization but was not part of it. In his own mind, he reconstructed the myth of Eden, preferring a version in which Adam abandoned his second wife as he had abandoned his first, to be given another of the same name on which to father Cain, while the one he left in Eden—*Genesis* being explicit in the statement that he was expelled alone—had entered into a more intimate relationship with the serpent, and had found a better fate than death in the fruit of the Tree of Knowledge.

Charles preserved that fantasy jealously, even after discovering, somewhat to his dismay, that undeath had not rendered him immune to aging, disease or death. He wanted to believe, even then, that Jeanne was different, and that her undeath really was undying. His friends, who had never been able to comprehend his interest in her, could not comprehend now why he maintained his relationship with her even though she was no longer his mistress.

"She is beautiful in her fashion," Banville told him, after encountering her in his presence in January 1848, "but beyond her relentless irritability she is remote and indifferent. There is no feeling in her for other human beings, no reward for attention paid to her. She might have amused you once, but I cannot understand your continued fascination."

Nadar, who was also present, concurred. "She's seductive, but insubstantial. She's long accustomed and inured to the fact that the men she fascinates move on. She understands that there is no future in any of her dalliances, and expects no more than desertion. In this instance, at least, you should indulge her. You'd do far better to let her alone, now that she's of no further use to you in bed."

"There is a sense in which she is my only true companion," Charles told them, "and always will be. There may be others like me, but I do not intend to seek them out; she is different, because she knew me before, and made me what I am."

"I know that you can never hear two men agree without wanting to argue the opposite case," Banville pressed him, "but I can see that there is more to your interest in Jeanne than a simple desire for dissent. Alas, your explanations make no sense."

"I can see the goddess in her," Charles told them. "I can see the sublimity of her conduct as well as the beauty in her face. There is always an element of horror in sublimity, as there is always an element of pain in beauty, but it only serves to sharpen the sensation for the connoisseur. Art comes from the Devil as well as from God, Theo, and the true artist must love and fear both virtue and its opposite."

"Now that *is* sheer perversity," Nadar opined.

Charles made no attempt to deny it. "When I call Jeanne my dark Venus," he said, instead, "I do not mean by that that I ever worshipped her, or ever desired to do so—but I always knew that there was something in her more or less than human. There is nothing that she can teach me about what I desire to become, but that does not alter what she is."

He said no more, because he was committed to playing the part of a living man, even with such friends as Banville and Nadar, let alone Murger and the Brasserie crowd.

Charles continued to see Jeanne, not to interrogate her or to worship her, let alone to sleep with her, but to study her as a specimen of his own kind and to imagine her as the better Eve. There was, however, one thing that did intrigue him,

17

almost to the point of asking her a question—one matter relative to which the products of his imagination seemed vaguely imperfect.

Obviously, she did not kiss all her lovers in the way that she had kissed him. Very few of those she took to her bed, he had to suppose, had ever seen her metamorphosis or calculated its significance. For the majority, she remained forever flesh, although she presumably drank their infant blood from its marrowbone cradle as thirstily as she had drunk his. He did not know whether it was her generosity that granted him the sight of her true self, or whether there had been some special capacity for sight in him. She had seen that he had seen and had known that he had known—and had seen and known, too, that when he saw and knew her as a snake and as a skeleton, he did not recoil, being entirely content with the confirmation of his fascination—but that in itself did not explain why she had kissed him in the serpentine fashion that had allowed him to survive the dagger's penetration of his heart.

Sometimes, he wondered whether she had actually intended it at all, or whether she was as helpless to determine the inheritance of her legacy as she was to determine so much else in her life.

Either way, he did not want to learn the secret of the kiss from her, because he had no intention of communicating it to any of his own lovers.

3. *L'Invitation au voyage: 1848-1855*

As Charles watched the barricade being constructed from his window, on the morning of the 15th, his first thought was: *This is nothing to do with me. Mine is only a pretense of life, a mere masquerade.* Then the National Guardsmen came, and tried to tear down the incomplete barricade. He saw one of the defenders run through with a bayonet—a man whose blood was all too ready to flow and flood, and whose flesh was entirely unresistant to the shock of fatality—and he went downstairs.

He took his place at the barricade, consenting to be armed with a rifle that had not been fired since July 1830, because he had something to defend, not on his own behalf, but on behalf of his fellow men, to whom injustice had been done. When he heard from Nadar that the rumor had been put about the Brasserie that he had donned a workman's blouse and run from barricade to barricade trying to raise a mob to assassinate General Aupick he was momentarily annoyed, but then consented to laugh, and even to wonder why he had not thought of doing exactly that. He left the barricade, though, when he concluded that it was doing more harm than good to those whose interests he desired to represent.

"You did the right thing," Banville told him, "not simply because the revolution has soured, as revolutions inevitably do, but because ours is a different and more effective path of rebellion."

"Not if it leads to your Parnassus or Gautier's *art pour l'art*," Charles told him, risking a quarrel. "I am pioneering a different way."

"By imagining yourself in love with my mistress?" Banville retorted, although Charles knew that he was far more intent on defending the New Parnassus than Marie Daubrun. "I wish now that I had never counseled you to abandon Jeanne Duval."

"All my life," Charles told him, pointing to the window so that his friend would know that he was referring to the barricade rather than Marie, "I have sought oases of horror in the vast desert of *ennui*, but when civil order disintegrates and human society is reduced to chaos there is no relief in horror—quite the opposite, in fact. The horror of the sublime requires a very different *mise-en-scène*. I require nothing of your mistress that need occasion your jealousy. She is a merely an example, an actress cast in a role; I view her as a writer, not as a seducer."

"Sometimes," Banville told him, "I think the Brasserie rabble might be right, and that you might be going mad."

Sometimes, as he dreamed while he was wide awake, Charles thought that might be possible, and he was not so foolish as to believe that undeath was any insulation against the dangers of madness. He had been undead long enough, by the Year of Revolutions, to know how imperfect its insulation was even against the diseases of the living.

The repression that followed the revolution did not please him any more than the monster the revolution had become, and such order as it restored seemed to him to have been bought at a terrible price. He had had to leave Paris behind to go to Dijon; he had work to do, not merely for the support of his remaining appetites, but in pursuit of the only utility left to him. Alas, he was ill, and found it as difficult to work, even in more pleasant circumstances, as he had often found it while he was alive.

"Those who are brought back reluctant from the tomb," he said, to the absent Jeanne, "rudely wrenched from the oblivion they would have preferred, are doubtless conformists in undeath as they were in life. It is small wonder that they often become angry and wretched when they discover that they have no more won immunity from pain and terror than they have won immunity from original sin. Legend doubtless speaks the truth when it portrays vampires pursuing what ends they may still find, by stake or fire or the guillotine, shunning daylight in the meantime as if it were the unquenching fire of hell."

Charles had never been overfond of daylight before he left life behind, but he found it just as endurable afterwards as he had before, even in Dijon, where the sun shone far more fiercely than in smoke-cloaked Paris. He did not seek it out, but nor did he live in fear of it. He dedicated himself to his learning, and his work, in spite of his fevers and his aches, and in spite of the deliria that disturbed his waking dreams.

He knew that the delirium was not caused by the venom that Jeanne Duval's vampire kiss had injected into his flesh and his soul, but he suspected that she might have communicated another poison to him as well: the poison of the pox. He did not blame her for that any more than he blamed her for the other—indeed, he blamed her less, for he had been warned of *that* sort of danger attendant on sleeping with whores.

"A voyage to Cythera must be taken at the pace granted by the wind," he told his father's ghost, "and whether there are gallows-trees standing on the shore or not, dream-vision will provide them. Dreams are essentially morbid as well as wayward, although they can be enlivened as well as tamed by rhyme and metre, shaped for the sympathy as well as the comprehension of the ear. I shall not mind their morbidity, any more than I mind their waywardness, because I know that it will merely be the dark component of their oxymoronic mask. I shall welcome them, for what they make of me. As my living body was once sculpted by disease and death, so my undying mind shall be etched by disease and dreams. I am content."

Even so, the first thing he did on his return to Paris was to visit Jeanne Duval. He did not question her directly, but he did go fishing for enlightenment "Undeath has spared me once" he told her, "but I do not believe that it can spare me forever. The interval it has purchased might be thirty years, or it might be a dozen, but the pox is within me, and is consuming me still You and I shall not be companions for all eternity."

"I never expected that," she told him. "The pox won't kill you, if you don't yield to it, but I don't think you have the capacity to resist. I never did think so."

Charles told himself that she could not know that, but he knew that she could and did. There were many things that she probably did not know—including her given name and how old she was—but she did know how to live with the pox inside her. She knew how to carry the disease without injury to herself, and she knew how to recognize those who could not.

There was no alternative for Charles but to race against time: to work, in spite of his deliria. He had worked even before committing suicide, but not as he worked thereafter. That was partly because the undead had to sustain themselves just as the living did, whether they pretended to breathe or not, and he could not have lived on the pittance doled out to him by Ancelle even if he had been prepared to abandon to the ideals of dandyism, but it was mainly because he had a far greater sense of vocation. He was, after all, the Lavoisier of undeath. As soon as he had become a vampire he had announced the imminent publication of his book of

21

verses in 1845, and he had continued to advertise it ever since. It had begun its imaginative existence as *Les Lebiennes*, had been transmuted into *Les Limbes*, and was now *Les Fleurs du mal*, growing all the while in its actual substance as he wrote poem after poem. In the meantime, he supported himself by publishing prose, commemorating the life he might have lived, had he not left life behind, in *La Fanfarlo* and encouraging his fellow artists as best he could in his essays on the *Salons* and other ephemerae.

By the time he had been ten years a vampire, Charles had left far behind him all the misconceptions regarding undeath that he learned on the stage of the Théâtre Porte-Saint-Martin and the pages of *romans feuilletons*. When the revolution of 1848 had given way to Louis Napoléon's coup d'état, and the consequent exile of Victor Hugo, Alexandre Dumas and Eugène Sue, he became convinced that there were more undead among the living than anyone had ever suspected, although their appetite for work had helped to hide their presence. Whether there might be any laboring in the fields or in manufactories he could not tell, but he suspected that an inability to lose consciousness would be less an asset than it might seem in such repetitive occupations. His judgment was that the great majority of the past's undead must have worked as he had worked, not necessarily with a pen in hand—and perhaps more likely with a paintbrush—but certainly in the production of art...and probably in the production of *modern* art, which sought to move the world into the future.

He was determined, though, that undeath should not make an obsessive recluse of him. He cultivated the new friends forced upon him by his poverty. He entered more fully into the Bohemia of those whose pens and brushes were all that stood between themselves and penury: those who wrote or painted *for a living*. With Ancelle as his guardian, he found himself caught in a strange limbo between two worlds—an heir without access to his fortune, a Tantalus whose hunger and thirst could never be appeased—equally far from home in the Café Brasserie and the *salons*, among those who counted their fortunes in *sous* and those who reckoned in *louis*. He was not unwelcome in either milieu, and such suspicion as he excited in both had little or nothing to do with having left life behind without having fallen dead. In spite of his conviction that the undead were far more likely to labor as artists than as agriculturalists or wage-slaves, though, he never met another of his own kind—not, at least, in person.

By 1855, it seemed to Charles, in retrospect, that the revolution of 1848 had not been the most important event of that year for him at all. It was in 1848 that he had translated Edgar Poe's "Mesmeric Revelation," although it was not until three years later that he realized the importance of the role that Poe was to play in his career and my life, and began to suspect that Poe too must have been undead for some years before finally departing the world in that same crucial year of 1848. Even in 1851, translation still seemed a mere side-line within his work, but he came to understand then that if he were to be the writer he wanted to be—the secret apostle of undeath—he need not, and perhaps should not, restrict his efforts to the definitive volume of his poetry that was still in gestation. If Poe too had been a voice of undeath, as seemed increasingly obvious, then he ought to do what he could to assist in the transmission of that voice, by importing it into his own language.

That too became part of his vocation, hampered but never stopped by the progress of the disease that was making undeath as impossible for him as life had been.

4. *The Phosphorescence of Putrescence: 1855-61*

By 1855, those effects of undeath that had proved cumulative, perceptible only with the passage of time, had revealed themselves in full. Charles understood by then that he had lost the faculty of forgetfulness along with the ability to sleep. His memory had become a store from which nothing was any longer discarded.

At first, he thought that this must be an envious situation, especially for a writer—but he realized soon enough that its advantages were undermined by darker corollaries. He found that, just as the living body is sculpted by death, so the active mind is sculpted by forgetfulness. He discovered that sleep—true, dreamless sleep—was no mere absence of mental activity, but rather a process of release and disposal. He realized that a mind that had lost the ability properly to discriminate between dreams and wakefulness had also lost the ability to reformulate and reorganize its memories. In the short term, that had caused him, and would continue to cause him, no acute difficulty—but he knew that in the longer term, it would surely engender a chaos of superfluity.

The realization of what was happening to him had grown in Charles by slow degrees, but by 1855 the evidence was irresistible. Jeanne, he saw then, had contrived to overcome the difficulty by learning to forget without going to sleep—but she had not been able to retain the *discrimination* that sleep normally exercises. Her forgetfulness was random, and it was powerful—except for the kind of unconscious memory that her body had, which required no input from imagination. She had become a creature of ingrained habit, with a layer of conscious memory so thin and delicate as to be hardly more than a gloss. She retained her language, well enough to memorize small theatrical parts, but she hardly knew who she was, let alone what elaborate combination of experiences had made her what she was. She could relate to other people, well enough to be seductive, but her seductiveness had no greater objective, no place in any plan for the future—and she was forever restless, without knowing why. That was the price she had paid for her immortality. That was how she had learned to live with the pox, to carry it without being consumed by it

It was not a price that Charles could ever be prepared to pay. He was an artist; memory was the core of his expertise. He had, therefore, to make the most of his gift-cum-curse while he still could. He had to take the tide of opportunity. He had to publish what he could, while he could, even if *Les Fleurs du mal* were not yet finished—and in spite of the gulf of incomprehension that still separated him from a more complete understanding of his own state of being.

"My undeath," he told his father's ghost, "is no simpler an opposite of your death than life was and is. The living are dying while they live, and the transition to undeath does not banish death entirely from the body, any more than it banishes sickness and disease. Undeath preserves—indefinitely, I must suppose, if one can adapt oneself fully to its requirements—but the immunity it confers is by no means absolute. Such freedom from age and decay as undeath confers is not only conditional on the cultivation in consciousness of a new kind of forgetfulness but on the cultivation in corporeality of a new kind of robustness. Jeanne has that kind of physical obstinacy. Perhaps I might train myself to it, if I wanted to, but my fate lies in another direction. What I am trained to do by my own experience of life is to become more and more conscious of the frailty of my flesh—not in the general sense of which the living are always aware of their mortality, or the specific sense in which the living feel particular aches and pains in response to particular injuries and diseases—but in a new sense peculiar to the state of undeath. I am becoming hyperconscious of my own inner decay: of the creeping chaos afflicting my various bodily tissues and mental capacities, under the dual pressure of mortal syphilis and fatal insomnia."

"If you do not have to die, my son," his father's ghost told him, bitterly, "then I would advise you against it."

"It is in the nature of the dead to envy the undead, even when they are sick," Charles told his father. "But I am free of that kind of envy now. Syphilis is the one disease whose possession in metaphor could not require the sufferer to envy others their own sicknesses, because syphilis is the great mimic among diseases. It is ubiquitous; there is no symptom it cannot present, no ignominy it cannot contrive."

"Perhaps," his father insisted, "you might yet be able to cultivate the faculty of forgetfulness without unconsciousness. Then, your flesh would surely acquire the same fortitude as Jeanne Duval's, without any further effort."

"I doubt it," Charles replied. "At any rate, it hardly matters. No matter how much I might resent the appalling profusion of my accumulating memory, or the extent to which that profusion is shot through with superfluity, I cannot do without it. Nor can I resist the ravages of death and disease as they became similarly profuse and disordered—or even the exaggerated consciousness of that increasing disorder."

It was true, or so he firmly believed. There was only one thing he could do in response to his slowly-discovered predicament, and that was to work. he worked as hard as he could, stealing poetic inspiration as and when he could, and filling the remainder of my time with prose, original and translated. When he could not work at all, he dulled his senses with laudanum, even though it could not deliver him to unconsciousness. All that it could do, at best, was to grant him a kind of separation within himself, so that he seemed to be existing on two planes at the same time, drifting between the ethereal and the mundane as he drifted between *salon* society and Bohemia.

He published *Les Fleurs du mal* in 1857, although it was not finished, and was rendered even more incomplete by the censors, who demanded that six poems be deleted. He published a new version in 1861, although it was still not finished. In the meantime, he began work on a second volume, which was to consist entirely of poetry in prose, and would be called *Spleen de Paris*. When General Aupick died he went to live with my mother at Honfleur for a while, fully intending to look after her, but it proved impossible; no matter how strong his desire was, his condition—physical, mental and spiritual—was no longer equal to the task. He had to abandon her for her own good, as she had once abandoned him for his.

His work suffered too, but not in the same way. He could write as never before, but only briefly and with increasing trouble in the formulation. Poetry increased in difficulty more rapidly than prose, and original prose more rapidly than translation—but he could not have tolerated the translation of any writer with whom he had a less manifest kinship than Edgar Poe. Poe became his *alter ego*, communicating order and discrimination when he could no longer find it in himself, calming him and giving him a focus that he needed as desperately as he desired it.

Year by year, the excess of memory corroded and corrupted his mind, while versatile disease corroded and corrupted his flesh. He could no longer have the least doubt that he would one day leave undeath behind, just as he had left life, faltering and groping to a far greater extent. He felt further and further removed from the world of living men, more and more alien to its habits and customs. He still went out to all his old haunts, but he began to feel that he was indeed a haunter rather than a participant in what went on there: a spectator who, while not yet disembodied, was nevertheless not wholly present.

Might he have felt the same had he still been alive? He could not tell for certain, but he could not believe it. Had he been burdened by a mere mélange of conventional poisons, he should have been able to enjoy the bounty of forgetfulness and the grace of ordinary pain. As things were, he remembered too much and felt too deeply. He could feel the disease working within his flesh, conducting an entire orchestra of petty miseries, and he could not rid himself of the ceaseless mental pressure of every vile nuance.

It was sublime, of course; it was beautiful too, in its fashion, but it was excessive, and it became increasingly problematic for him to select out moments and ideas for preservation and analysis in written form.

Charles could not have been free of Jeanne Duval even if she had not come to see him to demand her petty tributes—but in truth, he would not have wanted to be free of her. She was still his goddess, his creator, and if she was also his damnation, there was some cause for gratitude even in that. Art, as he had assured Banville and Nadar, came from the Devil as well as from God, and undeath had brought it forth in him more extravagantly than life...if only for a little while.

"All those who find life unendurable are likely to find undeath no less so," he told Jeanne, when she came to visit him one day in 1861, "but all those who find life woefully inadequate to feed their dreams will find in the dread excess of undeath an immeasurable, if temporary, exaltation. There are many kinds of people who would derive nothing from a lamia's kiss but catastrophe, but there are a few kinds, at least, who might find it rewarding. I belong to one such kind, Jeanne, while you belong to another, but there must be others who could find a means therein to supply their own wild hunger. You must continue your quest, Jeanne, when I am gone. You must not give up. You must learn to love again, for ever and ever, and you must use your kisses wisely, however sparingly."

"I have no quest," she told him, cruelly. "Nor wisdom, nor economy."

The next time she came to see him she found him in a very poor state, but she did not look at him with pity, and demanded her tribute regardless. He gave her what he could—more grateful now than ever before for the modesty of her needs and demands.

"I love you, Jeanne," he said to her, as she made to leave. "I worship you. I always have."

"I've heard that before," she told him, "more times than I remember." She seemed to be making light of the matter, and gave the impression that she had no idea of the import of her words.

"You are an archetype of irony, as I am," he told her, "but your undeath really is incurable. Mine, alas, is not, although I have another disease, which certainly is. Nature favors discreet diseases, which allow their hosts abundant time to communicate the infection, and yours is very discreet indeed. I hoped at first that mine might be as clever, in its own way, but it was too profligate and too impatient, and it will cauterize my soul before the pox sends my flesh to its final ruination. Now, I hope for a different kind of immortality."

"You're mad, Charles," she told him, mildly. "You always were, but now it has run away with you. Who will keep me when you're gone? What will become of me?"

"You'll survive," he assured her. "You might lack a worshipper, for a while, but you'll not lack lovers. In time...you'll kiss another at least as worthy as me. In time, you must."

"Some might think my life disorderly," she said, as she placed her hand on the doorknob, "but it isn't."

"Mine is," he told her, "but not entirely—and I am glad that I did not die when I first repented its impossibility. I hardly knew what disorder was, in those days. I do now."

"Goodbye," she said, as if it were forever—but that was the way she always said goodbye.

"One day," her victim told her, continuing even when she had closed the door behind her, because it did not matter in the least whether she could hear him or not, "a future Lavoisier will teach everyone in the world the trick of leaving life behind without actually dying, and your kind of poison will be mixed by apothecaries in their mortars for sale as a tincture. One day, we shall all be able to toy with memory and damnation, conscious of every movement of decay that moves within our diseased flesh. Then, we shall see what can be made of undeath by artists who can master every skill and conquer every thirst."

Instead of saying goodbye, he reached for his pen. Jeanne Duval could not understand him, any more than she could understand herself, but Charles assured himself that there would come a day when *everyone* could understand him, and would.

"There will come a day," he said, to the smoke-fogged air in his dingy room, as he set his nib to paper and began to scratch away at the illimitable irritation that would not let him rest, "when you, my reader, my hypocrite brother, will understand everything that I have recorded here. There is a time to every purpose under heaven, and beyond the corrosions and corruptions of our petty envies and haphazard diseases, you and I are of the same sad kind."

He fell silent then, but his pen continued to scrape away, extending its broken trail of scrupulously-stolen blood across the jaundiced page.

JUSTICE

In the days when Swabia was one of the five grand duchies and the *Schlegerbund* were a great power in the land there came to the town of Ravensburg a man named Nikolaus Makri, who had fled from Lombardy upon a tide of dark rumors, which alleged that he was overactive in the cause of change and progress.

Swabia's nobles considered theirs a more advanced realm than decadent Lombardy, and so Makri was made welcome there—all the more so because he claimed to be a wise and artful physician, and also to be expert in the amputation of limbs. In Swabia the work of surgery had long been the prerogative of barbers rather than physicians, but the march of progress had reduced the barbers' guild to a mean and powerless thing. The status of barbers was so reduced that they had little enough success in persuading certain stubborn souls that it was evil for a man to cut his own hair, so their protestations failed to inhibit the ardent Nikolaus from plying his saws and razors as he wished. He became a well-respected man in Ravensburg, and became enthusiastic for the improvement of his adopted town.

There was in Swabia at this time a very violent highway-robber who had also come to the duchy from Lombardy. His name was Zorillo, and the depredations that he practiced around the shores of Lake Konstanz had become the stuff of legend. The *Schlegerbund* finally condescended to send a company of mercenaries to pursue him, and he was eventually seized by them while hiding in a cheesemaker's shop on the outskirts of Ravensburg. He was quickly brought to trial before the three magistrates of the district.

30

Knowing that he was doomed, Zorillo confessed all his crimes and pleaded guilty. This was a wise move, for Swabia was at that time the most civilized region of the Empire, and the law of the land was meek enough to license torture only in cases where the guilty would not admit their crimes.

The presiding magistrates labored long and hard to find a way in which they could increase the robber's punishment, for he was guilty of many heinous crimes against the property of noblemen as well as the murder of a few lesser folk, but the law was quite clear. They could pass no harsher sentence on a robber who confessed his guilt than to order that he be hanged by the neck and choked by slow degrees. No doubt they considered the possibility of an accusation of heresy, which—if substantiated—would permit Zorillo to be burned alive, but however reluctant the robber had been to abide by the laws of the Church, he had never openly questioned their propriety; nor had he ever been so vile as to play the cutpurse with men of the cloth.

Thus it was that Zorillo was sentenced to go to the merciful gallows with his limbs unextended by the rack and his joints uncrushed by the boot. The voices of his victims, whose gold had never been recovered, were loud in proclaiming that such gentle treatment could not be an effective deterrent to other Lombard thieves, who would surely flock across the border in ever-greater numbers. The fact that Zorillo had become something of a hero to the poor folk who were not worth robbing only amplified these fears.

* * * * * * *

When Zorillo's trial was over, however, Nikolaus Makri visited the frustrated magistrates, and told them that he knew of a way by which the bandit's suffering might be prolonged within the letter of the law. He said that he had been encouraged to speak in the interests of serving justice, and in the interests of encouraging the thieves of decadent and hateful Lombardy to stay at home.

Makri proposed that the magistrates should allow him to make a small incision in the lower part of Zorillo's throat before the robber was sent to the scaffold. This, he ex-

31

plained, would allow a trickle of air into the felon's lungs even when the rope was drawn exceedingly tight, and might prolong the hanged man's agony for an hour or more.

The magistrates were skeptical at first, objecting that a slit throat was the easiest way of all to die, but when Nikolaus Makri had demonstrated his technique on a stray dog they were convinced, and gave him license to proceed, so that the vengeful ends of justice might be seen to be properly served in spite of the gentleness of the law.

When the time came for him to meet his destiny Zorillo objected most strenuously to the making of this incision, declaring that it amounted to unlawful torture, but the magistrates gleefully replied that Master Nikolaus was a certified physician, whose vocation was to discover how life might be prolonged. They pointed out to the miserable villain that wise men everywhere were quite agreed that the actions of physicians—no matter how painful and nauseating they might sometimes seem to the ignorant—could not possibly qualify as torture.

The robber could not be persuaded to agree with this judgment, and he appealed to the Bishop of Ravensburg, asking that the Church should intercede on his behalf. Alas for Zorillo, the bishop—whose own wealth had been somewhat reduced by Zorillo's zeal for theft—agreed with the magistrates that the ends of justice would best be served by letting Makri proceed with his experiment.

When he heard this, the condemned man fell to cursing everyone in sight—but he dared not call upon the Devil's name lest he provide grounds for his own burning. The magistrates, being good and pious Christians, had not the least fear of his feeble invocations. Indeed, they were convinced that God would wholeheartedly approve of the lesson which they were about to offer to all those who might contemplate interference with the divine ordering of men's estates—which clearly insisted that the best of men were destined to be rich and the worst of them poor.

* * * * * * *

When the appointed hour came, the incision in Zorillo's neck was duly made by the ingenious Makri, before the hangman's rope was made secure. Then the robber was hauled most carefully upwards, and made secure to the gibbet, so that the weight of his body might cause the noose to tighten by patient degrees. The whole town had heard of the physician's bold scheme, and everyone was there to see how long it took for the condemned man to die, and what wrigglings and writhings he might contrive to make in the meantime. How many there were who wished to see the experiment fail—in addition to Ravensburg's three barbers, who had an understandable prejudice in the matter—it is impossible to judge.

There was much discussion regarding the longest time that it had ever taken anyone to die upon a Swabian scaffold, and veterans of a hundred public executions were earnestly consulted as authorities upon the matter. Some said fifteen minutes, others twenty, and one ancient crone swore by her rotting teeth that she had seen the infamous murderer Hornstein kick his legs for half an hour before the inevitable stink gave evidence of his dying spasm. Wagers began to be laid as to how long Zorillo would last, and there was such excitement generated by these speculations that marked candles were brought from a nearby Benedictine monastery in order to measure the result—for all of this occurred in the days before the invention of mechanical clocks.

The most popular predictions were clustered between forty minutes and an hour, and within five minutes of Zorillo's suspension more gold had been wagered upon the length of his life than he had ever stolen. Whatever redistribution of Swabia's wealth he might have contrived by the manner of his life paled into insignificance by comparison with the redistribution which would be accomplished by the manner of his death.

When the first of the twenty-minute marks upon the candle-timer was passed, a great cheer went up from the crowd. Zorillo was still writhing and kicking his feet in a thoroughly vigorous fashion, and though his eyes were bulging from their sockets he was still capable of looking wildly about. He was still trying to speak, although the cord about his neck would not permit it, and a sorrowful priest was heard to remark that this enforced silence would at least keep his soul safe, by preventing any weakening of his resolve to refrain from calling upon the Devil for aid.

As the second twenty-minute mark was passed in its turn there was a greater cheer, and loud applause for clever Nikolaus Makri—especially from those who had wagered on a longer interval. Zorillo was quieter now, and his bulbous gaze had ceased to roam the crowd, but his fists continually clenched and unclenched in a strained and calculated manner which was clearly not the work of some posthumous agitation, and his bowels had not yet let go of their burden to signal the moment of expiry. The gamblers were counting the seconds now, calling them in scrupulous unison, held taut by the knowledge that fortunes might be won or lost on the passing of each moment.

By the time that the hour mark was passed the chanting of the seconds had begun to waver, because the greater proportion of the wagers laid had by then been settled or given up for lost. Only the boldest of the speculators had put pledges of times in excess of the hour; although another cheer went up at the melting of that mark, it was somewhat muted by comparison with the last. The crowd were no less inclined to marvel at what Makri had accomplished, but there was now less praise and more anxiety in the exclamations, for Zorillo had once again commenced to struggle fiercely against the rope which held him, as if he sought by furious effort to hurry on the moment of his release.

If the robber's efforts were indeed directed to that end, they failed him. He continued to dance, and his dance now seemed as uncanny as it was desperate. Although his eyes were blank and fixed, his blackened tongue still moved like a slug within his gaping mouth, and in the quieter moments there were those in the crowd who believed that the hanged man was somehow contriving to make audible sounds. More than one was later to claim that they heard words, but German is the kind of language that, when whispered, can easily sound like the gaggings, gaspings, and gurglings of a strangled throat.

34

* * * * * * *

When another hour had elapsed, and Zorillo still moved on the end of his rope, the wonderment of the crowd was beginning to turn to horror. None had dared to bet on such an interval as this, and the minds of the watchers began to turn—as the minds of men inevitably do when they are faced with the unprecedented—to the fear that some awful magic might have been involved in procuring Zorillo's amazing longevity. Nikolaus Makri was still standing by the magistrates, as proud as a peacock in seeing what he had achieved, but he was now the target of uneasy glances from many of the humble folk—who were ever inclined, in their ignorance, to suspect physicians of secret sorcery.

When a further twenty minutes had elapsed without Zorillo being reduced to stillness or incontinence, the magistrates conferred, and then sought a second opinion from the bishop, who was also in attendance. They decided, though not without a certain reluctance, that enough was enough, and that justice had now been seen to be done. The public executioner was commanded to go forward and grip Zorillo's body firmly round the waist, while lifting his own feet off the ground, so that his extra weight would further tighten the noose and hasten the robber's demise.

The executioner obeyed, but he quickly let go, saying that he could not bear to feel the hanged man struggling so fervently to throw him off. While he was making this excuse he suffered the consequence of standing too close to the gibbet, for Zorillo caught him with a well-directed kick, which knocked him sprawling on the ground. Some of those in the crowd cheered, but the greater number were too anxious to be amused. The suspicion was abroad that the Devil's hand was in the business now, and there were many who were willing to suppose that Zorillo might have secretly turned heretic after all.

"You have done your work well enough," said one of the magistrates to Nikolaus Makri. "Now will you tell us, if you please, how much longer it will take this wicked man to die?"

But Nikolaus Makri did not know, and he could only shake his head. An anxious frown had appeared upon his face.

All of a sudden, the hanged man began to shake and quiver in a new way, as if he had been seized by a bout of wild laughter, which, because it could not escape from his sealed throat, was forced to eddy and echo inside him.

"Well," said the bruised and bitter executioner, picking himself up from where he had fallen, "there is one sure way to put an end to the farce." So saying, he took a dagger from his belt, and thrust it hard into the hanged man's breast, intending to puncture the heart that was still beating within.

But the wound inflicted by the executioner refused to bleed, and the hanged man skillfully kicked his persecutor in the head again, sending him sprawling in the dirt for a second time.

"It is not Zorillo!" cried a voice from the crowd. "It is a demon sent by the Lord of Hell to possess his body, and there will be a dire time in Swabia while it hangs undying there!"

When this was said, the priests and friars who were present became angry, for they alone had a license to detect the hand of the Devil in earthly affairs, but they made no shift to offer an alternative explanation. Even the bishop seemed fearful, and he was evidently beginning to regret that he had given his approval to an action that, however virtuous it might seem, had no obvious precedent in the scriptures.

The crowd began to melt away, as the common people began to run to their homes, anxious for the consequences of what their masters had wrought.

Now it proved quite impossible to approach the hanging body, for if anyone stepped towards it, its booted feet would lash out very fiercely—and Zorillo did not seem to be in any way aware of the fact that the hilt of a dagger stood out prominently from his breast, set firmly in a deep but unbleeding wound.

The face of the hanged man was very dark and bloated now, but the protruding eyes did not seem sightless—instead, they seemed possessed of a stare more wrathful than could ever have been worn by a man who had not a strangling noose about his neck. While the sun stood high in the sky the baleful glare was difficult enough to bear, but, when sunset stained the western sky blood-red, Zorillo's eyes became so fierce and fiery that there was not a man in Ravensburg who dared meet that stare. In the end, even the priests and magistrates went away, and the watchmen set to guard the gibbet stood with their backs to the unsleeping man who still danced beneath it.

* * * * * * *

When night had completely fallen, the hangman was instructed to creep up on the gibbet under cover of darkness, with the object of cutting Zorillo down, so that his body might be dealt with in another way. He agreed to try it, for he was a man of courage and he had not forgotten or forgiven the indignities to which he had been subjected. But when he approached the scaffold, as stealthily as he was able, he was kicked yet again, more savagely than before. He instantly resigned from his position.

All through the next day, and the next after that, Zorillo hung unquietly where he was, with his bulging eyes staring horribly at everyone who passed him by. Although his face began to show signs of corruption, with white maggots creeping upon his darkened flesh, still his body squirmed and still his legs lashed out if anyone approached. No one any longer doubted that the adversary who took delight in all the sufferings of men had been moved by Nikolaus Makri's cunning ploy to take too keen an interest in the duchy of Swabia—and if any proof were needed that Satan was abroad in the land, fevers broke out in the town, and the animals in the fields began to sicken.

When a week had passed, and the rotting body on the gibbet still gave every indication that there was unnatural life in it, Nikolaus Makri was seized by the constable and taken to the prison, where he was swiftly tried for sorcery, and convicted in spite of his denials.

He complained very loudly that he was a physician and a devout follower of Christ—and this refusal to make a proper confession of his foul sins entitled his judges to torment him until he acknowledged the justice of their action. His limbs were stretched until the joints popped, his skin was vigorously raked with iron combs, and his eyes—when their stare began to remind his uncomfortable questioners of the staring eyes of the undead Zorillo—were melted and sealed by boiling tar.

When this business was concluded, Makri should by law have been taken to the place where Zorillo's scaffold stood, and properly burned in order to make certain that his soul could not be darkened by any failure of his hard-won repentance, but this was not possible while the demon-inhabited corpse still hung there. So Ravensburg's churchmen and lawyers were forced to continue their lately-established tradition of innovation; in view of the fact that the position of public executioner remained unfilled, they ruled that the guild of barbers must supply a razor man to cut the physician's throat.

The guild of barbers was only too happy to oblige, and the three candidates drew lots to see which one would be afforded the honor of carrying out the execution.

* * * * * * *

When the act had been done—more neatly than any mere physician could ever have managed it, the perpetrator proudly claimed—the bloodstained body of Nikolaus Makri was taken to the gibbet, and laid down nearby. All the free citizens of the district were called to public prayer, and the bishop piously led them in imploring Jesus the merciful to undo what his dire enemy Satan had contrived, allowing Zorillo to go to that eternal rest—or perhaps eternal torment—from which the people of the town had tried so foolishly to keep him for a while.

In the morning, however, it proved that the hanged man was still staring and squirming, and that the plague had still to run its horrid course throughout the region; and so the people of Ravensburg learned that, once the common order of things has been deliberately upset, it is not so readily restored.

This single example of the dangers of tampering with tradition was doubtless of little significance in the greater scheme of things, but it contributed in its own small way to that great tide of misfortunate events which eventually caused Swabia to turn its back on the dubious causes of justice and progress, and which ultimately swept the entire duchy on to the rubbish-heap of history.

THE COPPER CAULDRON

If anyone living within the Ultimate Empire's bounds should ever doubt the wisdom and necessity of political union they need only travel abroad to some benighted region of the world where a central organizing force is lacking. In the archipelago of Ambriocyatha, which stains the New Tethys Sea like a rash, every island is a petty kingdom perpetually at odds with its neighbors and ever-liable to spoliation by the cankers of its own internal disputes. The ruling houses of such estates are like pimples that never quite heal, always flaring up again no matter how many times their internal infections might cause them to burst asunder. The insidious forces of corruption may lie dormant for a while within such an isolated community, but, where there is neither a higher law nor the power to enforce it, such forces can never be quieted for long. After a time, intrigue and treason begin their pollutant work again; the body politic festers and swells until the lifeblood of the kingdom turns into rank pus and catastrophe becomes inevitable.

The ports of Ambriocyatha's smaller islands usually take longer to complete this cycle than those capitals hidden in the arid interior of larger and more independent landmasses, because the necessity of trade is always a healthy influence, but the good effects of intercourse with other islands are sometimes offset by the depredations of pirates. The most unruly pirates in the region, and perhaps in the entire world, are those whose secret harbors are excavated in the crumbling cliffs of the Karnatan Peninsula, the only part of the Tropical Continent that remains outside the benign span of the Ultimate Empire.

40

Almyria is one of the smallest and southernmost islands in Ambriocyatha, whose location places it in unfortunately close proximity to the Karnatan Peninsula. Legend informs us that it has been conquered more than once by Karnatan pirates, who have established their own ruling dynasties there, and now that the world has run out of historians we have no alternative but to put our trust in legends. At any rate, Almyria is certainly well-equipped to serve as a pirates' nest; it has a deep-water harbor whose entrance is inconveniently narrow, and the remainder of the island is fringed by precipitous cliffs. The warm winds stirred by the dying sun have long since scoured the topsoil from the island's central plateau, so it has no agriculture at all; those of its inhabitants who do not care for fish have no alternative but to live by plunder.

To the best of its inhabitants' recollection—which is admittedly hazy, since they are entirely ungifted in the fine art of legend-making—no king of Almyria has died of natural causes for a hundred generations. Popular opinion differs as to the number of kings who have reigned in the interim, the more conservative estimating two hundred, the moderate three hundred and the reckless few five hundred, but the general principle is universally admitted: each and every one of them was either slain in battle or murdered.

Popular opinion is also divided as to the exact number of kings of Almyria who died in any particular fashion, but those disputes too are trivial with respect to the general pattern. All the accounting-schemes agree in asserting that, for every king who died in honest combat, ten were treacherously done away with, and for every one who was killed by a resentful and rebelliously-inclined subject, five were assassinated by members of their immediate families.

Assassinations, like all family matters, tend to become matters of local tradition; whereas some families much given to murdering one another favor the dagger and others the strangling-cord, the first weapon of choice of the royal house of Almyria has always been poison. The Ultimate World, seen as a whole, offers an extraordinarily broad spectrum of opportunity to would-be poisoners, but in this matter the would-be kings of Almyria are a trifle narrow-minded. With only a few exceptions, their instruments of choice have been the venom of the horny asp, the fruit of the spineless cactus and the mucus of the glistening toad.

All three of these compounds have the advantage of being quite tasteless and odorless, easily concealed in any kind of food or drink, and they remain effective when spread on an ingeniously-placed needle, a convenient undergarment or a dice-thrower's cup. Scholarly wisdom has long held that there is no specific antidote to any of these three poisons, and even though isolated and insular islands know so little of scholarly wisdom that their inhabitants tend to treat it with principled disrespect, what passes for common knowledge in Almyria concurs with this view. Even the meanest island state is, however, capable of producing the occasional daring innovator, and a royal family subject to a stern selection process over many generations is likely to play host to a steady progress of ingenuity.

More than one of Almyria's kings, therefore, having disposed of his predecessor by poison, has entered into his career with a firm determination to equip himself with the means to ensure that he would not suffer the same fate himself. The one who did so most determinedly was Zurara VI, who—following his coronation and the customary round of celebratory tax-increases and public executions—immediately set out to amass an armory of antidotes to *all* known poisons, including those which had hitherto been thought to have none. Since no specific antidotes were known to the venom of the horny asp, the fruit of the spineless cactus or the mucus of the glistening toad, the bold Zurara set out to discover some by experiment.

* * * * * * *

King Zurara's first step in this quest was to recruit a dozen healers who were supposedly expert in the medicinal qualities of plants. They were set to work distilling potions from all manner of exotic roots and blooms. His second step was to buy a few hundred worn-out slaves at rock-bottom prices, paying no attention at all to their capacity for further labor. Then he told his healers that every time they offered him a new potion, he would test the supposed antidote by examining its effects on a group of three poisoned slaves. Each healer would be permitted three failed attempts to produce a worthwhile antidote before being required to test his fourth offering on himself.

This scheme was agreed by all Zurara's freshly-appointed ministers—and, indeed, everyone else in the capital, with the possible exception of the healers—to be a prudent and profitable way of spending the new tax revenues. Unfortunately, it took less than a year for the entire company of healers to follow nearly a hundred dead slaves to the barge outside the harbor-mouth from which corpses were tipped into the retreating tide. Zurara was forced to order the captains of Almyria's tiny merchant navy to find more healers, and even took the trouble to offer bribes to a few Karnatan pirates who had prospered sufficiently to reckon themselves adventurers rather than mere villains. Alas, the supply could not keep up with the demand, and another year passed without any specific antidote being found to the venom of the horny asp, the fruit of the spineless cactus or the mucus of the glistening toad.

By this time, Zurara VI knew only too well that his popularity with his people was on the wane. He had, of course, murdered all of his immediate family along with his predecessor, but the inevitable effect of that precaution had been to elevate to the rank of would-be-heirs-presumptive half a dozen distant cousins he had never met—who promptly went into hiding—while making the former dancing-girls who now constituted a harem of beloved queens unduly anxious for the fate of their as-yet-unborn children. Obsessed with the necessity to protect himself against the conspiracies that might already be forming around him, the king of Almyria did what many men in his situation would have done, and turned to sorcery for aid.

The first three sorcerers employed by Zurara VI went the same way as the healers, thus proving either that they were charlatans or that they did not stand very high in the estimation of the evil gods they served. The fourth, however, was a man of a different kind. His name was Bernardo Cassingena, and he was a much-traveled man, whose knowledge of the northern regions of the Tropical Continent was as unparalleled as his expertise in evil magic.

"I fear that you are going about this project in entirely the wrong way, your highness," Cassingena told King Zurara, as politely as he could. "Even if you were to amass a large enough collection of specific antidotes, you would still face the prospect, in the event of your being poisoned, of having to determine which one was required in time for it to take beneficial effect."

"What do you suggest I should do instead, Master Sorcerer?" Zurara demanded, slightly resentful of the implicit criticism of his intelligence.

"It would be better, would it not, your highness," the sorcerer replied, "if you were able to discover a specific treatment for your own body, which would make it invulnerable to *all* possible catastrophes and misfortunes?"

"I suppose it might," Zurara agreed. "But who ever heard of such a thing? I never did."

"Actually, your highness," Cassingena said, "I happen to have come across one myself, while I was exploring the uplands of Karnatan."

"Nobody goes into the uplands of Karnatan," Zurara told him, flatly. "They're far higher than our own accursed plateau, and even more barren. Nothing grows there, so nothing lives there, and no one but a lunatic would try to go up there in the first place, given that he'd have to get past the pirates to do it."

"Your highness is *very nearly* right," the sorcerer conceded, judiciously, "but even the pirates who hollow out their refuges in the soft cliffs know next to nothing about the territory above them. They have spread the rumor far and wide that they alone have any kind of tenure in Karnatan, and that their positions are unassailable, but they are more thinly spread than they would like their enemies to suppose and a man who knows the way into the uplands can easily evade them.

"The highlands of the peninsula are by no means as level as your bleak plateau; the rain of millennia has eaten deep into the rocks, making precipitous clefts where silt accumulates into soil. The paucity of sunlight makes such valleys difficult to cultivate, but there are tribes of hillmen who have been isolated from the greater human society for longer than any legend could possibly survive, and who have therefore been forgotten by all their civilized fellows. Their own traditions may well be entirely compounded out of lies, but even if their tales of having once been in contact with long-lost starfarers are false, they do possess certain magical artifacts for which it is difficult to account in any other way. Who else but our starfaring ancestors, who left the world forever when they decided that it was no longer in their interests to shunt it around the heavens in response to the transformations of the dying sun, could have made the elixir that simmers eternally in the copper cauldron?"

"What elixir? What cauldron?" Zurara VI wanted to know.

"The elixir of invulnerability to all disease and poison, your highness. A secret tribe of hillmen, whose deep-set valley had remained unvisited for hundreds of generations until I stumbled across it a thousand days ago, keeps a fire that is never allowed to go out, upon which sits a copper cauldron, whose contents have been simmering for a least ten thousand years.

"By virtue of this prolonged excitement, the liquid in the cauldron is now alive, and more insistently so than any mortal creature in the world. Anyone who drained that cauldron to the dregs would be possessed of all its virtue. The flesh of the living liquid would dissolve the flesh of the host, little by little, replacing it with more solid flesh of its own manufacture, while never disturbing the intelligence seated within. The individual thus remade would be invulnerable not merely to all toxins known and presently-unknown, but to all infections known and presently-unknown. Moreover, his new flesh would have such awesome powers of self-repair that no ordinary dagger-thrust or strangling-cord would ever be fatal to him."

Because Zurara VI was an exceptionally ingenious man, at least by the meager standards prevailing in Almyria, he was inclined to be suspicious of this tale on several accounts. First of all, he knew that the so-called mountains of Karnatan are modest in height by comparison with the World's Spine or the Mountains of Mourning, and thought that even their remotest regions were unlikely refuges for a "secret tribe". Secondly, ten thousand years is a very long time for temptation to be resisted, and it seemed exceedingly unlikely to him that, even if the tribe really were unknown to all outsiders save one, none of its own people would have taken advantage of such a treasure. Thirdly, if no one in all that time had ever drunk the copper cauldron to its dregs, how could anyone be sure what the effects of such a draught might be?

Zurara VI demanded clarification of all these issues from the sorcerer.

"First of all," Bernardo Cassingena replied, "the height of mountains is irrelevant; the point is that no one ever goes there because no one expects to find anything there. The cliffs fall so steeply into the sea that the pirates resident along the coast would need a very powerful reason to scale them; in the absence of any such motive force, they have never made the slightest attempt to invade the mainland— and the same was true of the people they displaced, and all their various predecessors. The uplands seem stubbornly unprofitable to anyone who looks up at them from the ocean, because their valleys are so well-hidden, and the tribes that live in them have, in consequence, been cut off from the rest of the world since time immemorial.

"Secondly, the people of all these hidden valleys are so tightly-bound by tradition as to make your most sacred customs seem like momentary whims. Their languages are not like ours, having no equivalents for terms that we would think utterly indispensable, like theft and treachery and selfishness. Having no words for such concepts, they lack the concepts themselves, and they are utterly incapable of formulating any intention to defy the mores that they have followed for thousands of years. None has ever drunk the contents of the cauldron because none could even imagine doing so.

"Your third objection is, admittedly, harder to counter. The potion has not been tested for ten thousand years, and no experiment can be tried in advance because the entire draught is required to produce the effect. My only recourse is to the same fact that defeated your second objection: the utter incapacity of the tribesmen for any deception. They have no concept of lying; everything they say they believe, and they certainly believe that the cauldron has this virtue. They might be wrong, but I believe that they are relics of a time when the world was a kinder and more orderly place, when many things were known for certain that are confused and mysterious today, and I am inclined to trust them. Given the way that events in Almyria have recently transpired, I suppose I am required to bet my life on it—very well, I do so, bravely."

While this long speech was being delivered, a fourth point had occurred to Zurara VI, and he was quick to put it to the sorcerer.

"If you alone have found this hidden tribe," he said, "and you alone have penetrated its secrets, why have you not appropriated the produce of the copper cauldron for your own use?"

"I am only one man, highness," Cassingena replied. "My sorcery is the inquisitive kind that lusts for knowledge and a little luxury, not the violent kind that revels in striking men dead and laying villages to waste. These tribesmen are sworn to defend their secret to the death; it will require a small army to defeat them and a small navy to land the army, even if I undertake to show the navy the best place to land, guide the army to the valley, and exercise my ingenuity to the full in orchestrating a sneak attack upon it. I know that I cannot win the cauldron for myself, and that my only hope of profiting from its use is to attach myself to a king who will use its gift wisely, serving him loyally as his chief minister and principal confidant."

At this point, a truly wise king might have asked Cassingena why, out of all the petty kings in Ambriocyatha—or, for that matter, the world—he had chosen Zurara VI. There is, however, a certain vanity that goes with kingship, which prevents even the wisest throne-squatter from doubting his own majesty. Zurara VI thought himself an exceptionally clever and altogether superior kind of king, and could see no reason why anyone else should think of him any differently. So what he asked instead was: "And how, in your opinion, should such a gift be wisely used?"

The answer that Bernardo Cassingena gave took advantage of the same blind spot that had made Zurara ask the wrong question. "To increase a ruler's authority and domains, your highness," the sorcerer said. "A king immune to poison, disease and all ordinary injuries would be a fearsome and charismatic leader—and it has been a very long time since Ambriocyatha could call itself an empire, rather than a patchwork of island states. Had I taken this news to the heart of the Ultimate Empire, the Emperor of the Last Days would have told me that he already has more land under his dominion than any ruler could meaningfully govern, but even in the evening of the world, Ambriocyatha is home to men of ambition—and Almyria is fortunate enough to be ruled by a man who has vision as well as ambition." Like all great sorcerers, Bernardo Cassingena knew the value of flattery.

"I will give you a fleet of fourteen ships, each one equipped with seventy marines," Zurara told his adviser, dazzled by sudden visions of glorious conquest. "Bring me the cauldron, sorcerer—and be sure to keep it simmering while it is carried down from the mountains to the sea."

And that was what was done.

* * * * * * *

According to the tales carried back by Zurara's marines, the scaling of the cliffs of Karnatan was a feat of unparalleled heroism, given that it had to be accomplished so stealthily. That achievement faded into insignificance, however, by comparison with the task of invading the valley where the copper cauldron was kept, and slaughtering the cauldron's guardians. The hillmen fought like demons, and more than half the company of a thousand brave men was lost before the cauldron could be secured.

Fortunately, there were more than enough men left to keep a very careful eye on Bernardo Cassingena, to make sure that his newly-formed loyalty to Zurara VI of Almyria did not waver before his mission was complete. While they were doing that they also kept an eye on one another, just in case some petty relative of the king might imagine himself a less remote cousin than he really was.

According to the same accounts, it proved by no means easy to carry the copper cauldron through the mountains to the secret harbor where Zurara's ships had anchored, while keeping a fire burning beneath it day and night. Fortunately, the sorcerer was very assiduous in his attention to the matter, and the living liquid never ceased its restless seething for an instant. Nor did the consequent sea-voyage contrive to extinguish the fire set beneath the cauldron, even though it had to be transferred to other vessels on two occasions after it spread to the underlying timbers.

When the cauldron finally arrived in the courtyard before the tower which Zurara VI liked to call his palace, the king looked it over very carefully.

"How am I to drink it down without scalding my throat and guts?" he asked Bernardo Cassingena.

"Alas, highness, you cannot," the sorcerer told him. "But even as your flesh scalds, it will heal. The pain will, I fear, be very intense—but only for a little while. Afterwards, no toothache or bellyache will ever trouble you again, nor will anything you eat ever have the temerity to disagree with you."

Zurara VI was by no means a coward, but the cauldron was as tall as the bone connecting his knee to his foot and as broad in diameter as the length of the one connecting his elbow to his hand—and it was very nearly full to the brim. He could not imagine how a mere human being could drink such a mighty draught of cow's milk or weak ale, let alone a boiling fluid, which might well taste utterly vile.

"It is impossible," he said. "It cannot be done."

"On the contrary," said Bernardo Cassingena. "The living liquid has appetites of its own. It has been waiting to be drunk for ten thousand years, and it is as thirsty for you as you are for it. It will help you in every way it can. To drink it down will be painful, I confess, but the liquid will hurry down with all the haste it can muster, and it will not let you choke. The distress will be momentary, I assure you, and the reward immense. Am I not betting my life on the outcome of the experiment? What your torturers will do to me if you do not survive the experience will surely be a thousand times more terrible than your own fate. Are not the inquisitors of

Ambriocyatha famed throughout the world for their skill and powers of endurance?" In actual fact, they were not—but Zurara had no idea how meager the archipelago's celebrity was in the heartland of the Tropical Continent.

Zurara VI had risked much to become king of Almyria, and he was prepared to risk even more to avoid the fate of his multitudinous predecessors. Summoning all his courage, he wound rags around his hands to protect them from the heat, then stepped forward and took hold of the two brass handles placed at either side of the copper cauldron's rim. It was by no means easy to lift such a vessel, but he was a strong and determined man, and he raised it from its resting-place.

Without further delay, the king set the inconveniently broad rim to his tremulous lips, and began to pour the boiling liquid into his mouth. It burned his tongue and turned his teeth to pillars of fire. It shriveled his epiglottis and roasted his vocal cords. It turned the conduit to his stomach into a cylinder of white-hot flame. What it did to his stomach when it arrived there was indescribable.

If Zurara had been able to prevent himself from quaffing any more, all the regal power in the world could not have overridden the reflex that would have made him choke the stream, but as soon as the flux was established the cataract became irresistible. It leapt from the vessel to which it had been too long confined into the comfort of its new host, and would not be denied its conquest.

The pain was awful, but it soon reached its limit and began to die. The few seconds for which it lasted seemed to Zurara to last a little longer than usual, but people who talk of seconds seeming to last for an eternity overestimate the power of the human imagination. Moments are not infinitely elastic; the dull truth is that, even in what one would normally think of as extraordinary circumstances, moments are not very elastic at all. So the pain went away quite quickly, if not quite quickly enough to suit King Zurara the Indestructible.

Zurara drained the cauldron to the dregs, and when he had performed this seemingly-impossible feat, he felt a great deal better than he ever had before. It was as if a raging thirst that he had always had, but had never noticed, precisely because of its everpresence, had finally been slaked.

He felt very well indeed: exactly as a man *should* feel who was ambitious to be a king of kings and a conqueror of conquerors. So confident was he that he had recovered the ability to speak, along with an unprecedented authority over his people, that he decided to make light of his ordeal. Smacking his lips, he looked around at his captains, his wives and his faithful sorcerer, then glanced casually down into the empty cauldron and said: "A very tolerable soup—the perfect accompaniment to a diet of fish."

* * * * * * *

In the days that followed, King Zurara VI grew stronger and healthier still. Several minor diseases from which he had always suffered—certain fungal infections of the skin, a little rheumatism in his joints and a persistent runny nose—cleared up completely, making him realize that he had never actually known what it was to be wholly well. He had always been a tall man, but now he grew by exactly the margin required to let him tower over all his subjects. All the petty sores and grazes accumulated about his body healed, and all his dull, unfeeling scars gave way to robust living tissue. Formerly, he had been in the habit of summoning each of his wives once a fortnight or thereabouts, but now he began to bring seven or eight from the harem every night.

Zurara set about testing the truth of Bernardo Cassingena's promises with a remarkable zest. When he cut himself with a dagger the cut closed with remarkable rapidity, leaving no scar. When he plunged the dagger more deeply into his flesh the pain was intense, but it lasted no more than a few inelastic moments before abating, and the wound healed easily enough. When he ate rotten meat, his stomach took it in without the least protest, and when he ate a cocktail of offensive vegetables, he digested them with ease. When he quaffed a full quart of strong liquor he did not feel in the least intoxicated, and when he ate a loaf of ergotized ryebread he suffered not the slightest hallucination. When he put his hand in a fire the agony was terrible, but as soon as

51

he snatched it away again the charred and blistered flesh began to repair itself; this last was not an experiment he was in any hurry to repeat, but he had to reckon it a success.

Eventually, he instructed his chief steward to bring forth a cup of wine in which a spoonful of the venom of the horny asp had been dissolved.

He drank it without the least trouble.

Then he demanded a pudding stuffed with thirteen fruits of the spineless cactus.

He cleared the dish without the least ill-effect.

Finally, he ate six blancmanges laced with the mucus of the glistening toad, and found them very good indeed, although the last one did make him burp a little.

He felt wonderful—so wonderful, in fact, that when the captain of the guard ran in to tell him that a foreign navy had arrived to blockade the harbor, having also sent a squadron of marines to scale the difficult cliffs in order to lay siege to the port on the landward side, he only laughed.

"Bring me my bow," he said. "They will soon discover what kind of hero they have come to face.

The invading army and navy had set out from the island of Calila, to the west of Almyria, despatched therefrom by King Nindowari XIV. Nindowari had heard a rumor, carried to Calila by a passing adventurer, to the effect that Zurara had lost half of his best fighting men in an expedition to the mountains, and had murdered every healer in Almyria. The first loss, Zurara's would-be rival thought, would severely weaken the island's defenses; the second would severely weaken the resolve of its citizens to withstand a siege. The adventurer had also mentioned that Zurara's men had established a new benchmark in heroism by scaling the supposedly-unscalable cliffs of Karnatan so stealthily as to evade the notice of the peninsula's ever-watchful pirates. Nindowari XIV did not want to be outshone in the twilight of the world by some third-rate poisoner, so he had decided that his own forces must emulate Zurara's by scaling the supposedly-unscalable cliffs of Almyria. They had accomplished this feat with sufficient ease to call into severe question the standards employed by the reputation-makers of Ambriocyatha.

Nindowari's brave marines made a camp, according to the accepted rules of strategy, just out of bowshot of Almyria's walls. Unfortunately, they had miscalculated the range at which the arrows of Zurara the Indestructible could find their targets, and they lost thirty men before rectifying the error.

The ships in Calila's navy did not outnumber those in Almyria's navy, but Nindowari had disposed them so that they had complete control of the bottleneck formed by the narrow strait giving entrance to Almyria's harbor. When Zurara took personal command of his flagship and sailed forth to attack them without an escort, Nindowari's captains were delighted, thinking that they had only to set up grappling lines and overrun the lone ship's decks. They sent two hundred men to board her, armed with cutlasses and cross-bows—and every last one of them was rudely cut down. No less than nine dozen were felled by a single fighting man: a giant of enormous strength, who seemed impervious to sword-cuts and arrows alike. With this colossus to lead them, Zurara's soldiers fought like men possessed, striving with all their might to emulate his magnificent example.

The flagship of Almyria's navy could not contrive actually to breach the blockade, but the battle served to demonstrate that an indefinite continuation of the stalemate might be the best that the invaders could hope to achieve. Nindowari knew—just as Zurara did—that an indefinite continuation of the blockade was not in his long-term interests; beyond Calila, further to the west, was the island of Jerena, whose king would learn soon enough that Calila's navy and marines were away from home, leaving Nindowari's own capital vulnerable to raiding-parties.

Zurara believed that once he had shown his mettle, the Calilans would simply go home. Perhaps they would have done so had they known exactly what they were up against, but they did not. Ambriocyathan expeditionary forces are as notorious for their impatience as their lack of military intelligence, and Nindowari's immediate reaction to his initial setbacks was to instruct his men to press forward more furiously than before.

The captain of the invading marines must have known, when he received this order, that it was an invitation to a massacre. He must have been tempted to lay down his arms and surrender to the port's defenders—but Almyria had the reputation in Calila of being a nation of cruel pirates, on whose dubious mercy no sane person would throw himself. The captain decided that it was a matter of do or die, and told his men as much, urging them to hurl themselves upon the enemy with all the ferocity they could muster. Fortunately for them, the defenders of the city had been celebrating Zurara's victories on land and sea with generous allowances of wine, and they had not expected such a furious attack.

Although the odds were heavily stacked against them, Calila's marines contrived to breach the outer wall with scant delay, and once they were in the streets of the port they had only to press on methodically to force Zurara's defenders back to the tower itself. Forewarned of the prowess of the mysterious bowman, they were careful to keep their shields high and not to fire any bolts themselves. As it happened, though, Zurara's excursion in his flagship had run his supply of arrows dangerously low, and without due replenishment he could not maintain his deadly fire for more than a few minutes.

All would have been well enough had the common people of Almyria remained loyal to their king and joined Zurara's soldiers in the defense of their city. Alas, they had taken due note of the king's unhealthy appetite for tax-increases as well as his extraordinary invulnerability, and they had begun to wonder whether they really wanted to be ruled by an undeposable monarch. Somehow, it seemed quite alien to their traditions. Given the relatively small number of the marauders, Zurara's forces would probably have turned the tables on them if the common people had only consented to provide adequate obstruction in the form of barricades, but no barricades went up.

To make the situation even worse, from Zurara's point of view, it now transpired that no less than six of his remote cousins—who would normally have been deadly enemies one to another—had banded together in a alliance whose like had not been seen in Almyria in a thousand years. They had raised a rebellious army of their own, which was far too small to have been effective under other circumstances, but now found a golden opportunity to carry forward its cause. When this force arrived in the rear of Calila's invaders, the captain who had commanded the attack immediately began congratulating himself on his military genius, and forged the hastiest alliance ever made on Almyrian soil.

Zurara the Invulnerable realized, a little belatedly, that as soon he had succeeded in draining the copper cauldron, his distant relatives had understood that their slender chances of future advancement had all-but-vanished. Desperate to claw back their lost opportunities, they had been driven to take steps that would normally have been unthinkable. Their conspiracy not only lent much-needed men and armaments to Calila's soldiers, but also provided valuable local knowledge. The rebels were able to tell Calila's captain how to gain entry to the underground workings beneath the tower, from which the Calilans immediately launched a sneak attack.

Even then the day might have been saved had not Zurara's beloved wives, still fearful for their unborn children and somewhat resentful of the recent increase in their marital duties, decided to add their own collective betrayal to that of the distant cousins. The numerous queens used their feminine wiles to persuade a considerable number of the tower's defenders to abandon their posts and make themselves scarce, with the result that the intruders met far less resistance than they could possibly have anticipated.

When Calila's valiant swordsmen finally began hammering at the barricaded door of Zurara's own apartment, which was the topmost in the tower, the king discovered that even his closest friend and most trusted adviser, Bernardo Cassingena, had mysteriously disappeared. All the gold and gems from Zurara's most secret treasury had vanished too—presumably spirited away by the insidious Cassingena, by means of some exceedingly cunning sorcery—thus depriving the king even of the last resort of bribery.

* * * * * * *

At first, Zurara was inclined to laugh even at such extreme circumstances as these. Was he not Zurara the Indestructible now? But the laughter died in his throat as he remembered the experiments by which he had tested his indestructibility. The dagger had hurt when he had plunged it into the flesh beneath the skin, and the fire had hurt a great deal. When he had withdrawn the dagger and snatched away his hand, the pain had faded and the wounds had healed—but what if he had not withdrawn the dagger, or taken his hand away? What if he had not been able to remove the blade from his body, or his hand from the fire?

Zurara knew that Nindowari XIV of Calila had torturers as expert as his own. He knew, too, that torturers are like all craftsmen, in that they are always enthusiastic to make new progress in their ancient trade. He realized that the torturers of Calila would be doubly glad to make his acquaintance: firstly, because he would provide an unusual challenge to their ingenuity; and secondly, because he would provide a wonderful opportunity for them to practice certain aspects of their art without using up their material.

Suddenly, death seemed the better option.

Death is a difficult eventuality for any man to face, although people who live in dangerous places at dangerous times really ought to able to take a fatalistic attitude to it—and if we who inhabit the twilight of the world cannot do that, who can? Zurara VI was, however, so wildly delighted with the notion of his own recently-acquired indestructibility that the sudden necessity of having to contrive his own death in spite of that invulnerability was neither easy to bear nor conducive to methodical planning. There was an understandable element of mad panic in his consequent actions, and more than a trace of ludicrous foolhardiness.

Zurara's apartments still contained a cupboard full of the deadliest poisons. While he was trying to think of something more effective he took every one, in the faint hope that the combination might succeed where the individual compounds would surely have failed. He was not at all surprised, however, when his stomach yielded not the slightest twinge, although he did contrive a few unsatisfactory belches.

In the meantime, a battering-ram began thudding away at the barricaded doors, as rhythmically as a drum beaten with mournful slowness at the funeral of a great man.

By the time the poisons were exhausted, Zurara had made up his mind that drowning was probably his best bet. Unfortunately, he had never bothered to install a bath in his apartments and he had already used the only drinking-water he had to wash down the poisons. Cursing his ill-luck, he wondered whether hanging might have the same effect, and soon succeeded in suspending himself by the neck from his sturdiest chandelier. Not until he had kicked away the chair did he remember Bernardo Cassingena's boast that no strangling-cord would ever be able to choke him.

So it proved; even though the cord around the king's neck became extremely painful, his mighty lungs continued to suck sufficient air through the constricted passage. In the end, it required a great deal of effort, and not a little ingenuity, to discover a way of squirming out of the inconvenient noose.

Zurara knew that he could be hurt by blades, and he now seized upon the idea that the hurt in question must be testimony to real damage done. If so, it must be the case that he could stab himself to death, if he could only be brave enough to press a stout blade as deeply as possible into his flesh. It would hurt, but was he not the man who had drunk the copper cauldron dry of its boiling contents?

As the doors to his apartment began to splinter under the relentless assault of the ram, therefore, Zurara threw himself precipitously upon his sword, taking care to ensure that the long blade went up into his belly, through his intestines and his diaphragm, all the way to his heart.

The sword-blade went in, and gave him a very great deal of pain, but it did not kill him. He began to thrash about, desperately. Alas, no matter how he contrived to twist the blade within his guts, Zurara could not make his unpunctured heart stop beating. He could not even contrive to fall unconscious.

As the disintegrating doors finally gave way, Zurara the Invulnerable was driven to the last extreme of desperation. With the sword still buried in his body and his mind maddened by the pain, he cast himself from the window of his apartment and fell upon the brutal stones that waited far beneath.

Although he smashed the greater number of his bones, twisting his limbs into improbable formations—which rendered him quite incapable of crawling away, let alone of standing up—Zurara VI was still Zurara the Indestructible. He did not die. The pain was unbearable, but he had to bear it anyway. As fast as his flesh was mangled, it healed, but the sword embedded in him continued to slice the repairing tissue every time he moved. His broken bones mended themselves too, but he was in such a state of anatomical disarray that they could not rediscover their former shapes. They knitted themselves together anyhow, not merely crookedly but in ridiculously incorrect formations and combinations.

The result of this misguided healing process was that Zurara's tendons were regenerated in an equally disordered fashion, at best awry and at worst entangled. The rejuvenated muscles lent their own reflexive efforts to the business of continuing to tear him apart from within. No matter how hard he tried to be still, he could not do it. A balance was quickly struck between destruction and revivification, but that balance secured the perpetuation of his pain, at an intensity that no ordinary man could have tolerated for a minute.

Unfortunately, Zurara the Almost Indestructible was by no means an ordinary man.

The superstitious soldiers of the invading army, certain that their arch-enemy must be possessed by some appalling demon, left the defeated king where he lay, bathed by the wrathful light of the sun by day and exposed to the baleful glare of the stars by night. He had all the time he could possibly have needed to wonder whether the most expert torturers in Calila could possibly design a worse and more ignominious fate than he had contrived for himself.

By the time Nindowari XIV, King of Calila, had landed to receive the gratitude and applause of Zurara's rebel cousins, Zurara decided that no torture devised by any merely human artist could possibly make his situation any worse. He was by no means an objective judge, of course, and might conceivably have been mistaken—but if he was, the margin of his error could not have been great.

* * * * * * *

Zurara VI lay where he had fallen for fifteen days before Nindowari and his allies finally decided that they could tolerate the sight and sound of him no longer.

Nindowari was not an unduly mild man, and he still remembered the havoc that the giant archer had wreaked upon his forces, even though they had been placed correctly according to all the rules and customs of siege-warfare, but Zurara's was a fate that not even his worst enemy could bear to watch or hear indefinitely. It was not mercy but simple self-interest that made the Calilan king call a conference of all the interested parties to debate the question of what ought to be done with the defeated tyrant. After long and very careful deliberation, Nindowari obtained the blessing of all the amicable contenders for Almyria's vacant throne to order that the living but horribly twisted body of the monstrous usurper should be set upon a pyre and burned, until every last vestige of his magical flesh had been consumed and annihilated.

Zurara VI did not scream for very long once the fire had been lit, but no one looking on could be certain that his life ended when his voice died. Nor could anyone be certain how elastic his remaining moments might have become, once he had passed into an existential phase that no other human being had entered for at least ten thousand years.

It is extremely unusual, in these unhappy days when every man knows that the sun is doomed and the Earth with it, for any story to have a happy ending, but this one does. Thanks to the fine example set by Zurara VI, the distant cousins and former inhabitants of his harem who had banded together to contrive his downfall did not begin plotting against one another as soon as he fell from his high window, nor did they start a war against their erstwhile allies from Calila. The would-be-heirs-presumptive decided, instead, that they would form a parliament—admitting even the former dancing-girls, on condition that they would no longer call themselves queens—whose future tax-increases would all be unanimously voted, a portion of which revenues would be paid to Calila as a fee for services rendered. The conference called to decide how Zurara the Almost Indestructible ought to be deprived of his unnaturally insistent life had given its members a taste for compromise, which now seemed to them the perfect accompaniment to a diet of fish.

NOBODY ELSE TO BLAME

When Bruce Halpern came home from work to discover that Marian, his younger daughter, had hanged herself from the banisters he went into the kitchen and put the kettle on.

He put a teabag into a mug decorated with his company's logo, poured boiling water over it, added a Canderel tablet, and stirred mechanically with a teaspoon for half a minute. Then he went to the fridge to get the milk.

There wasn't any. Marian had used the last of it before killing herself. She hadn't bothered to do the shopping, even though it was Thursday. Bruce supposed that he couldn't hold that against her, even though her mother had set a better example.

Actually, he'd been very careful of late not to hold anything against Marian, in the hope of avoiding this very eventuality. Obviously, it hadn't worked.

He fished the teabag out and took a sip. Black tea wasn't his sort of thing, but in the circumstances he felt that he could make an exception. Tipping it away would be a waste, even though teabags were cheap, because Canderel wasn't.

People would blame him, he knew. They had probably grown so used to it by now that it would be a reflex.

It didn't take much to train a reflex in Wokingham. The people of Wokingham were relentless conformists and creatures of habit; they had only to repeat a notion or an emotion once and it was theirs for life, automatically summoned up by any vaguely similar circumstance. Maybe it was different in the country, where the dearth of central heating meant that people were still vaguely in touch with the changing seasons, or in the inner cities, where the dearth of neighborliness meant that they weren't even vaguely in touch with one another, but Wokingham was respectable. People liked to agree with one another in Wokingham. Once they thought they knew what other people were likely to think and feel and say, it became second nature to think and feel and say the same. Bruce still understood that, in spite of everything he'd been through. He understood exactly how and why they would blame him.

He even blamed himself.

There was, after all, nobody else to blame.

He had been the first to see all three of them, but that had been a mere matter of the force of circumstance. The bathroom door was only fitted with a small brass bolt, no more than four inches long, secured by half a dozen tiny screws. Anyone could have forced the screws out of their holes by leaning on the door for a couple of minutes. It hadn't required a melodramatic shoulder-charge or a kung fu kick. But it had been a man's job. Bruce understood that perfectly well. So he had been the one who went in first while Joan and Marian stood back, their fretfulness edging towards hysteria. Most girls, when they cut their wrists, were only uttering cries for help, but not Helena. Helena had made the cuts vertically, all the way from her elbows to her wrists—although it must, of course, have been a tricky job slitting her right arm with her left hand while her left arm was already flooded with blood.

The policewoman had tried to persuade them that it might have been a cry for help gone wrong, but Bruce couldn't see that it made much difference either way. Serious suicides usually left notes, the policewoman had said, and there was nothing of that sort to be found in Helena's bedroom. Whereas Bruce had been the first one in the bathroom, Joan had had a clear run at the bedroom, and Bruce had read somewhere that the majority of suicide notes disappeared before the police began to look, because they tended to attribute blame to the people most likely to find them, but it really didn't matter either way. The blame was there, after all, floating around in search of someone to whom it might attach itself.

He was always going to be the one who found Joan, of course, because he was the only other user of the double garage. Marian had been too young to learn to drive, in Joan's opinion if not the law's, so it was always going to be Bruce, coming home tired from work, just as he had tonight, who found the garage full of fumes and the hose connecting the exhaust-pipe of the Ka to the front seat, where Joan lay, with more color in her cheeks than ever before, safe at last from the harassment of insomnia.

Joan hadn't left a note either—although it was possible that Marian had been in their bedroom before the police took a look—but she had hoovered round, emptied the laundry basket, and stocked up the fridge. It wasn't so much that she had always been a conscientious person, although she hadn't been as bad as some even when they were still in Northampton, but that living in Wokingham had increased her sensitivity to the social niceties almost to concert pitch. In Wokingham, a good mother was a mother to the end, and a good wife always kept up appearances until death or divorce brought her to the actual parting of the ways.

When he had finished his cup of tea, Bruce went up to Marian's bedroom to search for a note, but he didn't find one. He hadn't really expected to. If she'd gone first, she'd probably have left a note, because she'd probably have had the vague idea that that was what suicides were supposed to do, but because she was following an example twice set, she had taken her lead from her sister and her mother. Marian had only been four when they'd left Northampton; she was Wokingham through and through.

Bruce couldn't see that it would make much difference either way. Even if the note hadn't blamed him, everybody else would. Even if the note had gone out of its way to absolve him from blame, he'd have blamed himself.

When he came back downstairs he turned the TV on. *EastEnders* was just finishing. He hadn't realized that it was so late, although he always stayed an extra half hour at the office in the hope of missing the worst of the traffic on the A329, and he always ran into problems anyhow, even when there weren't any road-works.

There was nothing on worth watching. Eight to nine was always a lousy slot because all the channels saved their good stuff till after the watershed. Joan hadn't seemed to mind sitting through godawful vet shows and those farces in which neighbors redecorated one another's front rooms in the most ghastly fashion they could imagine, but Bruce had always found them utterly unrealistic. In Wokingham, everyone had healthy pets and no householders would ever dream of letting their neighbors take over their front rooms, or their back rooms, or their darkest, dingiest and chilliest cellars.

When the ads came on Bruce figured that he had put it off long enough, and he went to dial 999.

He wondered briefly whether he ought to cut Marian down before the ambulance arrived, so that he could pretend to have made a futile but understandable attempt to revive her, but he didn't want to touch her. Although the fact was never mentioned in polite company, suicide was a filthy business because the dead lost control of their sphincter muscles. No matter how well-scrubbed their faces were, or how rosy their cheeks, suicides always stank to high heaven.

Things like that weren't supposed to matter when it was someone you loved, but they did, and not just in Wokingham. Some things were universal.

He didn't hold it against Marian, of course. She couldn't help it, and even if she had been able to he wouldn't have held it against her. He had got into the habit lately of not holding anything against her, in the hope of avoiding this very eventuality.

Obviously, it hadn't worked.

So Bruce left Marian's body untouched, hanging in mid-air. It wouldn't make any difference to the way the ambulance men looked at him, or the police, or his neighbors, or Marian's school friends, or Joan's mother and father, or his own mother and father. They would all look at him in exactly the same way, as if they all knew exactly what everyone else was thinking and feeling and saying, and wanted to make perfectly certain that they thought and felt and said the same. They would pretend to be nice, but they wouldn't be able to sustain the illusion.

They wouldn't suspect him of foul play, because anyone could see that Marian had been dead for hours, just like Joan, and the office was full of people who could give him an alibi, but they wouldn't be able to keep up the pretence of being sympathetic, of sharing in his tragedy.

They would blame him.

Even though there were no notes at all, they would blame him.

There was nobody else to blame.

HEARTBEAT

When I found out that my heart had stopped beating my first thought was that I must be mistaken, but after twenty minutes of searching for a pulse I was convinced that there was none to be found.

Then I thought that I must be mad. I thought my senses had to be deranged, that the fault was in my head and not in my heart at all. But then I realized that there was no more rational response to such a situation than to wonder whether I might be mad. The very suspicion was secure proof of my sanity.

After that I was terrified that someone might find out. I knew that I could keep it secret for a while, but not for ever. It wasn't so much the doctor I was worried about—no, that wasn't it at all. I supposed that I could easily steer clear of doctors, unless I got knocked down by a bus or something, in which case nobody would be overly surprised to find my heart not beating. It was the thought that I'd have to be careful about getting too close to people. No more snuggling up to the wife, no more cuddling my little daughter. I couldn't take the risk that they might find out—because, out of all the people in the world, they were the two who absolutely mustn't find out. After all, if a stranger were somehow to find out, it needn't be the end of the world. He might not care, and might be perfectly happy not to tell other people, ever, what an unnatural creature was walking in their midst. And if I thought he might tell someone, I could always kill him. I'm sure I could kill a stranger, if the need arose, although I'm the most mild-mannered of men.

Perhaps, if I'd been a little less mild-mannered, it wouldn't have happened at all. More assertive men probably have more assertive hearts.

Anyhow, I took good care that nobody found out. I stopped cuddling my wife and I stopped hugging my daughter—and when the divorce came through I told myself that it was all for the best, because now they would never find out what a monster they'd been close to for all those years.

I never attempted suicide. What would have been the point?

I stayed well away from doctors. In fact, I stayed well away from anyone who might get close to me. I went to work every day, of course—that wasn't a problem. At work everyone's too busy to notice whether the man at the next desk has two heads, let alone no heartbeat.

It took me quite a while to come to terms with my condition, but I had to do it. I had to learn to love myself again. I had to recover my lost self-esteem. I made a resolution to tell myself that not having a heartbeat was nothing to be ashamed of, that in actual fact it made me very special indeed. I told myself that a man was better off without a heartbeat, because a non-beating heart could hardly be in danger from hardening arteries or coronary thrombosis. I told myself that I might well be the first of a new and better breed of men, and that, if I ever did decide to let my secret out, the scientists who studied me might be able to make a breakthrough that would free the entire human race from all the burdens of heart disease. Day after day I told myself that I was a walking miracle, a precious natural resource waiting to be discovered.

In the end, I convinced myself.

I convinced myself so thoroughly that I decided to go public. I made an appointment to see the doctor—but on the morning of the appointment, my heart started beating again.

Just like that! Years and years of pulselessness, and then: *bingo!*

Life can be so bloody unfair, sometimes.

At first, of course, I thought I might be going mad, but I knew that the suspicion itself was proof of my sanity.

I rang my ex-wife and asked her to come home, but she said no.

There's nothing left, it seems, but to walk down to the main road and step out in front of a bus. I don't suppose anyone will ever understand—but at least they'll never know that anything was ever amiss with my heart.

UPON THE GALLOWS-TREE

Hanging here, hanging here, upon the gallows-tree, my lumpen legs swaying in the bitter wind—I thirst! O how I thirst! Half way to hell should I be by now, deep in the dark abyss beneath the world...but instead I am becalmed, held fast to my leaden corse, which hangs upon the tree, colder than living flesh could ever be....

* * * * * * *

Why? Why am I not in hell?

Is that the church bell sounding the hour? What hour? How long has it been, since the breath was squeezed from my throat, and the life from my flesh?

Nine...ten...eleven! It lacks an hour of midnight, curse the clawing, bitter wind...it lacks an hour of midnight, when they will come to take my body down, and cut it into quarters, and take my heart to the crossroads, lest my spirit should reawaken in the prison of my flesh, and fly upon the breezes of the night in search of blood....

Once I cursed their stupid superstitions and their feeble magic, but now...do they have the right of it, Dark Lord? Must I haunt my own dead flesh until they set me free, and banish me forever?

Perhaps so. After all, my soul is here, not fallen into the dark abyss, not taken into any of the seven hells, not claimed as yet by the Dark Lord who was and is my master....

Am I here, as they would certainly believe, so that I might join the legion of the undead? If so, they will surely see to it that I do not.

What will it feel like, I wonder, when they cut me in quarters and steal my heart away? Shall I die twice for all those sins they charged me with? Have I one more measure of earthly suffering to take, ere I go to the eternal flames?

And will *he* come, with all the rest, to keep one last tryst before his wedding day, to see me damned as well as killed? Is he not finished with me yet?

He will come. Most certainly, he will come—but not as eagerly as once he came, for the animal spirits which stir in him now are guilt and terror and unease, not lustful fever.

Perhaps I have one wish still owed to me...perhaps the Dark Lord owes me that, for all the pain I have suffered on his behalf...perhaps this one last meeting is a kind of gift, that I may have one last sight and one last touch...perhaps...although the gift I ought to crave is not the sight or touch of him, but to see him suffer as he made me suffer. If there is hope left to me now, it should be the hope that there is some fate which binds our souls together...that he might destined to share with me that fall into the dark abyss...that there is mercy in the world after all, which will make us one for all eternity...in Hell!

Perhaps....

Dark Lord, is there no end to doubts and dreams? Is that the truth of hell? Are the rumors of fire and torment naught but a jest, whispered to the ears of men and mages by bothersome spirits? Is this hell? Is hell not knowing what we are or why...for all eternity?

Dark Lord, how I thirst!

Death is no release—that much I know for sure. As my cold, cold flesh receives the bitter kiss of the wind while I swing beneath the gallows-tree, I know one thing for certain: death is no friend to my kind. I freeze but cannot shiver; I thirst but cannot drink; I languish in uncertainty, and have no knowledge.

Where, oh where, is my reward for the service that I did thee? What use am I now upon the earth, Dark Lord, that you refuse me my appointed place in hell?

Why am I here, alone?

Or am I not alone...?

70

* * * * * * *

Beneath the gallows-tree, shadowed there, shadowed from the starlight, there is a well of darkness which I took for the lip of the abyss. Someone is there: still, stiff, silent, but ne'ertheless there. I cannot see him with my dead and ruined eyes, but he is there.

I wish it might be *him*, but it is not...indeed it is not.

Ned Teach, the crofter's son, is here, and only the gods know why. Did he love me, like the others? I dare say he did. Who could not love me, when I had the glamour in my eyes and the bloom of youth upon my cheeks, and the perfume in my hair?

They all loved me...but only Ned Teach is here, squatting on the ground beside the gallows-tree. Has he not seen that they have shorn my sleek black locks, and put the scorching-iron to my luminous cheeks, and lashed the glamour from me? Was he not there when they strung me up, lightly, so that I might dance the more ere the life was choked from me...? *Dark Lord, how I thirst*! Did he not hear the chattering priests imploring the better gods for aid, begging them to hurl my soul into the blackest pit which eternity has to spare?

What business has he with me now?

I am dead, after all, and my soul should be in hell....

Perhaps he is sick with memory, molested by regret. If he had ever shared my bed—once only would surely have sufficed—he'd have turned away with all the rest when the hangman called out his joyous news: "The witch is dead! The witch is dead!" But I had no time for the likes of him...and now, perchance, he has lost his senses in dreams of might-have-been.

How stupid men must be, to be so stricken with illusion! And yet...I've seen pretty girls keep vigil beneath this very tree, for ugly cutpurses and dour highwaymen...

But not on such a night as this!

Perhaps he was ordered to sit and watch, to keep me safe until they came with their binding spells. Perhaps....

How I thirst with that harsh and hempen cord about my throat! Who'd have thought that a corse could feel so cold!

Why? Why am I not in hell?

* * * * * * *

"Ned...Ned Teach...canst hear me, Ned Teach?"

He turns; I have a voice! My tongue is stiff and my throat is tight, but I may whisper on the wind!

I have a phantom's presence: a phantom's voice; a phantom's sight.

I see him well enough, although the night is dark and he is shadowed from the starlight by the boughs of the murderous tree. Though he is but a shadow among shadows I see him clear. He stares at me, not believing his ears. He cannot believe that I spoke...and why should he, since my lips are black and cracked and dry?

The marvel is that he does not run. He stares, but he does not run.

It is easy enough to speak, easy enough to be heard—but what should I say to him?

"Ned...Ned, I thirst! Wilt fetch me water, Ned? Wilt do that for a witch? Wilt give me one last sip of water from the brook, ere my soul takes ship for the shores of hell?"

His eyes are full of fear; were his soul naked, 'twould be shivering in terror. But he does not run.

Brave lad, he does not run!

"Morwen?" he whispers. It was my name, though not my true name. He seems to speak it with love—can I blame him, then, for being slow of wit? Is this why I am here? Am I here to keep a soul's tryst with poor Ned Teach?

"I thirst, Ned. Fetch me water from the brook. Put it to my lips, dear Ned."

He should refuse. Even though he will not run, he should refuse. He should know me for the evil spirit which I surely am; he should call me witch and curse me. But he looks at me so strangely....

He stands up, and lifts his hands, flexing the impotent fingers. I believe I know what is in his mind. His first thought, on discovering that I have a voice, is to bring me down, to loosen the rope about my neck...he thinks to bring me back to life! Poor Ned...he cannot begin to know what is happening or why. But he has no knife with him. All he has is a cudgel, which he keeps by his side.

A cudgel! Is he mad enough to appoint himself my guardian, despite that I am dead?"

"Take me not down, Ned. Let me stay where I am...but fetch me water from the brook, Ned, for I thirst. *I thirst!*"

Dark Lord, why am I here? Why is this stupid youth content to do the bidding of the damned?

He goes bravely and obediently to the brook, and cups his great hands to take up water. He's a big lad, nearly twice the size of dainty Donal, though Donal always wears a blade, and takes a pair of handsome hunting dogs whene'er he goes abroad. The water must be near to freezing...it must hurt his hands, but he cups them so carefully, and carries the water up the slope, to me.

My feet are half a yard from the ground, but Ned's a tall lad. At full stretch, even with his hands cupped, he can reach my lips...and he does. His hands are steady as earthenware mugs...and they are not shy of my black and shriveled lips....

Dark Lord, the water is so cold! What would I not give for hot mulled wine, or brandy warmed before a roaring fire?

Is this what hell is, to have all the longings of the living flesh, and yet be impotent to salve the least of them? Have I fallen after all to my appointed place? Is this the bottom of the vast abyss, and not the earth at all? Is my attendant demon made in the image of poor Ned Teach, to mock me with absurdity?

If what men say of hell is true, I'll be warm soon enough...at the bottom of that dark abyss, a promised fire awaits me...but whatever else I may doubt, I cannot doubt that I am cold....

He is waiting: bravely, stupidly, madly waiting!

"Thanks, Ned...a thousand thanks...."

A curse upon this necklace, which will not let me swallow. I thirst, Dark Lord how I thirst...but I have the taste upon my tongue.

I have the taste, and cannot be in hell. Ghost I may be, or prentice vampire, or spirit stranded 'twixt earth and the eternal, but I have the taste of water on my poor stiff tongue, and that is mercy of a kind. Whatever god did this for me, I thank.

He spills the remaining water on the ground, and wipes his hands on his jerkin. His eyes are upon my ruined face: his horrified, worshipful eyes. Ned, I should have spared a night for thee!

Had I but known....

I must repay his kindness. Even a witch acknowledges a debt.

"Go now. Thanks, Ned—but go now. There's nothing for thee here...naught but grief and pain. They cannot hurt me more, no matter what they do. Go, before the bell tolls twelve."

He does not speak at once, and when he does, he simply says: "Art thou living still?"

I cannot call him fool, for I do not understand myself.

"Nay Ned, not living. Canst see my dead lips move? Canst hear my still heart beating? The worms are at work within my flesh...but I'm a witch. I'm a witch, confessed, convicted and condemned. I'm a witch, and my hell-bound soul hath some score to settle before it sails upon that dank and dour wind which blows the phantoms of the dead to their predestined ends."

The sound of my phantom voice should shrivel his courage and turn his legs to jelly. He should run away—but he stays.

"They mean to take thee down," he says, as though I might not know it. "They mean to quarter thee, an' burn thy bits...all save the heart, which they will bury beneath the crossroads, ne'er to know peace...but I will not believe that thou'rt a witch. Thou'rt innocent—that I know! They have killed thee, but they shall not keep thy soul from heaven— that I have sworn."

Innocent! Can he really think me innocent? Can he really think that my soul might be saved, for *peace*? Can he really think that he—or anyone—might do it?

Poor fool!

"I'm a witch, Ned—confessed, convicted and condemned."

He will not look away. I am horrible in death, but he will not look away. He is sick with memory...maddened by the knowledge of what I was.

"We are all witches," he tells me, bleakly. "When they flay the skin from our backs and put the irons to our flesh, we cannot help but confess and be condemned; torture makes witches of us all. What did they charge thee with, save for tempting men to sin? They have blamed every death in the district upon thee, as though sickness never claimed a life before thy coming! They have blamed thee for the harshness of the winter, as if the wind from the north has naught to do but hasten to your call! As for tempting men to sin...rather they should blind themselves, ere they banish beauty from the world."

Who would have thought that a crofter's son could find such words? And yet, he is all the more a fool for finding them. What does he think he can do, when they come to take my heart? What can it possibly matter, what they do to me now?

What can I say to him, to make him go?

"I dare say they've hanged their share of innocents in times past, Ned...but this was no mistake. I tell thee now, Ned, and tell thee true...I'm a witch, and always was."

I can see, even as I say it, that it will do no good. The truth will not move him; I should have found a lie to wake his disgust.

"They have made thee believe it," says the stubborn lad. "They have made thee mad with their questions and curses, their whips and their burning irons. I tell thee now, thou'rt not bound for any of the seven hells, nor shall they steal thy heart to keep thee from thy rest. Ned Teach will see to that."

What a lunatic he is! How well I tempted him, and did not even know it! He thinks they have maddened me, but I have only maddened him, and that without ever trying to, or even deigning to notice him. Dark Lord, I beg thee, send him home to sleep! One night is surely all he needs to repair his scattered senses. What need hast thou of the likes of him?

"Go, Ned. I implore thee, go!"

"Dost want more water?" he says.

I thirst. Dark Lord, how I thirst!

Perhaps it is not water that I crave.

"Nay, Ned. It is not water that I crave, but blood—the blood of little children, of innocents, of noblemen, of priests. I am undead, and crave the milk of the undead. Wilt give me blood, Ned? Wilt do that for me?"

He looks up into my dead and glaring eyes, as though the glamour were still in them.

"Had I a knife," he says, "I would cut the heel of my hand for thee. But I have not. Be still, I beg thee. I will answer for thy safety, body and soul. If thou'rt innocent, as I believe, I'll save thy heart for heaven!"

It is not hearts which go to heaven, but souls—and not the souls of witches. My heart is dead and useless, and might as well be buried at the crossroads as elsewhere. Let them cut me up and burn my quarters—what difference can it make to a hell-bound soul?

They are coming. I can see the light of their torches in the distance. I have one last chance to save the fool—one last chance to spare him. Surely that is why I am here, and not in the depths of the abyss.

"Let them do what they have to do, Ned. I command thee, let them have their way. They cannot be prevented, and they are right—were I left unquartered, and my heart unburied, I would return as a vampire to suck the blood of their children.

I can almost believe it—Dark Lord how I thirst!

He looks at me uncertainly...he does not believe me. Perhaps he thinks I am some demon, pretending to be the Morwen that he loved...or imagines that he loved. But I have sown the seeds of doubt. Surely he will stand aside, and let them have their way.

* * * * * * *

Beneath the gallows-tree Ned stands; he stands his ground while the rest of them approach. Lord Donal is at their head, with his two sleek hounds straining at the leash.

"Here already, Ned!" cries Donal. "Cut her down, lad, cut her down! We've work to do, if her witchcraft's to be finished forever."

76

Ned Teach makes no move at all; he stands like a statue with his cudgel in his hand, half as huge again as slender Donal, and bigger than any of the others...but they are thirty strong, and he's alone, save only for a thirsty ghost.

Donal stops, ten feet away from Ned, holding hard to his dogs.

"What's up, Ned?" he says, softly. "Her body must be divided and burnt, and her heart buried at the crossroads, else she'll haunt the night as a demon bloodsucker. Dost not know the law?"

"Thou shalt not have her," says Ned.

Donal smiles, and in his smile I see that he understands—perhaps better than I—what madness has brought Ned here.

"Why not?" says the young lord, lightly. "What use is she now, to anyone?"

"Thou shalt not have her," says Ned, again.

Donal's smile turns into a frown, as I have seen it turn half a hundred times before. Lord Donal does not like to be thwarted, even in the least of his many whims, and likes it least of all when there are thirty men at his back.

"Stand aside!" says the chief of the priests, raising his staff. "What must be done must be done."

Does it matter whether it is done or not? I do not know—how can he? We have no guides but rite and rumor, custom and conviction. My magic was stronger than his while I lived, and I have better proof than he could ever find that the spirit of a witch survives her death...but what, in the end, does it matter?

I have a phantom's sight and a phantom's voice. Have I, I cannot help but wonder, a phantom's strength? What power have I to interfere in this contest? Dark Lord, how cold it is, and *how I thirst!*

"Ned," says Donal, not so lightly now, "I command thee do as thou art bid. As thy liege-lord, I demand it. We must cut the witch down, and lay her soul properly to rest."

To rest! If that were so, how I might yearn to be quartered and split!

"Leave her be," says Ned.

"He is mad!" says the priest—and must be right. If I am
what they say I am, then they must do what they intend; if I
am not, whatever they do cannot hurt me. He is mad!

"She has cast a spell on thee," says Donal, sternly.
"Dead she is, but her power yet remains. Thou art bewitched,
Ned Teach—she means to use thee, that her foul black soul
might cleave to the earth and harry the living. Some demon
has been sent from Hell to possess thee, and turn thy hand
against thine own kind. For the love of all the good gods,
Ned, stand aside!"

"She ne'er cast a spell on anyone," says poor deluded
Ned—has the Dark Lord really sent some minion to seize
him for my sake? "She became an inconvenient mistress
when my liege-lord sought to marry, and so my liege-lord
branded her a witch, and gave her to the torturers that she
might be forced to condemn herself. I should have stood
forth then and said what I believed, but I was too slow of
wit. 'Twas not until I knew the measure of my grief that I
knew what I must do, but I know it now. Thou shalt not have
her!"

Donal is surely right—this is some demon sent to possess poor Ned. How else would a man be brought to condemn himself for the sake of a cold and ruined corse?

Donal curses, and lets loose his dogs, both at the same
time. He points to Ned and urges them forward. They do not
hesitate; it is not the first time they have been sent to pull
down human prey.

Jaws agape they hurl themselves at Ned, one at the
throat and the other at his ankles—but he does not give way.
His left arm reaches out, and his huge hand grasps the loose
fur at the first hound's throat, lifting the beast into mid-air.
His right hand brings the cudgel down upon the skull of the
second hound, which drops dead at his feet. The other, with
that choking hand at its throat, cannot cry out, but it thrashes
madly with its hind feet while the life is squeezed out of it,
as cruelly as the life was squeezed from me.

When Ned throws down the second beast Donal is already coming forward, sword in hand. Ned's cudgel is only
half as long as the blade, and Ned is but a commoner, never
schooled to fence—even so, when the blade licks out at his

breast, Ned catches the flat of it with his wooden stave, and turns it easily aside. The advantage now is to him, could he only go forward to take the attack to the lighter man...but still he does not move an inch.

Donal dances back, collects his wits, and comes forward again, this time more stealthily. He moves with the grace of youth and schooling—he always did, e'er as easy in the arts of love as in the arts of war. He has a handsome face, prettier by far than coarse-featured Ned's...I loved him once, ere I ever thought to put a spell on him...would that the spell had been stronger!

The point of the sword strikes home this time, but Donal is at full stretch—he has not dared to throw himself forward with all his strength. He draws blood, but the wound is not deep. Indeed, as the young lord moves back there is fear in his face.

"Stand aside, Ned!" he says. "I do not want to run thee through. Thou canst not stand against us all."

"Stand back thyself!" says Ned. "Or come as thick and fast as thou durst—I can crack a man's skull as easily as a dog's."

Donal looks about him, at the watching crowd. Thirty strong they may be, but a dozen are old and among the rest there is none to be seen who seems over-anxious to lead a charge. 'Tis true that my brave defender cannot stand against them all—but 'tis equally true that the first who comes against him will likely have his skull caved in. As Donal looks to them for aid, so they look back to him—for is he not their liege-lord, and has he not the sword in his hand? His dongs were bold enough to go before him to the fight, but these are not dogs.

Donal's eyes flare with wrath, and his gaze is drawn to Ned's breast, where blood is oozing from the cut he made. The sight of it inspires him, and he comes again, flashing his blade with all his might and all his art. His thrust is a feint, and Ned's attempt to turn it with the cudgel comes to naught. Donal pivots on his heel, sways and comes again, inside the bigger man's defensive blow. The blade strikes home again, and this time Donal does not dance away—he presses on with all his might, to run his victim through.

It is as though Ned's massive body sucks in the blade and swallows it entire. There is no great gout of blood, and Ned does not fold at the waist or fall to the earth. Instead, as though it had waited for exactly such a move, his great left hand seizes Donal by the throat as it had seized the dog.

Donal, though most certainly taken by surprise, has too much sense to let go the sword—but when he tries to yank the blade from side to side, it will not budge. The weapon is stuck hard within the big man's body, and cannot be forced to slice through his lights.

Ned squeezes, and his grip is merciless.

Donal would surely be screaming, were he able, but he has no voice.

Then, at last, Ned moves. He lifts Lord Donal's feet well clear of the ground, and he turns, with the sword still in him. He turns his back to the thirty men who might at any moment strike him down, and he holds Lord Donal out to my dangling corse, like some dainty morsel brought to the feast.

Ned drops the cudgel, and puts his right hand to his breast, where the sword-hilt stands. He does not try to draw the blade from his flesh, but simply lets the sluggish blood stain his fingers. Then he lifts his hand, and holds it out to my dead lips.

"Drink, Morwen," he whispers. "Drink, if this is thy need."

Donal is not yet dead. I can see his staring eyes, looking into mine. And I can see that he sees—*he sees me*! Phantom sight I have, and phantom form for those who've the knack to see such phantoms. I cannot see my own ghostly form, but I reach out anyhow with invisible fingers, and feel the softness of his cheek against them.

"Oh my love!" I say to him, as softly as I ever whispered in his dainty ear. "Was it really such an evil spell I cast? Could thou not have loved me still, betrothed or no...married or no...I could have made thee a widower very soon, were that thy true desire. Why was my magic not enough for thee?"

I could forgive him, even now, were there the least hint of remorse in his frightened eyes...but there is not. His soul is full of an agonizing fear, which is the fear of death...and something more....

And something more!

Why, poor foolish Ned has the truth of it, after all! Donal never knew, until this very moment, what I was and what I am. He never believed! He condemned me as a witch without ever knowing that in truth I *was* a witch, merely because I had become an inconvenient mistress....

Now he knows. Now he sees. Now he understands!

They come to strike Ned down now, hitting him from behind with all the force they can muster, like the cowards that they are. But they are too late. Lord Donal's throat is crushed, and though he writhes upon the ground for three full minutes when they pull him free, he cannot draw another breath.

I can still feel the softness of his cheek. My body hangs still upon the gallows-tree, but I am not bound by the limits of its cold, cold flesh. I have no form that I can see, but I can feel the silken skin of his cheek upon my phantom lips.

Oh, my love! Would that the Dark Lord had given me magic enough to make you mine forever!

Donal is dying...dying beneath the gallows-tree.

So is poor Ned Teach, beaten down by a dozen men, pummeled and kicked and cudgeled, with that deadly blade still stiff and sharp inside him.

I know now that no demon possessed Ned Teach, save the madness of my enchantment, which I never knowingly put upon him. 'Tis a sad fate to be a witch, and to see the best-cast spells go awkwardly awry, while those I never sought to cast bring those I never sought to hurt to dire destruction. Has his soul quit his body yet? Might I have seen it fly away had I spared a glance from poor pale Donal's agony? They say there is a special hell, with torments worse than all the rest, for those who slay their liege-lords.

The light is fading from Lord Donal's eyes—where, oh where will *his* soul go, I cannot help but wonder, now that he understands that the crime he sought to do was no crime at all?

Is that his soul I see, behind his eyes? Is that his fragile phantom, struggling free from the prison of his flesh? Is that, perhaps, what he saw when he looked into my poor dead eyes? I cannot think so, for this is something delicate and numinous and silvery, which has no eye to see or tongue to speak, nor anything human in it at all—it is like a little lake of light...and when I reach out with my ghostly, invisible hands to touch it, it is curiously warm....

See! I can cup it in my fingers, and hold it, despite that it is not solid at all....

It is the stuff of Heaven! *This* is virtue and nobility, naked and unclad...pure spirit...and yet a murdered witch can hold it in her phantom hands, and lift it to her lips for one last kiss....

Dark Lord, how I thirst!

* * * * * * *

The husk that I once was is cut in quarters now, and the wreckage of my pretty flesh is burnt—save only for my heart, which is buried deep beneath the crossroads, not alone.

I am not fallen into the dark abyss, nor delivered into any of the seven hells whose natures the priests are ever anxious to describe. What the future may hold I cannot tell, but the earth around me swathes me like a great dark cloak, and I am no longer cold. Nor shall I ever ride by night upon the angry wind, to hunt the blood of little children and faithless wives, for I have slaked my thirst....

Whether poor Ned Teach has found such rest as this I cannot tell, but I know full well that my dead and handsome lover ne'er won the Heaven that he sought...*for I have slaked, have slaked, have slaked my horrid thirst....*

THE DEVIL'S MEN

When they came to apprehend him he knew that it must be a mistake, and told them so: that he was naught but a schoolmaster, and a respectable man, and that his name was not Fian at all but only John Cunningham, and that he did not know Geillis Duncan—who had named him a witch—at all. When they threw him into prison he was certain in his own mind that they would quickly discover their mistake and release him.

When rumor was carried to him that the king himself had taken an interest in those whom Geillis Duncan had accused he felt certain that justice would soon be done and that all would be well. When further rumor reached him that one Agnes Thompson had told the king that Satan himself had appeared at North Berwick kirk, in order to instruct the witches gathered there to make stormy mischief against the king, he declared that the king could not possibly believe such mad fancies. Even when they told him, gloatingly, that the king himself had said as much, but that Agnes Thompson had then offered firm proof, he could not credit it.

"The witch took the king aside," his jailer explained, "and whispered in his ear the very words which passed between his majesty and his queen on the night of their marriage. The king swore by the living God that all the devils in hell could not have discovered as much."

"Nor could they," he replied, contemptuously. "But a king is surrounded by servants even on his wedding night, expert eavesdroppers all; they might easily do what no demon ever could."

"But the king's servants are very loyal," the jailer told him, "for this same witch confessed that she had been intimately acquainted with one of them, John Kerr, and had tried to persuade him to obtain an item of the king's linen, which she might anoint with the venom of a toad, thus to place a curse—and he would not do it!"

"Would that Master Kerr had kept such discretion with his flapping tongue," he remarked, not knowing how utterly the irony would be lost.

* * * * * * *

First of all, they questioned him as they had earlier questioned Geillis Duncan, by knotting a rope tight about his head and wrenching it back and forth, tearing the skin from his temples.

He gave them no answer save to protest his innocence of all wrongdoing.

After that they talked to him softly and persuasively, telling him that he must see how things would go henceforth, and that he ought to save himself further agony by a confession that would justify their efforts.

Still he could not believe that an innocent and respectable man could be condemned on the word of a tortured servant, and he refused.

Then they put his feet into the iron boots, and struck the wedges three times with a sledgehammer, the awful agony of which rendered him unconscious.

When they had brought him round they told him that he must see by now how things were, and explained again that once they had begun such treatment they could not possibly end it without obtaining the result which they desired. Because he was a man and not a hagwife, they said, and a man of good standing too, they would make a compromise with him. They would say, if he consented, that he had not spoken before because his tongue had been held fast to his palate by two great pins put there by the magic of the old hags, thus making him as much a victim as a criminal. Nor would they require him to confess that he had tried to kill the king by magic, but only that he was guilty of the acts specified in the rumor that was commonly told against him, which everyone had heard.

"What is it that everyone has heard?" he wailed, quite mystified.

"That you required one of your scholars to obtain hair from his sister's private parts," they said, "in order that you might possess the gentlewoman by magic, having earlier cursed her husband so that he was overtaken by a fit in the king's presence. When the mother of the gentlewoman, seeing what was afoot, plucked hairs from the udder of a heifer and told the scholar to bring them to you instead, the heifer came to the door of the school, and followed you therefrom to church, revealing to the world your pact with Satan."

He began to understand, then, what must have happened. Some aggrieved schoolboy had invented a wild tale, so amusing that it had been repeated and repeated, eventually passing for news instead of malice, traveling so fast and so far that Geillis Duncan, asked to name witches, had drawn on it for inspiration. But he understood also that what his inquisitors said to him was true, and that matters had now developed to the point that such ludicrous tales could no longer be seen for what they really were.

The master of the prison promised him that if he confessed to the lesser crime, he might be excused as an unlucky dupe of those witches who had confessed to far more heinous crimes—but that if he did not, the wedges placed in his iron clogs would be driven further and further, until his feet were crushed to pulp.

He signed the paper that they offered him, admitting the crime laid against him by rumor and conceding that he had been seduced by Satan—but declaring withal that he now renounced Satan and all his wicked works, and would henceforth lead the blameless life of a pious Christian.

That night, he was released from the prison and he returned to Saltpans, where he lived and worked.

* * * * * * *

The next day, they came for him again, and brought him back to his cell. The jailer explained to him that the king's men had waxed indignant when told of his release by the master of the prison, and had ordered that it be put about that he had escaped, for they were not prepared to have any man set free who had been implicated in the affairs said to have taken place at North Berwick Kirk.

"I was never at North Berwick Kirk!" he protested. "Nor were those who claim that they were, for their tales are all wild fantasy!"

"It matters not," the jailer said. "They are determined to place you there, and they will do whatever may be necessary to make you say so."

"God will not allow it!" he said, although he knew in his heart that if God were disposed to prevent such things the world would be a very different place.

On the next day they twisted his fingernails with pincers, and drove needles under them, and finally tore them away, asking him all the while to confess that he had been won back to Satan's cause after signing the paper they had first given him, and that Satan had in consequence set him free.

He would not own to it, saying over and over again that *they* were the Devil's men, and that *their* work as the Devil's work, and that they knew full well that they themselves had set him free—but the greater his wrath became against them, the greater theirs became against him.

They brought out the boots again, and this time did not hesitate to drive the wedges in to their extremest limit, crushing the flesh and the bones within the flesh until the blood and the marrow flooded out.

They demanded, meanwhile, that he confess that he had betrayed their kindness by returning to the Devil's cause after his apparent repentance—but he would not do that, insisting that they had betrayed him, and that no power on earth could make him declare that he had been fairly treated, and that his first confession had been wrung from him by means of lies and false promises of exactly the kind that Satan might design.

When there was no more that could be done to his hands or feet the master of the prison accepted that no confession would be forthcoming, and berated him for his stubbornness.

"We cannot let you make liars of us," the master said, "and you are exceedingly unkind to try. If you were a good

Christian, and a loyal subject of your king, you would understand that the king's peace and the Almighty's authority
must be preserved at all costs, against all manner of treasons.
You should do your part, as even the witches Geillis Duncan
and Agnes Thompson consented to do. What manner of man
are you, to be so resolute in foolishness?"

Had he been capable of clear speech, he would have answered, but the pain was too great. Indeed, the pain was so
great as almost to deny him further thought—but while he
lay sleepless all night on the cold stone floor of his cell, trying with all his might not to move a muscle lest he destroy
his mind with pain, he made the most strenuous efforts to
understand exactly what had been done to him, so that he
might make his reply when the occasion presented itself
again. He knew now that he was doomed to die, and that the
only consolation or achievement left to him would be to tell
the truth to anyone who might hear him.

Item by item, harried all the while by terrible pains, he
put together his indictment:

*There are no witches save those made by malicious ru-
mor and vicious torture. Were men not so ready to listen to
malicious rumors, and repeat them laughing, there would be
no accusations of witchcraft. Were men not so ready to take
savage delight in torture, there would be no proof of it.*

You, not I, are the Devil's men.

*Yet the danger is that in treating their fellows thus—in
being led by malice and tyranny to call their fellows servants
of Satan—men will soon create witches where none exist:
witches who will say, "if these are men of God, then Satan
must be far the better master," and will gladly embrace any
and all causes which set themselves against cruel authority.
For this reason, all who are complicit in doing to any man
what has been done to me are doing the work of Satan, re-
cruiting armies to his cause.*

You, in sober truth, are the Devil's men.

*And who shall say that the witches thus created have not
justice on their side? For who among the servants of God,
the servants of the king and the servants of the law, have
ever endured what witches are forced to endure in the cause*

of preserving innocence? We who are called witches are surely to be reckoned martyrs, as true to our cause as any listed in the Golden Legend.

You, not we, are the Devil's men.

By the treatment you meet out to us, you damn yourselves; in using us as scapegoats you increase the burden of your sin.

You, and you alone, are the Devil's men.

Before his ordeal, it would have been easy enough for him to formulate a speech like that; he was, after all, a schoolmaster. As things were, it was a very remarkable achievement.

* * * * * * *

The next day, they took him to be burned on Castle Hill in Edinburgh—but first they strangled him, so that he would not be able to speak to anyone about what had been done to him and why. Then they caused his story to be published, offering the extent of the tortures he had endured without confessing as firm proof of his commitment to Satan, and representing the fact that they had strangled him before putting him into the fire as incontrovertible evidence of their merciful disposition.

THE ELIXIR OF YOUTH

Frederic Paschel, a wine merchant who lived in the town of Sylah in the valley of the river Dordogne, was left a widower when his two sons, Gilbert and Benedict, were in their infancy. The younger son, Benedict, was as dutiful as any father could ever have desired; he was amiable and pliable, ready and willing to be molded in the image of his sire as a respectable tradesman. Gilbert, on the other hand, was surly and rebellious; he swore that he would do anything in the world to spare himself the necessity of following in his father's footsteps.

When asked what he intended to do instead of working in the family business, Gilbert declared his intention of becoming a knight of the realm in the entourage of the Duc de Romanin, whose domain included Sylah and three other small towns as well as thirty farms, a dozen vineyards and a forest that provided some of the best hunting in southern Aquitania. Frederic laughed when he heard this, saying that the most Gilbert could ever hope for was to be taken into the Duc's service as a common man-at-arms—and even that privilege would be withheld at Frederic's request, because Lord de Romanin was one of the winery's best customers.

Gilbert flew into a temper then. He said that if his prospects of following the best traditions of chivalry were to be thwarted by his father's petty spite, he would become an adventurer, hunting for treasure in Arabia and the dark heart of Africa. That declaration made Frederic laugh even louder— with the result that Gilbert left home on his seventeenth birthday, swearing that he would not return until he acquired such immense wealth that Frederic Paschel would seem a pauper by comparison.

Ten years passed while nothing was heard in Sylah of Gilbert Paschel. Frederic's business flourished, but not to the extent that he grew conspicuously richer. The number of barrels that his laborers filled increased year by year, but the price he obtained for each barrel did not increase at all. His wealth grew slowly, moderated by the increased wages he had to pay the laborers, but he was able to make some economies in the latter respect as Benedict grew older and stronger.

Unfortunately, Benedict became rather resentful of the fact that he was expected to work harder and harder as each year passed in order to allow his father to spend less on hired labor. While the vintage was brought in he had to work from dawn till dusk in the winery, and he continued to work long hours while the grapes were trodden and the wine fermented. He had to take more turns than any of the hired men in guarding the vats until the wine was ready for casking, and when the barrels had all been filled he had to load them on the carts that carried them to Frederic's customers in the neighboring towns. He was sometimes allowed to accompany his father on the most important deliveries, including excursions to the Château de Romanin, but he always had to take longer turns than his father driving the cart, and he was the one who had to carry the barrels down to the cellars while Frederic enjoyed the fruits of his customers' hospitality.

"You work me like a donkey so that you do not have to pay wages to hirelings," Benedict complained, when they returned from one such trip, "but I see nothing of the money you save. By rights, the greater portion of it should be mine."

"The money I save on wages goes to buy more grapes and better equipment," his father explained. "It is reinvested in the business so that the business will continue to expand. One day, it will all be yours, so the money you do not receive now will benefit you in the future."

"That is all very well," Benedict said, "but in the meantime, I am dressed as poorly as any common laborer, and I work even harder for longer hours. I would prefer to have the money now, so that I might dress in the manner appropriate to an Aquitanian gentleman, and entertain myself as a gen-

90

tleman does instead of rising at dawn every day and working long into the night."

"That would be a foolish way to conduct yourself, my son," Frederic told him, severely. "Money invested reaps greater rewards; money spent is gone forever. You are young, and you have a long life ahead of you. Don't be envious of the young popinjays who parade themselves about the château and its gardens, or the wastrels who hang about in the taverns; the former will spend their inheritances soon enough, and the latter will end up bearing spears and longbows in the Lord's troop. You will have a comfortable home and a life of ease."

"It is because I am young that I want to make more of myself," Benedict countered. "How shall I enjoy a life of ease when I am old and my appetites are blunted?"

"I am growing old myself," Frederic pointed out.

"My point, exactly," Benedict murmured—but he waited until his father was out of earshot, because he was a dutiful son, long accustomed to yielding to the pressure of Frederic's will.

Benedict's duties grew more varied by degrees as well as more extensive. In addition to filling and loading the barrels, he was gradually entrusted with the delicate operations required to bring the wines to perfection in their vats and prepare them for casking—with the result that the long shifts he worked standing guard over the vats became even more demanding. He often had to work around the clock, sleeping for short periods in the loft above the winery rather than returning to the house where his father was now able to spend more and more of his own time.

"I am growing old," Frederic told him, when Benedict complained again. "I need more rest than I did when I was young. You will be able to set your own hours soon enough, and hire men to do your work for you, if that is what you wish."

"Sometimes," Benedict replied, "I wish that I had gone with my brother to seek my fortune in foreign lands. I am certain that he has had a much more interesting life than mine."

"Ha!" said Frederic. "The ingrate will likely be dead by now, and if he is not dead he will certainly be utterly wretched. There are no treasures to be found in Arabia and the lands beyond the Sahara, no matter what traveler's tales may say. All travelers are liars."

It turned out, however, that Gilbert was not dead—although he did seem conspicuously wretched when he suddenly reappeared, at the dead of night, in the winery where Benedict was working late, patiently overseeing a vat of rich red wine that was just approaching the condition in which it would require to be casked.

"Hello, little brother," Gilbert said, as he laid down his meager pack. He sat down on a stool and took off his worn-out sandals so that he could inspect the sores on his feet, adding: "Still the dutiful son, I see, hard at work on our father's behalf."

"I am delighted to see you, brother," Benedict replied—politely enough, although a bystander might have thought it odd that he did not rush to embrace a brother he had not seen for ten years. "I presume, judging by your rags, that you have not found the treasure that you sought."

"As a matter of fact," Gilbert said, "I did."

"Then it must consist of diamonds and rubies," Benedict said, sarcastically, "for I could tell by the way you laid your pack down that it is not full of gold."

"What I have is more precious than diamonds and rubies," Gilbert told him.

"In that case, perhaps you should have sold a little of it to buy stout shoes and a pair of trousers that had more cloth than thread in them," Benedict observed.

"That would have been difficult," Gilbert told him, "for what I have is divisible only once, into two portions. No lesser dose would be fully effective."

"Dose?" Benedict echoed. "Have you brought back nothing but medicine? After ten years of wandering in the wilderness, have you found nothing worth bringing home but some quack cure for warts or baldness?"

"It is an elixir concocted with water from the fountain of youth," Gilbert told him. He opened his pack and produced a small stone flask, which might have held a single gulp of brandy, although it seemed to Benedict more like the kind of vessel in which poison might be kept.

"The elixir of life?" Benedict scoffed. "Are you immortal, then?"

"I have not drunk it yet," the older brother said, patiently. "Nor will it make me immortal. But what it can and will do is to restore my health to the finest pitch of perfection, and make me feel as well as any man can feel, for as long as I may live. It cannot give me eternal life, nor can it protect me against the danger of a sudden violent death, but it can double the usual allotment of a man's potential years, and make the century I might yet live, if I am careful and fortunate, a hundred years entirely worth the living. Once I have drunk it, I shall no longer age, I shall be full of vigor, and my spirits will be permanently uplifted. The measure I possess is said to be adequate to do the same for one other person."

"So brotherly love has brought you here, in order that I might share in your good fortune?" Benedict was hesitant now, no longer daring to be quite as sarcastic as he had been before.

"You are absolutely right, dear brother," Gilbert said. "But I fear that I must ask a price for what I intend to give you."

"A price?" Benedict said. "That seems a trifle unreasonable, given that we are brothers. What price do you want for your supposedly miraculous potion?"

"I want your inheritance," Gilbert said, frankly. "I want all *this*: the winery, and everything accessory to it. The carts and the horses, the barrels and the tools, the suppliers and the customers."

"You mean that you want your half," Benedict said. "The half that you gave up when you went a-wandering."

"No," Gilbert said. "I want it all. I was the one who took the risk. I was the one who traveled far, who staked his life and future on the hazard of discovery. If I drink one dose of the elixir, I shall have every advantage of indefinitely-protracted youth save one: an income that would allow me to make the most of it. If I can trade my second dose for the income, I shall have the full extent of my desire. Ergo, dear brother, I offer you the choice: you may have youth without wealth for as long as you may live, or wealth without youth. It is a fair offer."

"A fair offer!" Benedict was astounded. "It is piracy! Can you imagine that I would trade my inheritance for a sip from a flask that might contain anything or nothing at all?"

"If you refuse, brother, I shall have to make my offer to someone else."

For a moment or two, Benedict did not see what Gilbert was getting at—but then he realized that, if he would not sell his inheritance, there was another who might be persuaded to sell it before he was able to receive it: his father. "But our father is already old!" Benedict protested.

"Exactly so," said Gilbert. "He will understand the true value of the elixir. Having already spent his youth, he will not obtain as much advantage from it as you might, but I dare say that he will settle for the protraction of his current state of being for another sixty or seventy years, and the sense of well-being the elixir will give him in the meantime. I am, in any case, his eldest son; he might take the view, as I do, that the inheritance is rightfully mine in any case."

"Over my dead body!" Benedict said.

"That will not be necessary, brother," Gilbert replied, calmly. "Quite the reverse, in fact. What I am offering you is the opposite of death: youth and good health, for as long as you might live. What do you have to lose? If you will not pay the price I ask, the winery will be taken from you anyway. You know as well as I do what kind of man our father is. I shall not demand that he deliver all his possessions to me. I only want the business—he can keep his secret savings, to spend in whatever way his newly-rejuvenated whims may take him. But I remember how he treated me when I was a child, so I have come to you first, in order that you can have first refusal of my offer. Am I not generous, brother?"

"Very generous, brother," said Benedict, his voice redolent with astonishment and a keen sense of injury, Nor was his tone a liar, for he picked up a paddle that he had been using to stir the wine in the vat, and struck out at his brother so forcefully that Gilbert would certainly have been killed had he not stepped sideways to avoid the blow.

94

If the older brother had had a weapon in his pack he would surely have fetched it out, or had there been something close at hand that would serve as a cudgel he would surely have improvised—but he had no weapon of his own, and there was nothing nearby that would serve such a purpose.

What Gilbert did instead, therefore, was to remove the stopper from the flask and put it to his lips, saying: "Strike at me again, brother, and I will down the lot—both doses in one. You will lose your opportunity!"

Alas, Gilbert had misread his younger brother's resolve. Benedict had not been fully persuaded that the flask really held the elixir of youth, but he had been persuaded that his father might be gullible enough to think that it might, and to disinherit his younger son in order to obtain it. So Benedict did, indeed, strike out again—alarming Gilbert sufficiently to make him carry out his threat.

Gilbert tipped the flask, and took its entire contents into his mouth. He held the liquid there, as if he thought that Benedict might relent when he saw the threat about to be carried out—but Benedict only took the opportunity to measure his victim for a third blow.

This time, Gilbert was not quick enough to get out of the way. The paddle descended upon the crown of Gilbert's head, with lethal force. The only action he had time to perform before he fell dead upon the winery floor was to swallow what he had in his mouth.

* * * * * * *

Benedict immediately regretted what he had done, and became exceedingly anxious to hide the evidence of his crime. It had been dark for some hours and Sylah was not a well-lit town, so it seemed unlikely that anyone who had seen Gilbert approach could have recognized him, even if anyone had been abroad at such a late hour.

"I must be grateful to my brother after all," Benedict muttered, as he wondered how to do away with the body. "If he had gone to my father first, I would certainly have been disinherited."

Benedict picked up the dead body and weighed it in his arms. Although Gilbert had by no means grown fat while he was on his travels, the corpse was no lightweight. Benedict did not want to risk anyone seeing him with a dead man slung over his shoulder—the Duc de Romanin was well known as a severe judge, very intolerant of all kinds of homicide except those ordered by himself.

The most obvious hiding-place that was readily available was the barrel waiting beside the vat to receive the matured wine, and Benedict wasted no further time before lowering his brother's body into the empty vessel. He considered the possibility of putting the lid on the barrel and moving it directly to the storeroom, but he knew that anyone who so much as tapped its wooden flank would realize that it had no wine in it. For this reason, he filled it up to the brim with wine from the vat before sealing it.

When Benedict turned the barrel on its side to roll it into the store he was glad to discover that it was only slightly heavier than it would have been had it contained nothing but wine. He placed the barrel in a dark corner, intending to leave it there until he could find an opportunity to dispose of it permanently. He rolled out another empty barrel to set beside the vat, so that he could continue his work as if nothing had happened.

Three days later, when the contents of the vat had been casked and another consignment of grapes brought in for treading, Frederic Paschel came to the winery in the early afternoon, in company with the Duc de Romanin's steward, Corentin.

"Good news, my son!" said the wine merchant. Duc Meldred's eldest son, Sir Blaise—the finest knight in the entire province—is newly betrothed to Lady Ghislaine de Thyresse, and there is to be a great feast at the Château in three days' time. There will be jousting and a circus, and a great deal of merry-making. My old friend Corentin wants to buy every barrel of this year's vintage on Duc Meldred's behalf, as well as the best we still have in store from last year and the one before."

Benedict was thunderstruck. "But father!" he protested. "This year's vintage is far too young to please an educated palate. Lord de Romanin would do far better to take every-thing else we have in store and leave this year's deposits to mature."

"Don't be silly, Benedict," Frederic said, impatiently. "All the Lord's vassals, of every rank, will be party to the celebration. This year's vintage is more than good enough for the lower ranks."

"Even so," Benedict objected, "We shall need to hold some barrels back for future years, when they will be much improved.

"Fool!" was Frederic's reply to that. "Lord de Romanin is very willing to compensate us for any loss we might sus-tain by selling the wine before it is fully mature. This is a great opportunity, you dunderhead. Bring out a score of spig-ots immediately, and start setting them in the casks so that Corentin and I can test their contents and agree a fair price for each one."

Benedict had no alternative but to do as he was told. He volunteered to help with the tasting, but Frederic told him yet again what a fool he was to think that his naive palate could possibly compare with the practiced expertise of a successful wine merchant and an experienced steward. Benedict knew only too well what a connoisseur his father was, and Corentin also had a great reputation as a wine-taster, so he had to give way on that—but he took what com-fort he could from the fact that the two wise men were con-tent to leave the business of rolling out the barrels and ham-mering in the spigots entirely to him.

One by one Benedict brought out eight of the barrels laid down in previous years to give their contents every chance to mature, and tapped them all. Every cup brought forth cries of delight from his father, but the Duc's steward professed himself disappointed with all of them, so the hag-gling process by which the prices were agreed was long and arduous. Nor would the steward agree to let the current crop go untasted, so Benedict had to roll out another seven casks and tap them all. Again Frederic Paschel professed himself very satisfied with his crop, but Corentin was a hard man to convince, and they managed to quaff more than enough wine to keep thirst at bay as the long hot afternoon wore on.

When the fifteenth barrel had been tested, Benedict told the steward that there were no more to be tested, but Frederic Paschel had not done as well as he had hoped in the haggling, and protested loudly that he had seen with his own eyes that there was one more barrel of the current vintage left, even though some fool had misplaced it by shoving it into a shadowy corner.

"I believe that one is spoiled," Benedict said.

"Nonsense!" his father said. "It has not even been tapped. Bring it out, boy, bring it out!"

Benedict had no alternative but to roll out the barrel and drive a spigot into its side. He filled the steward's wooden cup for the sixteenth time, and passed it to him with a trembling hand.

Corentin had already begun to frown before he set the cup to his lips, in preparation for the customary battle over price, but as soon as he took a sip from the cup his expression changed. He had earlier been very scrupulous about spitting out at least half of the wine he had tasted, lest the expertise of his palate be confused by intoxication, but he swallowed this mouthful entire, and followed it with another that was considerably more generous. Then he looked down with evident disappointment into his empty cup.

"Now that," he said, forgetting his prepared script, "is a truly excellent wine."

"Is it?" said Frederic, thrown off his own stride by this unexpected development. The merchant handed his own cup to Benedict, who took it to the spigot—but before it could be filled the steward's bony hand clamped down hard on Benedict's wrist.

"No, no," he said, regretfully. "That's too fine a vintage to waste on the likes of us, I fear. That's the sort of wine that must go to my master's table, for the benefit of his most intimate guests." And he offered a price for the barrel that was half as much again as the highest price he had ever previously offered for a barrel of Frederic Paschel's wine.

Frederic was a trifle disappointed, obviously regretting the loss of an opportunity to taste such a wonder, but he was a man of business, and he accepted the offer gracefully.

"You can deliver the other fifteen barrels at your leisure, Master Paschel," the steward said. "Have your boy put this one into my carriage; I shall take it to Romanin today."

Benedict opened his mouth to protest, but realized that he had no possible grounds for so doing. Corentin's carriage was designed to carry passengers rather than cargo, but there was certainly room in it for a single barrel, provided that the steward was prepared to sit beside his driver. Benedict had no alternative but to rope the barrel and lift it with the aid of the windlass, and it was only with the utmost difficulty— even though Gilbert's corpse weighed only a little more than the volume of wine it had displaced—that he managed to inch the load on to the floor of the carriage. He recovered his breath while the steward drove away, having promised to settle Frederic Paschel's account as soon as the other barrels were delivered.

"This is a great day, my son," the wine merchant said. "Your inheritance has had a great boost—and to judge by the way you were sweating as you lifted that barrel, Lord de Romanin will have a very ample measure of wine therefrom. I do hope that you have not been making a habit of over-filling the barrels."

"No, father," Benedict said, sadly. "If that cask contains more than it should, you can be assured that it is one of a kind."

* * * * * * *

That night, Benedict went to his father and said: "I have had enough of the wine trade, father, and have decided to follow my brother's example in going abroad to seek my fortune. I would be very grateful, though, if you would pay me the wages due to me for laboring these last ten years in the winery."

Frederic Paschel was obviously astonished by this request, because he became quite purple as his temper rose. "You ungrateful swine!" He cried. "How dare you! Every farthing that the winery has earned these last ten years has been reinvested in the business for the benefit of your inheritance. Everything I have done in my entire life I have done for you."

"Well," said Benedict, "I suppose you might see things that way, but I cannot. It seems to me that everything I have done in my entire life I have done for you. While I have toiled by day, you have been idle. While I have labored by night, you have slept in your comfortable bed. And as for all your talk of reinvestment...well, I count every bunch of grapes that goes into the vats, and every barrel and spigot we buy, and simple arithmetic assures me that you must have considerable savings in gold and silver stored away as part of my so-called inheritance. I do not ask for all of it, but I do want my fair share."

Had Benedict not grown so wiry while manhandling barrels Frederic Paschel might have been tempted to turn his son over his knee and give him a good thrashing—but when his father's furious gaze had measured him from top to toe, Benedict watched that resolution falter and shrivel.

"Don't be stupid, my son," the wine merchant said, in a more conciliatory manner. "You've invested far too much yourself to throw away your inheritance now. Yes, I could give you a little coin—but if you take it away it'll soon be spent, and the winery will go to rack and ruin in the meantime, for I can't be expected to continue running it when my heart is broken. If you will not keep it going, it will have to be sold, and what a pity that would be, when we've just been producing the finest wine we've ever made...did I say *we*? I meant *you*, of course. It's obvious to me that you've always had the wine-maker's gift, and only needed practice to bring it out. I've stood back to let you obtain that practice, my son, and my discretion has paid off. You don't need to go away to make your fortune—you can make it right here."

Benedict was slightly taken aback by this change of attitude, but he knew that he could not give in. He dared not wait in Sylah for one more day. Indeed, he had already waited longer than he should, for he was spared the necessity of answering his father by a loud hammering on the door. When he answered it, he found a contingent of Lord de Romanin's spearmen outside, who had been sent to arrest them both on a charge of selling wine in short measure.

"Short measure!" Frederic Paschel reported, when he received this information. "Impossible! I saw the barrel loaded myself, and was only now admonishing my son for overfilling it. If it was short when it arrived at the castle, that rascal of a steward must have piped half of it away for his own use."

The soldiers were, however, merely following orders; their sergeant assured the merchant that he could lay his counter-accusations before Lord de Romanin. So Benedict and his father were put in irons and taken to the Château.

When they arrived, the merchant and his son were immediately taken to Duc Meldred, who was in his banqueting hall with his son, Sir Blaise, and his steward Corentin. The barrel was set beside the head of the table. The prisoners were thrust down on to their knees.

"If the barrel is light, my lord...," Frederic Paschel began, bowing until his forehead was almost touching the floor.

"The barrel is not light, Master Paschel," the Lord said. "Indeed, that is the mystery. When my loyal steward told me what a wonder he had found I could not wait until the feast; I had to test it for myself. Having found it every bit as delightful as he promised, I offered a cup to my son, and then invited the Comte de Thyresse, the father of my future daughter-in-law to sample it. We had a second round, and then a third...and our enjoyment increased so dramatically with every draught that we were extremely disappointed when it ceased to flow from the spigot, even though the barrel still had so much weight that the level could not possibly have sunk below the tap."

"Perhaps, my Lord," the wine merchant said, "you might tilt the barrel...."

"Of course we tilted the barrel," Lord Romanin said, "fully expecting more wine to flow—but no wine flowed. Plainly, there is something else in this barrel as well as wine: something solid, which has shifted to block the spigot. Now, what do you suppose that might be?"

Frederic Paschel looked at his son then, with accusing eyes. "Benedict?" he said, unsteadily. "You were the one who filled that barrel, were you not?"

"I fill all the barrels," Benedict replied, bitterly. "Whatever is in this one is to my credit—that I admit, since I cannot possibly deny it. Remove the lid, by all means. Take a look for yourself, my Lord...then do with me what you please. At least I have filled my last barrel for this old skinflint." He did not attempt to rise to his feet, but he held his head high as he met his liege lord's eyes.

Lord de Romanin looked at Benedict curiously, and then instructed his steward to hand over the claw-hammer he had thoughtfully brought to the meeting. Benedict shrugged his shoulders and accepted the instrument. It only took him a minute to pull out the staples securing the lid. When he thrust the lid aside the Duc de Romanin and Sir Blaise both peered in, very curiously.

"Why," said Sir Blaise, "it's a dead man. It seems that we've been drinking blood with our wine."

"So it is," said Lord de Romanin, thoughtfully. "And so we have."

Benedict had expected them to grow pale, perhaps even to vomit, but the aristocracy of Aquitania was obviously cut from finer cloth than the nation's common men.

"But it *is* an extremely fine wine," Sir Blaise added, "and it might not be a good idea to let my future father-in-law know what we have been feeding him, even if we were innocent of any knowledge of it."

"I am proud to have such a wise son," Lord de Romanin said. "A keen sense of the diplomatic niceties is the most valuable gift a future Lord of Aquitania can possess—and it is, as you say, an extremely fine wine. There will be a good measure still to be drunk, once we have moved the dead man's back away from the tap. Perhaps you can explain, Master Paschel, how the vintage turned out so well, given that the pickling of a corpse would normally be expected to spoil it?"

Frederic Paschel could only look back at his lord and master in frank amazement—but Benedict was quick to take his opportunity. "My lord," he said, "my father has not the slightest idea how the vintage turned out so well—but I know the secret."

Lord de Romanin raised his eyebrows in a delicately aristocratic fashion. "Which is?" he said.

"Mine to keep," Benedict said, boldly. "But I can assure you that the wine has a preservative effect as well as a wondrous taste. It will be of great benefit to you if you keep on drinking it, provided that you do not share it too generously—but only I have the secret of making it, so you will need to look after me well."

The Duc de Romanin looked long and hard at Benedict then, but in the end he only said: "Will you need more dead men?" he asked, politely.

"No, my lord," Benedict said. "That one was unique. But the body has virtue enough to improve several more barrelfuls of wine—perhaps many more, if it is supervised with the proper skill." This was, of course, a guess—but Benedict had reasoned that the elixir of youth must be seeping from the body that now contained it at a relatively modest rate, and might yet add a piquant bouquet to a luxurious harvest of wine.

Lord de Romanin made no immediate reply to this, but Sir Blaise said; "If it is only a matter of pouring in more wine, we could do as much ourselves."

"Wine-making is a skilled trade," Benedict pointed out, "and the best wines require the most artful makers. You might try, I suppose, to stretch the crop yourself...but if you were to fail, there would be no further opportunity. You would do better to put your trust in me."

Sir Blaise seemed a trifle offended by this slur against his competence, but Lord de Romanin was quick to intervene. "What about you, Master Paschel?" he said to Frederic. "Are you not a very artful wine-maker?"

"I am no murderer," the kneeling wine merchant was quick to say, "and no sorcerer either. No dead man was ever been found inside any barrel loaded by me."

"Your father has a point," Lord de Romanin said to Benedict. "The presence of the dead body in the barrel does suggest foul play, of more than one kind. Justice insists that murderers are hanged, and sorcerers burned. I'd be reckoned a poor lord of the realm if I did not put the demands of justice before those of my palate, would I not? Wine is only wine, but crime demands reparation."

"It is true, my lord," Benedict said, calculating that he had nothing to lose by being bold, "that if wine were only wine, it would be a poor thing to weigh against righteousness in the scales of justice. But you have drunk from that barrel, have you not? *Is* it only wine, do you think, or the veritable elixir of youth?"

Duc Meldred de Romanin nodded his noble head thoughtfully. "You told my steward that the barrel was spoiled," he observed. "You did not want your father to sell it—but he had no idea what it contained...."

He was interrupted by Frederic Paschel's cry of anguish. While attention had been diverted from him the curious merchant had climbed discreetly to his feet and tiptoed to the barrel, then leaned over to see what was inside it for himself. "Gilbert!" he moaned. "My beloved Gilbert!"

Lord de Romanin did not spare the merchant a glance. "Who is Gilbert?" he asked of Benedict.

"My brother," Benedict answered.

"You killed your brother?" Lord de Romanin said, raising his eyebrow again. "May I ask why, Master Alchemist?"

Benedict had been thinking furiously, and took his opportunity without delay. "Because that is what the recipe called for, my lord," he said. "That is why no other corpse would do—and even then, it required ten years of careful preparation."

"Sorcery, my lord!" cried the steward, who now seemed to repent having drunk from the barrel. "He must be burned!"

"Be quiet, Corentin," said Lord de Romanin, before addressing himself to Benedict again. "Are we in danger of damnation, then, Master Paschel, for having drunk your concoction."

"Not at all, my Lord" Benedict said, without hesitation. "I suppose I might be in some slight danger, but you and your son—and the Comte de Thyresse too—are knights of Aquitania, perfect models of virtue and chivalry. How could you possibly be in any danger, given that your hearts are absolutely pure? Men of your kind, I feel perfectly sure, could drink barrel after barrel of the elixir without incurring the slightest stain on your souls. But if you would rather not...." He left the sentence dangling provocatively.

"I have long been of the opinion that we ought to have our own winery here at the castle," Lord de Romanin said, after a moment's thought. "We would need a good man to run it, of course. Your father is obviously too old, but he seems to have taught you everything he knows, and you have evidently done a little studying on your own account. Would you be prepared to accept such a position, if it were offered?"

"I would be very disappointed to leave my beloved father," Benedict said, "but if my liege lord needs me, it is my duty to respond. I will gladly take the job."

"I am delighted to hear it," the Duc de Romanin said. He turned to his steward. "See to it that Master Paschel and his father receive suitable accommodation."

* * * * * * *

Benedict was elated when he heard the Duc's instruction, but his delight was short-lived. Instead of being taken to one of the workshops clustered in the château's capacious courtyard he was taken into the cellars beneath one of the towers, to a chilly subterranean chamber with a single barred window and a door with a heavy iron lock. It had no furniture, although it did have a hole in one corner whose connection to the château's main sewer was a little more immediate than any occupant of the room could have desired.

"This is a dungeon!" he objected.

"Oh no," said Corentin. "Our dungeons are much narrower, and have no windows at all. Your father's new apartment is a dungeon. This is a winery. At least, it *will be* a winery when the Duc's men have brought barrels and vats from your former establishment."

The room had not seemed very large when Benedict first measured it with his eye; when his imagination imported a vat and a dozen barrels—which was less than half of the apparatus presently contained in Frederic Paschel's winery—he realized that he would hardly have space enough to stretch himself out to sleep.

"The conditions are hardly conducive to good wine-making," he complained. "I need light, and air, and...."

"Then you will have to earn them," the steward said, "by the quality of your labor." And with that, he went out, locking the door behind him.

Benedict's imagination proved perfectly reliable. Even though the Duc de Romanin's men only set up a single vat and stacked up ten barrels of wine—in addition to the one containing Gilbert's body—there was hardly enough floor-space left in the underground room for a man of Benedict's size to lie himself down.

It only required a few minutes to refill the barrel containing Gilbert's corpse from one of the others, so Benedict had plenty of time thereafter to consider his situation. He had no idea how long the supply of elixir contained in his brother's body would continue to invigorate the wine, nor how long it would take for the elixir to seep out of the dead flesh. There was no guarantee that the next cupful drawn from the spigot would be as good as the last, and no way to calculate how many more cupfuls would follow in its train if it were. He would have to rely on trial and error to discover the optimum rate of improvement, and the one thing of which he could be certain was that the effect would not last forever.

Eventually, the elixir would run out and the wine would cease to derive any further benefit from the body. By that time, Meldred de Romanin and his son might have supped enough to preserve themselves indefinitely—although the fact that Corentin and the Comte de Thyresse had each taken a little, and given that Benedict would have to taste future barrels to judge their readiness, might ensure that none of them would gain the full benefit of the elixir. Benedict was not certain what difference, if any, that would make to his own situation.

Given that Gilbert had only had the evidence of hearsay to advise him as to the properties of his treasure, Benedict could not be absolutely certain that there had been exactly enough elixir in the flask to preserve two men against the effects of aging for an indefinite period. There might have been less, or more. On the other hand, Benedict thought, given that he had not the slightest idea how the elixir had been manufactured in the first place, it was at least conceivable that he might have stumbled upon a process by which it could be indefinitely renewed. If that turned out to be the case, there had to be a possibility that he could continue in the Duc de Romanin's service for months, or years...and perhaps, if he cared to sample his own wares, a century and more.

Alas, none of these prospects could be reckoned pleasant while he was lodged in his present accommodation.

Once the sun had set, Benedict discovered that his situation was even worse than he thought, because the hole that led down to the sewer was a two-way thoroughfare. It would undoubtedly be very convenient for him to be able to expel his bodily wastes from the chamber, but the cost of that convenience was that inquisitive rats were able to intrude upon his privacy. Mercifully, the few that emerged during his first night of captivity found nothing to encourage them to linger, and fled readily enough when he lashed out at them. Even so, he placed three barrels in a line so that their tops formed a platform of sorts, on which he could sleep without fear of rats running over his body or nibbling the leather soles of his shoes.

Benedict was grateful for the fact that the breakfast sent to him on the following morning was appetizing as well as plentiful, although he knew that any crumbs he spilt would encourage the rats. He was grateful, too, when the Duc de Romanin, who seemed to be in a reasonably benevolent mood, came to see him.

"When will the new wine be ready for tasting, Master Paschel?" Lord de Romanin asked.

"Ten days, perhaps," Benedict guessed.

"Oh no," his master replied. "That will not do. I shall come to test it the day after tomorrow, on the morning of the great feast. I must admit, though, that I have been thinking very carefully about what you told me yesterday. I take your point about your brother's body having some particular virtue, and requiring long preparation for its current function, but I cannot help wondering whether it might be worth our while to try a experiment or two, in a spirit of open-minded enquiry."

"What do you mean, my lord?" Benedict asked, although he knew perfectly well what the Duc must mean.

"It so happens, Master Wine-maker, that my faithful steward Corentin had an accident last night. He fell down a flight of stone stairs and broke his neck. It was most unfortunate—the poor man had been in my service for many years, and my father's service before that. Now, I understand perfectly that you could not work your magic with any run-of-the-mill dead man, but I cannot help wondering whether the steward—who had, after all, drunk a measure of the wine while he was testing its quality—might be able, so to speak, to *export* its effect. What do you think?"

Benedict's first thought was that if he did not agree to collaborate in the experiment, Lord de Romanin would certainly try it himself—and that if it happened to work, he would immediately become redundant. He therefore made haste to say: "I cannot be certain that my artistry, though considerable, will be able to accomplish much with a body so ill-prepared—but I am willing to try, my lord, if that is your wish."

"Excellent," said the Duc. "I shall have the body brought down to you."

It was not until the steward's body had been set in a barrel, and the barrel filled with wine, that Benedict began to wonder what the consequence might be if Lord de Romanin's experiment did work. The steward had undoubtedly supped more of the wine than was strictly necessary while he had been tasting it, and might have stolen a few further sips while he as transporting it back to the château, but he could not have drunk very much of it. Any elixir his body contained would be very dilute indeed by the time it had dissolved in wine—but it might, even so, make the wine more palatable. Benedict had not yet sampled the wine himself, but he knew that he would have to test his vintages while he was bringing them to their optimal condition; the health and pleasure thus gained would undoubtedly make his imprisonment more bearable, but his ingestion of the elixir would,

over time, increase his value to the Duc in an altogether undesirable way—thus making the problem of finding a way
out of his present predicament much more difficult and considerably more urgent.

With such weighty matters on his mind, Benedict might
not have found it easy to sleep even if the rats had not been
so active, but the news that something new and interesting
was happening in the world above had obviously spread
through the underworld during the day, and he was convinced that the number of furry visitors scampering about the
floor on the second night of his captivity was considerably
more than on the first. On the third night, if his ears could be
trusted, there were hundreds swarming below him while he
stretched himself out across the flat tops of his three broad
barrels.

Lord de Romanin was as good as his word, reappearing
in Benedict's gloomy chamber almost as soon as he had
breakfasted.

"What a great day this is!" the Lord declared, merrily.
"A marriage-contract to be signed and countersigned, a sol-
emn mass in the chapel and a nuptial ceremony conducted by
the Archbishop of Bordelais, a huge feast to be enjoyed, and
a fine tournament to be watched. Who could ask for anything
more? I am only sorry, my dear Master Paschel, that you will
be too busy to join in the festivities—but I know that an artist like yourself cares nothing for the joys of ordinary men,
and would far rather devote your time entirely to your vocation. Have you sampled the refilled barrel, or the one in
which my old steward was interred?"

"Not yet, my lord," Benedict said, truthfully. "I am sure
they are not yet ready...."

"You are probably right," the Duc agreed, "but I am so
enthusiastic to keep track of our experiment that I cannot
wait to take a sip from each of them."

Benedict had not hammered a spigot into the barrel containing the steward's body, but he had to do it now. First,
however, Lord de Romanin took a cupful from Gilbert's barrel.

"It is good!" he exclaimed. "Very good indeed! Perhaps
it will improve even further, given time, but I think you un-

derestimate your talents, Master Paschel. As an artist, of course, you think only of quality...but now that you are in my service, I must try to be the best master I can, and it is my duty to think of quantity. Let me try the other."

Benedict let out a cupful of wine from the steward's cask and handed it over, hoping that it would be foul—or, at the very least, unready as yet to be drunk.

"Not as good," was Lord de Romanin's verdict. "Not nearly as good...but on the other hand, not as bad as one might expect from a polluted barrel. I cannot reckon the experiment a total success, but it is not a total failure either. Would you care to give me your opinion of the two vintages, Master Wine-maker?"

Benedict recognized the polite request as a firm command, and took a sip himself. He took a sip of Gilbert's vintage first, and immediately understood why the Duc and Sir Blaise had taken the view that there were more important issues stake in this affair than punishing murder. The taste was divine, and the exhilarating effect it had on his consciousness was nothing short of miraculous—and yet he was as certain as he could be that this solution was considerably more dilute than the one that the Duc and his son had tasted on the previous evening.

"It needs more time," he said, trying not to let his sudden lack of sobriety show. Then he took a sip of Corentin's vintage.

The wine in which the steward's body had been soaked was not nearly as bad as Benedict could have hoped, but it was by no means as good as he had feared. He was glad of the opportunity to say: "This is not nearly ready, my Lord. Perhaps I was over-cautious to think that it would require ten years to mature, but it will certainly require one, or even two...."

"Perhaps you are right," Lord de Romanin said, judiciously. "You are the expert, after all, and it would not do to be too hasty...especially as we have the other, which will be ready far more quickly, and might be eked out for months or years...but I must go now. I have a million things to do—but you may be certain that I shall return."

"There is no hurry, my Lord," Benedict assured him.

110

"None at all," the Duc agreed—but he came again much sooner than Benedict had anticipated, before the sun had set.

"There has been a terrible accident, Master Paschel," Lord de Romanin said.

"Not my father!" Benedict protested.

"Oh no," his master said. "Your father is perfectly safe in his cozy dungeon. The accident occurred during the jousting at my son's betrothal feast...."

"Not your son!" Benedict exclaimed, in frank astonishment.

"I wish you would not keep interrupting," Lord de Romanin said. "My son is perfectly well. It is the Comte de Thyresse, the father of his contracted bride, who has suffered a terrible misfortune. His daughter begged him not to enter the lists, and I advised him myself that it was an unwise thing to do, given his age, but he said that he felt ten years younger than he had three days ago, and insisted on strapping on his armor for, as he put it, *one last fling*. How right he was! He toppled two of my best knights, and then insisted that I sent my champion against him. Somehow, in all the confusion, the weakened lance that my champion should have been carrying was set aside, and a sound one handed up to him instead—and the blow be struck was so well-judged that it went clean through my new brother's breastplate, and his heart too. What a tragedy!"

"A tragedy indeed," Benedict agreed, although his own heart was all a-flutter. "I suppose the Comte's men will carry him home to Thyresse for burial."

"So custom demands," Lord de Romanin agreed. "Clad in full armor, mounted on a shield drawn by his favorite horse. But the weather has been rather hot of late, and he came from such a distance, that I have agreed with his widow and daughter that the armor should be taken back empty for ceremonial burial, while the body is discreetly disposed of here. We must, of course, be very discreet. A matter of diplomatic nicety, you see."

"Yes, my Lord," Benedict said. "I see exactly what you mean." He recalled that the Duc de Romanin and his son had shared their wonderful wine, though not its secret, with their honored guest.

By the time that Benedict stretched himself out that night, precariously perched upon his three barrels, the contents of another three were slowly leaching whatever virtue they could from the corpses of men who had tasted the elixir of youth. By rights, he supposed, the most recent vintage should turn out to be the noblest of them all—but he suspected that rights had little or nothing to do with the matter, and that the elixir had not the slightest respect for the unsubtle gradations of Aquitanian society.

After that, Lord de Romanin came down to his new winery twice a week, in order to sample all three of his experimental vintages and obtain Benedict's expert opinion as to their progress. Neither the Duc nor Benedict made any further mention of Frederic Paschel, but they did spend a certain amount of time discussing one another's health. The Lord declared freely that he had never felt better, and was improving all the time, but he expressed some concern for his faithful servant.

"You are too pale, Master Paschel. I certainly would not want you to become addicted to your produce, but I do think you might be exercising a little too much abstinence. I was rather hoping that you and I might enjoy a very long partnership, if our experiments should happen to work out as well as I dare to hope. I have considered the matter carefully, and it seems to me that if the virtue of your brother's corpse can only be preserved, careful husbandry might allow us to exploit it for a long time...and if the virtue imparted to the other bodies can increase our stock...well, suffice it to say that I shall value your art more highly than I can say."

"It is not lack of wine that is paling my complexion, my Lord," Benedict told his master, "but lack of light. I could be a far better servant to you, for far longer, if I had better quarters. These are cold, dark and damp, and very uncomfortable."

"Are they?" said Lord de Romanin, as if the thought had never occurred to him—and Benedict had to concede that, having never visited them by night, his master might well have no idea how bad conditions then became. The Duc's own quarters were undoubtedly placed so high in a tower that he never saw a single rat, and had no idea how abundantly they swarmed in his cellars and his sewers.

After a few moments consideration, Duc Meldred went on: "Well, then, I suppose I must consider the possibility of moving you to more comfortable lodgings—always provided of course, that our work goes well. All three of the barrels are improving slowly, are they not? Indeed, your brother's vintage has almost recovered the full flower of its original bouquet—do you not think so?"

"You are right, my Lord," Benedict said, "as one would expect of a true connoisseur. I believe that particular harvest might be ready in a week or so to supply another evening's bountiful carousal...although it might be wise to exercise a little more caution. I am sure that the other two barrels will produce something drinkable eventually, although I fear that they will never match the quality of the original."

"Good enough," said Lord de Romanin, nodding his head sagely. "One more week, then...and if the evening in question lives up to my expectations, you'll have the kind of winery of which you've always dreamed, for as long as you can keep your elixir flowing. We shall become a legend in our own lifetime, Master Paschel—and if you are the artist I think you are, it will be a long lifetime."

* * * * * * *

Benedict went to his improvised bed that night thinking *One more week...just one more week*, confident that it was a thought that could sustain him at least that long. He still had no idea how long his produce might sustain him thereafter, but he had to admit that the drops of wine he had taken from the barrels containing the Duc's steward and Sir Blaise's father-in-law had shown a steady improvement in quality over the past few weeks. Although they were, as he had told Duc Meldred, highly unlikely ever to emulate Gilbert's vintage for taste or quality of invigoration, they did seem to have acquired a certain modest virtue—and who could say how much more they might yet acquire?

Benedict permitted himself to wonder, again, whether he might have had the extraordinary good luck to happen upon the secret of manufacturing the elixir of youth. Perhaps, he thought, Gilbert's return had been engineered by some higher power. It was surely conceivable that Gilbert had actually been the instrument of some generous spirit, commissioned by that spirit to bring the elixir to a place where it might not only renew itself but increase itself vastly—in which case, what had happened in the winery on that terrible night had not been his fault at all, but merely the working out of some divine plan. Rather than feeling guilty about his crime, in fact, he ought to reckon himself an instrument of destiny, chosen to bring a new fount of miracles into the land of Aquitania—a fount whose effects would surely spread beyond Romanin as the Duc became more ambitious.

Once his own supply was absolutely secure, Benedict mused, Lord de Romanin would undoubtedly begin thinking in terms of trade, but as an aristocrat he would not think of trade in the same vulgar terms as Frederic Paschel. No—the Duc de Romanin would think in terms of advancement at court, and the favor of the king...and when he went to the king's court in distant Aix-la-Chapelle, the Duc would doubtless take his faithful artisan with him, and raise him up from the station of wine-maker to that of Alchemist, or Master Magician....

While he indulged these flights of fancy, even Benedict contrived to forget the rats that swarmed below, scavenging every last crumb that he had dropped from his plate at breakfast and supper, and lapping up the spillage from his cups and ladles.

The next morning, he received a different visitor: the scion of the de Romanin family.

"You do not seem pleased to see me, Master Paschel," the visitor observed.

"Not at all, sire," Benedict said. "I was taken by surprise—I was expecting the Duc."

"Alas," said the former Sir Blaise, "I am the Duc. There has been a terrible accident. Last evening, while my father and I were out hunting boar in the forest, his horse stumbled and he was thrown. Mercifully, he broke his neck—otherwise, he would have died a lingering death, gored by his quarry's tusks and savaged by the beast's teeth. He was

114

so badly mutilated that I dared not allow my mother or my wife to see the body, but had it safely stowed away for discreet disposal. There will have to be a funeral, of course, but a suit of armor will suffice for all ceremonial purposes. It is a frightful thing to happen, of course; he had seemed so well of late, younger than ever. A good son cannot help but think of his beloved parents as if they were invulnerable, of course, but in my father's case there really did seem to be a possibility that he might go on forever. I had not thought of coming into my inheritance for years yet—decades, even— but when fate intervenes, priorities must change....

"At any rate, Master Wine-maker, you have a new liege lord now. Fear not; I have every intention of looking after you just as well as my father did, if your produce is as good as he had begun to hope. My father seemed very well pleased with the results of his experiments, but I should like to try a few sips of each of the vintages myself—it would mean a great deal to me to know that he did not die without making a worthy contribution to the sum of human knowledge."

"Yes, sire—I mean, my Lord," was Benedict's inevitable response. He drew a small measure from each of the three laden casks, one by one, and gave the three cups to his new master.

"Now that is excellent," the new Duc said, of Gilbert's vintage. "That is the vintage in which I shall toast my late father's memory—privately, of course; it does not do for an aristocrat to exhibit his grief in public. The other two will never match it, and are clearly unready even by their own low standards, but they are not entirely without virtue, are they? Please taste them, and give me your expert opinion."

"You are right, my Lord," said Benedict, when he had obeyed the command. "The other two will never match the first, but they are not utterly insipid."

"Given that the steward and my late father-in-law supped so little of the wine," the new Duc said, thoughtfully, "we cannot expect too much from them, but my father must have quaffed a great deal more during these last few weeks. Even he might not produce a harvest to compare with your own dear brother, but I think we should make the most of him—don't you? It's what he would have wanted, after all."

"I am sure that it is," Benedict agreed. "Am I to understand that I may still move into the new quarters the old Duc was making ready for me? I am certain that I could work far more profitably there than I can here, and the necessity of tending yet another special cask will make my work even more difficult than it was before."

"I will, of course, honor all my father's promises," Duc Blaise said, "but preparations for the funeral will take up a great deal of everyone's time in the next few days. We cannot possibly hold the memorial mass until Thursday, given that we shall have to bring the Archbishop all the way back from Bordelais so that he may officiate. We shall, of course, require a suitable interval thereafter for mourning, so you must be a little more patient. Your new quarters should be ready in fifteen days—twenty at the most—and you need not fear that you will be neglected in the meantime. I shall visit you again, as often as my father did, to keep track of all our experiments. You do have an empty cask to spare, I hope, and some wine with which to fill it up."

"My supplies have run very low," Benedict said, hesitantly. "They would have stretched for seven more days, had I not had any extra work to do, but now that I must prepare another cask and my relocation is to be delayed...well, my Lord, the vat is empty, save for the lees, which need to be cleared out. I need more grapes to tread, and new supplies of all the compounds necessary to aid their fermentation. If you would allow me to take a carriage down to the old winery, and then to the vineyards which supply our grapes...."

"Oh no," said Lord de Romanin. "You have more than enough to do here. Give instructions to my men, and they will fetch everything you need."

"It is not as simple as that, my Lord," Benedict said. "The grapes must be selected by an expert eye, and the compounds need to be assembled by someone who knows exactly what is what. I fear that I was never as careful in labeling as I ought to have been—even my former laborers would be all at sea if they tried to follow a list."

"I understand your reservations," said the young Duc de Romanin. "I am a great believer in having jobs done properly. Fortunately, there is a compromise available. I shall send your father to buy more grapes and gather all the necessary apparatus. That is doubtless why my father decided to keep him close at hand."

Benedict was by no means convinced that this strategy would solve his problems, but he could not think of an adequate objection, so he nodded his head meekly.

The old Duc's body was brought down to the cellar within the hour, by which time Benedict had figured out how to rearrange the casks in such a way as to have adequate access to the four experimental vessels. One unfortunate side-effect of the rearrangement, however, was that the row of three casks that he had been using as a bed had to be broken up, and the only way that he could contrive a similar surface was to place three empty casks on top of three full ones, lined up behind the four experimental barrels. This would force him to sleep no more than a few inches from the ceiling, but he judged that it would be far better to be too close to the ceiling than too close to the floor.

He had just enough wine to spare to cover the old Duc's body—a necessary precaution, given the tendency of bad odors to rise even in a cool cellar.

On the next day, the young Duc came to see Benedict again, in a very bad temper. "Your father is a damnable rogue," he said, "and he obviously has not an ounce of paternal affection in him. As an honorable man, I had naturally imagined that he would not do anything to annoy me while you were safe in my care, but I had forgotten that the high standards of duty observed by the aristocracy are not reflected in the lower orders of our society. It appears that the old man had considerable savings in silver and gold hidden in his house—enough, at any rate, to afford the extortionate bribes that he required to make his escape from my domain. He will have to run all the way to Castile or Normandy to find security, but he obviously believes that he can do that. I pity you, Master Paschel—it must be a terrible thing to have labored so long for such an ungrateful man, and to know that the fruits of your long labor have been the means of your own betrayal."

This was probably the truest thing that the young Duc had ever said—as Benedict freely acknowledged with a long cry of anguish.

"But you need not worry about your own future," Blaise de Romanin went on, "for I shall do everything in my power to protect you and keep you safe. I shall have every single item brought from your old storehouse to the castle, and I shall order my new steward to buy up every grape within a day's ride, so that you may have your pick of them. Next year, we shall do the same. Worry not, my faithful servant—I shall not hold your father's treason against you, and will look after you even more carefully because of it. Now, shall we see how my father's vintage is coming along? I must admit that I am keen to find out how much life there is in it, even though it will not be truly mature for a very long time."

This final judgment was, of course, correct—but Benedict only required a single sip of his new vintage to know that there was indeed life in it. The elixir of youth was obviously a very hardy liquor, which did not easily decay even if its host fell prey to dire misfortune. Even if the amount retained indefinitely within the four corpses reduced the reclaimable stock to a dose that was not quite sufficient to preserve two men indefinitely, Benedict guessed, there would be quite enough within the four casks to keep one man young for an exceedingly long time.

Well, Benedict thought, *I suppose my fate is decided now, and at least I shall get my new winery, in fifteen or twenty days. It will doubtless have a stout lock on the door, but I shall be free of the rats.*

Although he did not know himself whether his intention was to celebrate his own preservation or to drown his potentially-eternal sorrows, Benedict decided that he might as well console himself with a drink, and that if he were going to have a drink he might as well be drinking fine wine, and that, whether he were cursing his father or congratulating him, he ought to let his brother partake of his toast—so he took a generous cupful of wine from Gilbert's cask, and drank it down; and then he took another, and another. He did not even bother to top up the cask before climbing up to his new bed.

At least, he thought, *I shall be safe from the rats.*

Alas, this judgment turned out to be a trifle optimistic. He would, indeed, have been safe from the rats had he slept as soundly as he intended and expected to, but the ceiling of his cell was infested with spiders, which scurried about by night, and it happened that one of them lost its grip and fell into his open mouth while he was snoring.

Benedict sat up abruptly, smashing his head on the stone ceiling, and as he recoiled he rolled off his improvised bed, falling several feet on to the four barrels neatly arrayed below. No harm would have come to them had they all been properly maintained and topped-up, but Benedict had been working without a full set of cooper's tools for some time, and he had not topped up the barrel containing his brother's body. That barrel splintered, and two of its hoops broke—with the result that its liquid contents burst out, flooding the floor.

Half a dozen of the rats that were swarming over the floor at that moment were drowned, but half a thousand more set about lapping up the spilled wine.

Rats are not renowned as connoisseurs of wine, but they would probably have enjoyed what they supped even if there had been nothing in it but the essence of the grape or mere dead flesh. As things were, they were so greatly invigorated by their consumption that it only took them a further half-hour to clean Gilbert's bones of every last vestige of flesh.

Further invigorated, the rats set to work on the unconscious Benedict—who woke up just in time to feel the worst of the agonies thus inflicted, but not quite soon enough to be able to cry out in alarm. Connoisseurs of wine or not, the rats were certainly connoisseurs of flesh, pickled or fresh, and they held a tongue to be an even greater delicacy than a meaty heart or a juicy liver.

By the time that Benedict's skeleton had been stripped there were more than five thousand rats competing over the privilege. Under normal circumstances, they would have stopped at that, but many of these were rats that had now supped their fill of the elixir of youth, not to mention the essence of the grape, and they immediately set themselves to the task of gnawing through the wood of the three full casks that still remained to be emptied.

The eager rats broke their teeth and bloodied their mouths, but the stoutest heartwood of the Romanin forest could not have withstood that collective assault. Long before dawn the rats had cleaned three more corpses of every last morsel of flesh, and lapped up every drop of the wine in which the bodies had been doused.

By the time the young Duc's servants brought Benedict's breakfast down on the following morning, there was not a rat to be seen, although the scattered bones of the six that had drowned gave some evidence of what had happened. That day was, however, the last day on which life in the Château de Romanin maintained some semblance of normality. On the next night, the rats returned, and this time they were not content to stay in the cellars. They ran riot through the entire castle, consuming everything that could not move fast enough to run away—not excluding humans, dogs and horses. Lady Ghislaine and the young Duc's mother were among those who failed to make their escape.

Duc Blaise de Romanin came back the next day with a company of men-at-arms and three full packs of hunting-dogs. They set traps everywhere, and waited in full armor for night to fall. When the rats came out again the battle was long and bloody—but it was the men who eventually retreated, and never returned.

* * * * * * *

Within a year, the Domain of Romanin was no more. King Charles had revoked the title—necessarily, it was said, because the family was extinct, consumed by agents of the Devil. The Archbishop of Bordelais had informed the king that he had pronounced an anathema against the rats of Romanin, and had sprinkled holy water all around the desolate château, but to no avail—which was, of course, absolute proof that unholy forces were at work there.

The towns, farms, vineyards and forests that had formerly belonged to the Romanins were redistributed among the neighboring domains—all except for the Château itself, and the surrounding estate, which were put under proscription and left to return to wilderness.

No one was supposed to live in the château or its grounds, and it is possible that no one actually did—but long afterwards, on stormy nights, for a hundred years and more, the tale was told around the hearths of all the Châteaux of the neighboring domains that the ruins of Romanin were haunted by a gaunt and wild-eyed human creature.

This madman, the storytellers said, called himself Blaise the Undying, and claimed to be a Duc—but he was evidently the lowest of the low, in the reckoning of Aquitanian society, for he dressed in rags in spite of his rude health, and never ate or drank anything but the flesh and blood of rats.

THE LAMIA'S SOLILOQUY

"Is it an explanation that you want? How dull! Had I thought you that kind of person, I might have preferred another. Are you sure that you'll remember it when you wake up? Human memories are so very adept at forgetting—that's what makes human minds so ruthlessly efficient, so narrowly focused on quotidian affairs.

"You trust yourself implicitly! Poor fool.

"Very well. First of all, the rumor is false which says that we lie in wait for the unwary, seducing them away from the path which they have set out to follow. It might be true, I dare say, that we are creations of Hecate and daughters of Lilith, for we certainly thrive in the dark of the moon—but the travelers who come to us are those who had no settled destination in the first place, and were disposed to wander by their own waywardness.

"The majority, of course, are poets; when we drink the blood of men we offer full recompense, in the form of inspiration. The nine who live on Helicon are empty symbols; we are muses of a more earthly stripe. We draw strength from all our victims, but the best of them draw genius from us.

"Secondly, not all who seek us, consciously or otherwise, are privileged to find us. We have never been profligate with our favors. It is true, of course, that we need the blood of men, but not as daily nourishment. I could go without blood for a hundred years, or a thousand, without perishing of want or becoming agonized by thirst.

"I think the need we have for blood must be more closely akin to the need that poets have for poetry; it makes life more vivid, more worth the living.

"Thirdly—and I pray that you will not take offence—the blood of human beings is not the finest vintage imaginable. There was a time, before the Age of Heroes, when I could sup the blood of fauns and centaurs, or even oreads and hamadryads were the mood to take me. Their ichor was sweeter by far than the stuff which flows in human veins; perhaps that was the reason why they ceased to be. We are not the only possessors of bloodthirst, nor are we the greediest.

"The virtue of human blood is not its taste but its profusion. Those species that were more spirit than flesh were slow to reproduce their kind and easily fell prey to murder and massacre; humankind thrived like the hydra—wherever ten men were cut down, twenty sprang forth to take their place. Nowadays, we drink human blood because it is all that we can get. It enhances life a little—but it also makes us sad, by reminding us of what once was possible, but is no more.

"Three items of explanation are enough. I doubt that you are capable of remembering even one. I must go now, and leave you to your rest. Make me a poem when you awake, and make it worthy of the blood that you have shed."

* * * * * * *

The young man awoke, and stretched his bony arms. For a second or two, he was possessed by the fleeting memory of a dream—but the moment he tried to grasp it, it was gone. The world came into focus, asserting its sharp reality upon his five senses.

There were so very many things he had to do that he had no difficulty at all in forgetting the most important of them all—and the blood that surged within his veins became a little more insipid with every hour that passed.

AND THE HUNTER
HOME FROM THE HILL

The rifleman, whose name was Tom Stackpole, found that if he lay perfectly still his wounds no longer hurt quite so much. He was not at all sure that it was a good sign. The officer, whose injuries were far worse, had seemed uncannily at peace with himself since Tom had first tumbled over the rim of the shell-hole to join him, dragging his ruined leg behind him.

"I believe I'm done for, Tom," the officer had said to him, with a reckless disregard for the proper form of address, almost immediately after introducing himself as Captain Desmond Campion, Royal Field Artillery. Tom suspected that the officer might actually have offered his hand to be shaken if it had not been so busy playing with something Tom could not quite make out.

"I believe you are, sir," would have been the honest reply, but what Tom had actually said was: "Don't worry, sir. If my West Yorks lads ain't back by tea-time the Staffs and Shrops will be moving up in support. Either way, we'll be picked up. As long as the guns don't start up again...."

"They won't," the officer had assured him. "The Germans had the sense enough to move them back to surer ground before they sank too deep. We're the only ones lunatic enough to stick fast in ground like this—and even we're not so mad as to open up while your fellows are slogging through the mud."

Tom wasn't so sure about that, but it wasn't the sort of doubt you could confide to an RFA officer, even if he had been the one to introduce the concept of lunacy into the con-

124

versation. He wasn't so sure, either, that the West Yorkshire Fusiliers would be instructed to withdraw before nightfall, or that the Staffordshire and Shropshire Yeomanry would be sent to reinforce them if they were ordered to hold the hill over whose ridge they had disappeared that morning. Even so, he felt obliged to be optimistic for the old man's sake. Tom was fairly sure that he could hold on till morning if need be, and maybe longer, but the officer wasn't going to make it, even if they did get picked up before nightfall, and Tom had been brought up to be kind to the dying. He was still prepared to assume that the rest of the division would move up eventually, once it became obvious even to the generals that the Boche had moved back, and that he would then be able to use his own ticket home.

If there had been a battle, in any meaningful sense of the term, then the Boche would be reckoned to have lost it, although a saner accountant might have reckoned that the shallow slope of glutinous mud that had previously been no-man's-land was something of a booby prize, if it were any kind of prize at all.

Tom looked up uneasily, wondering if there was still a chance that he might begin his long journey before dark, but the signs weren't good. Sunset had already stained the sky red, as it always did in the wake of a heavy bombardment. Most of the dust and smoke expelled by the shell bursts settled back to earth, but there was always a residue that continued drifting upwards to catch the sun's dying rays, all aflare with mockery and defiance.

Tom lowered his eyes again, but didn't turn and raise his head to peep over the rim of the crater. To do so would have renewed his pain, and he knew full well that there wouldn't be anything to see.

The sky changed color a dozen times a day, if night were counted in the day, but the ground changed not at all. The ground was always grey. Sometimes it was a desiccated desert, sometimes an ocean of mud, but it was always the same dead hue, devoid of all radiance. When it was dry, the men who moved upon the face of the blast-ploughed surface imposed color upon it with uniforms whose camouflage had been designed for a universe that still played host to vestiges of life. When it was moist, on the other hand—let alone sodden, as it was now—it painted its own drear decay upon every inch of their bodies, and their faces too.

Had the war been fought by marching men, Tom thought, they might have remained aloof from the filthy stain, but this was a war in which every living thing must crawl or perish; no matter how deep the mire might be, the fighters crawled. You crawled from slit to slit and hole to hole, finding shelter where you could in the scars the guns and spades had opened up on the face of the earth, like an infestation of gangrenous bacteria clustering within wounds. You never welcomed sunset, even when the artillerists took it as a signal to cease fire. If you had any imagination at all, you saw your own blood written in the heavens, your own guts displayed in the ragged clouds.

* * * * * * *

Even in the fading dusk, Tom could see easily enough that the officer was dying by degrees. The blast that had carried away the lower part of Captain Campion's right leg and peppered his thighs and backside with shrapnel had disobligingly cauterized the nastiest of his wounds, sealing the remainder of his blood within his veins, but that only meant that he was condemned to die slowly. Even if the stretcher-bearers did arrive before the twilight faded, they could only carry the poor fellow away to die in another place, still fidgeting madly with whatever it was he had in his cupped hands. This was Flanders, after all, where the fields had been liberally fertilized with animal shit for nine hundred years, and where the blood of hundreds of thousands of the slain had built Jerusalem for every kind of lethal germ.

Tom's worst wound was also in the right leg, likewise caused by flying shrapnel, but the foot was still there and the boot too. It looked as if it might be saved, and if it couldn't...who wouldn't pay the fee of a leg below the knee, for a ticket out of Hell?

If the officer asked for a cigarette, the rifleman resolved, he would say that he had none. There was no point in extending polite kindness to the extent of giving something to a dying man that he would be able to use himself. On the other hand, he decided, he ought to refrain from smoking himself, because it wasn't right to add insult to injury. There was also the possibility that the Boche had not retreated quite as far as he supposed. A sniper on the crown of the hill might be able draw a bead on the glow.

"How old are you, Tom?" the officer asked him, in a voice not much more than a whisper.

"Nineteen, sir," the rifleman replied.

"Honestly?"

"Honestly, sir." Tom was not such a fool as to have lied about his age in order to enlist before his time.

"What were you, before?"

"In service, sir, "Tom admitted. Discovering that talk did not increase his pain, and that it provided a distraction of sorts, he continued. "Stable-hand and gardener's laborer on the Earl of Lonsdale's estate—but I was schooled first and I'm no Tomfool. You?"

"I was a sculptor," the officer told him, "and a Tomfool, alas, for all my schooling."

"Yes sir," Tom said, reflexively, "but what was your work?"

The officer tried to laugh, but couldn't. "I was a man of means," he said, quietly. "Not so meaningful as the Low-thers, mind—had I only been so fortunate I might have gone into the church. Isn't that how the great and good deal with the fool of the family?"

"No sir," the rifleman replied. "The church is for sissies. The navy's for fools."

The officer tried to laugh again, and failed again. The blood in the sky had darkened from purple to black, and so had the blood that stained the mud beneath the officer's missing knee like an evil shadow.

"I wasn't as far out of step as I imagined, then," the officer murmured. "I shipped out for Burma once on a time, to take a position in Rangoon that might have made my fortune, but I got no further than the Andamans. The ocean and I could not get along. The only training in adversity I ever had before this nightmare began was that voyage. I once thought a passage through a tropical storm was a season in Hell, but I know now that it was only purgatory, far more merciful than my opinions could then entertain. I was never truly grateful for what my tribulations taught me until I saw the Somme."

"My grandfather's brother ran away to sea," the rifleman said, struggling to remember the cautionary tale he had been told. "Couldn't stand it and ran back to land in America. Settled in Baltimore and died wifeless of typhoid fever."

"I was cast back upon the shore myself," the officer remarked, in a teasing fashion. "The ocean devoured me, but found me disagreeable and vomited me out."

The rifleman turned to look at his companion, but the light had all but faded out. The sky was black and the few stars visible among the parting clouds were faint. The officer's colorless face was fainter still. Captain Campion had raised his hands now, as if in prayer, but it was far too dark for Tom to see what it was that his restless fingers were fondling.

To have been so far forward before the West Yorks were ordered up, Tom thought, the captain must have been spotting for the guns. There was no trace of the landline that had carried his intelligence back to the gunners, so he must have been forced to abandon his original position before his legs were blasted.

For the first time, the rifleman thought to wonder whether the hole they had landed up in had been blasted by a British or a German shell.

* * * * * * *

"Never heard of the Andamans," the rifleman confessed.

"Cannibals there, I was told," the officer said. "No idea whether it was true, but if it was I was lucky. My ship rode out the typhoon, but I was fool enough to be swept overboard. Wound up on an islet eighty or a hundred miles west of Port Blair, more dead than alive, and sick in the head. Natives found me, fed me, kept me safe until I could be carried back to Blair. Signaled a pearl-fisher to pick me up, along with the price I had to pay."

"Price, sir?" the rifleman said, as he had plainly been invited to do.

128

"Quid pro quo. A favor for a favor. A village entire accepted the burden of my upkeep for a month or so and gave me a blind child to remind me of my debt. Didn't know I had her till I got a little of my sanity back in the hospital in Blair. Took her to Madras, then home to Manchester via Liverpool. My not-so-foolish brother took care to remind me that slavery had been abolished in England, but he didn't know the truth of it. He thought of me as the slave-keeper, and I wasn't.

"I was a burden on the family for years afterwards, though they wouldn't let me live under the same roof for fear of my so-called madness. Wasn't till the war broke out that they found a way to recover their moral credit. Lucky I was well by then, or they'd never have found redemption. There'll be nothing left of me by morning, I suppose, but my soul hewn in wood and clay and stone. It doesn't hurt near as bad as I thought it would, you know. You hear poor devils hooked up on the wire, screaming in agony, and you think *that's what death is like*, but I don't feel that way. Am I mad again, do you think, Tom?"

"No sir," said the rifleman, softly, as he wished that his own legs didn't hurt quite as much as they did and wondered whether every sculptor of means labored under the delusion that he was paring his own soul. "Not mad. Sometimes, I reckon, the flesh knows. It knows it's done for, and it just gives up. Pain's a warning, sir, and the flesh ain't always so stupid that it keeps on howling when all hope is gone. If you'll forgive me saying so, sir, you can't be such a Tomfool if your flesh has that kind of wisdom."

"Is that what it is? Well, perhaps. Or maybe it's just that I split my soul between two hundred parcels of wood, clay and stone, back home on St Mary's Hill. That's in Moston, above the Oldham Road. It's a steeper hill than this one, but far more forgiving. There's a pithead at its crown, but the terraces on the lower slope were built for mill workers, not for miners. Perhaps it's the honor of the primitive gods that protects me from my agony, but it may be just that there's nothing left of me to perish but a husk without a nut, emptied of everything that makes a man a man. Do you believe in the One God, Tom, the Lord of All?"

"No sir," said the rifleman, feeling no need at all to elaborate.

"I used to try," the officer told him, "but it was always a fight I couldn't win. No point trying now—wounds too deep. If you did believe, I suppose charity might require me to be quiet, but as you don't, I wonder if I might tell you a tale."

The question was couched so oddly and so politely that the rifleman was genuinely intrigued, but he hesitated anyway. He knew that he shouldn't even try to sleep, and that anything that might keep him awake ought to be welcomed, but he had heard as many tales as he could bear from men who had died. The last thing in the world he wanted right now was to hear the beginning of a tale from a voice that had not strength enough to reach the end.

The clouds were clearing now, and the stars were shining more brightly, but their comfortless light was cold.

"Everything I have is yours," the officer reminded him. "Unless, of course, you'd rather leave my corpse to be looted by the other side. Won't you take the tale as well, in case you survive? You wouldn't want to hand my trinket to your son without the details of the curse it carries."

"I don't believe in curses, either," the rifleman told his dying companion, without bothering to call him sir. He took leave to stare at the "trinket" the officer's hands were caressing with such tender fervor, now that it had been clearly stated that it was his to inherit, but there still was not light enough to make it out.

"Wouldn't you like to?" the officer asked him. "Wouldn't you like to believe that this is all a curse, and not our fault at all? That, even in the absence of Almighty God, we really aren't responsible?"

Tom Stackpole didn't reply to that, although he was too good an atheist to be in the least afraid of blasphemy. His unresponsiveness was invitation enough.

"Well then," said the dying man. "This is how it goes...."

* * * * * * *

130

I wish I knew how much of what happened on the island was real, and how much a dream, but I don't. It wouldn't matter overmuch if this were just a traveler's tale, but the greater part of it concerns what I did on dry land, in a house in England's second city. I heard plenty of tales of the other sort while I was outward bound on the *S.S. Sandoway Star* for Burma. Every crewman seemed to have one, though most were so old they were from a different world: a world where there were no steam engines and no ironclads, in which the south Atlantic still played host to a vast sea of weed. If that's true for a third-rate steamer like the *Four Esses* there can't be a vessel afloat without a hundred fanciful tales unlisted in her bill of lading, and the oceans must be full of tiny islands never seen again since someone's father or mentor dropped anchor there after their vessel wandered off course.

Maybe it was the stories I'd heard that shaped my dreams, and there's still too much in my own tale that's naught but the legacy of tales already told. I'd certainly heard of Easter Island, where the natives took to carving great heads from stone as a tribute to the gods whose favor they'd lost, but those were human heads, images of the kind of God in which all Tomfools are schooled to believe. That wasn't the kind of god I saw in my delirium.

Even Christians are sometimes wont to suggest that it might be a terrible thing to fall into the hands of a living God Almighty, but it's ten times worse to fall into the hands of one of a million primitive gods, for primitive gods have more bestial models than any divine emperor made in the image of man. Primitive gods have faces like swine or baboons, vultures or sharks. Primitive gods are inarticulate, incapable of dictating scriptures, but they rail against their own inarticulacy, and seize what opportunities they have to make themselves clear.

When we dream—and we are all equal when we dream, Tom Stackpole, no matter what means we may possess when we are awake—we open doors to the most primitive gods of all, and offer them nightmares for their work of revelation. When we are drawn to the very edge of our existence by disaster, dreams themselves may acquire the force of a typhoon, and our nightmares become crowded with the faces of a mil-

131

lion voiceless gods, every one of them passionate to make itself felt, to make itself clear.

I thought I was in Hell when the storm took me, but I know now that it was only purgatory, and that the faces I saw bore me far less malice than I thought at the time. I expected that my body might be devoured by cannibals, but the islanders who pulled me out of the surf were good and generous folk, after their own primitive fashion. I expected that my mind might be devoured by swinish and shark-like spirits, but I know now that the gods which visited me in that month-long nightmare were better and more generous than I dared believe at the time. They were horrid, and they were hungry, but they were only what they were, and not deliberately evil at all.

That might be a more comfortable revelation than I deserved, but it is not as hopeful as I might have desired, because it follows—does it not?—that if the primitive gods are not merely evil, then the goodness of the civilized God has no duty to suppress them.

While I was a castaway, I saw the whole universe in my delirium, and I saw the gods which inhabit it—but they did not make a meal of me, any more than the primitive folk who found me. As the islanders nursed me back to health, so the gods released me back to sanity. I can only suppose that it was my own fault that I took so long to reclaim it in full.

The islanders who saved my skin were blacker than you might expect, given that most Indians and Burmese are subtle brown. They were darker than the average Sinhalese, but they were gentle folk nevertheless. They fed me roasted fish, and the meat of turtles baked, and boiled beans, as well as plenty of fruit. I doubt that I ever ate so well. I do not believe that there was anything in what they fed me that nourished my visions more than my body, although that was what my brother William and my sister Caroline claimed, with that miraculous power of inference which arises from the arrogance of false sophistication.

There was no volcano on the island belching horrid fumes, although there were forested hills. Nor was there a temple in which virgins were sacrificed to a heathen god of wrath. As far as I could tell, the islanders had no temples at all, because they kept their religion in their homes and in their boats, always close to hand. As to whether there were any virgins past the age of puberty, I was in no condition to judge or care.

To the best of my recollection, it was the oldsters that looked after me. Perhaps they tried to tell me their names, in the beginning, but if so they soon gave up. They accepted that I wasn't going to be able to learn their language, and they certainly weren't about to try to learn mine, so they settled for wordless communication that was mostly reassuring gestures of the hand. They were comfortable with wordless communication, because words were merely a social convenience, and all the communication they judged truly important was channeled through the sense of touch. Their hands were always busy, with play if not with work.

They were very insistent that my own hands should be busy too, if not with work—of which I was plainly incapable—then with play.

* * * * * * *

When I was in Blair my doctors told me that the objects with which I had learned to play were "fetishes". I was never convinced that the doctors in Blair had the faintest idea what they were talking about, but I was not well enough to argue. On the island I had done as the islanders desired me to do, and in Blair I did as the doctors desired me to do. I allowed the islanders to make my hands busy, and I allowed the doctors to make them idle again. I allowed the islanders to communicate without words, and I allowed the doctors to label everything.

"Fetish" is a word that white men use to collapse hundreds of different kinds of native beliefs, trying to make out that they're all symptoms of a single simple-minded way of thinking. Fetishes, it's said, are images that possess magical properties, usually by virtue of being the symbolic abode of a protective spirit. Maybe the statues the islanders kept were fetishes and maybe they weren't, but that certainly wasn't the notion that came to mind when I first encountered them. I took it for granted, in my god-haunted delirium, that they

133

were objects made for the straightforward purpose of being handled. Some were carved in wood and others in soft stone, and the images in which they were made were just as multifarious, if not more so, than the objects of the emperor God's Creation.

I can't be absolutely sure now, but while I was on the island I simply took it for granted that the people looking after me gave me objects to caress in order to soothe my deliria, not to enhance them. I still incline to that hypothesis, in spite of what others have tried to tell me. At the time, I did not think of what I was doing as any kind of magic or worship, or even as medicine, but simply as a kind of distraction—and because there seemed to be such simple pleasure in the tactile sensation, I thought it one more kindness, one more politeness to add to all the rest with which I was favored by my hosts.

Even in Port Blair the suggestion was never made that the carvings over which my fingers roamed, ceaselessly and reassuringly, might actually have been the cause of my nightmares—but when I began to tell the tale in Madras, and on the ship that brought me home, some of those who heard it were quick to turn the experience on its head and perceive my saviors as my tormentors. More than one man of more than one race was enthusiastic to suggest that the figures delivered into my hands had not merely been put there with magical intent, or as objects of worship, but that the magic had been intended to harm rather than heal, and that the gods to which I had paid unthinking tribute were evil gods which would not gladly let me go.

I could not and would not believe that. I quickly learned to deny it, sternly and fervently—and by the time I completed the final stage of my homeward journey, traveling by rail from Lime Street Station to Manchester Victoria, I had built a fine edifice of counter-argument.

"We literate folk have grown so heavily dependent on the sense of sight," I would say, "that we tend to overlook the simple rewards of tactile sensibility. The Catholics among us cling to their rosaries, and I have seen Moslems use prayer-beads too. Even Protestants and Puritans, who pretend to have set aside such baubles, often play—

sensuously, for all that it may seem absent-mindedly—with all kinds of objects that they carry about their persons: watches and their chains; knives and pens; coins and luck-pieces.

"Whenever we are anxious, our fidgeting always increases its urgency, and we really ought not to feel so guilty about the relief it may afford. Such therapeutic effects arise from an aesthetic appreciation that need not be reckoned primitive, and ought to be as capable of sophistication as the finest of our arts. It is folly to leave such appreciation entirely to the blind. In the days before gaslight, darkness cast us all adrift in a world we knew primarily and most intimately by touch, and we should not let the electric bulb steal the virtues of that half-forgotten world as well as its inconveniences."

Such explanations might have sufficed to explain my attachment to the objects I had brought way from the island with me, and even my determination to make more—for everyone agreed that my works felt beautiful, even if they seemed odd and ugly to the eye—but they could not, alas, begin to explain my companion. I could not explain her fully even to myself, although I knew that I had to keep her with me at all costs, as a matter of the very highest duty.

* * * * * * *

I called the blind girl Sanya, because I had to call her something, but it was not her name. She was not dumb, but she rarely spoke because she never had the slightest interest in learning my language, and I often allowed people to believe that she was mute as well as blind. She certainly was not deaf, but we communicated almost entirely by touch. She had a remarkable knack of deducing my meaning from the slightest brush of my fingers on her forearm, and her own small hands were as adept in instruction and suggestion as they were in collecting information.

Sanya must have known my features exceedingly well by the time we reached England, but she continued to explore them nevertheless, presumably to calculate my shifting moods. She was always eager to explore the faces of others,

135

but there were few who suffered such investigations gladly; from the Andamans to Manchester and at all points in between the great majority of men—and all women, without exception—found her profoundly disconcerting.

Sanya's own eyeballs had been removed, presumably because the injury that had disabled them had also disfigured them, but her own people had fashioned substitutes from a jet-like stone. These did not seem so distinct when set against the almost-Negroid skin of her face as they would have had she been white, but they were obvious nevertheless. She was, I thought, about twelve years old when she left the island with me. I sometimes referred to her as my guide—which description many people took, wrongly, as an ironic jest—but it was safer in England to refer to her as my ward.

There was talk, of course, when Sanya and I set up house in Moston, even though I had a housekeeper on the premises. I took some comfort from the supposition that there might been even more talk had Sanya not been there, given that Mrs Hopkinson was a widow of twenty-nine, not five years older than I. Victoria was still on the throne then, of course, and talk of the yellow nineties had not yet begun.

I suppose my family and my new neighbors might have forgiven me for the new vocation I was eager to adopt had I declared an intention to work in bronze or marble. Had I committed my effort to that solid grey stone of which bulky civic statues are made to set outside the grand town halls of the northern cities, I might have been accepted as an artisan, if not as an artist—but nothing could have been further from my desire. I made no portraits of local dignitaries, or images of soldiers on horseback. I made my images in hard black wood and soft creamy stone, and the shapes I coaxed and caressed from my media resembled nothing that my relatives and neighbors could recognize, and nothing of which they could approve.

"If you must make chimeras," my brother said to me, when he favored me with the first of his rare visits, "can you not concentrate on those which are sanctioned by the classics? Fauns and centaurs would not be commonly decent, but they would have a certain esoteric respectability. Even mermaids might seem charming, but whenever you favor piscine imagery you seem perversely determined to concentrate on the wrong end of the fish—and I dare not even guess what manner of shaggy sea ape or swinish seal it is with which your sharks are hybridized."

"You are judging by eye," I told him, "when you should be judging by touch."

"They feel like tropic wood and far-from-precious stone, dear boy," he assured me. "If they are less of a insult to the fingertips than to the eye, the advantage is unclear to me."

"Perhaps it is your prodding and poking that constitutes the insult, William," I suggested. "Were you to explore them more tentatively, they might yield their virtue." But he was a man who paid two shillings for Piccadilly whores, and would probably have treated his wife no more lovingly, for all his reputation as an eligible man.

I had higher hopes of my sister Caroline, but she could hardly bear to lay a gloved hand on any of my works. She was as nice as William was crude, and her book-based theories of art could not help her to understand what I was about.

"I cannot see what you are aiming for," she confessed. "I cannot find the ideal to which your work is directed."

"Of course you cannot see it," I told her. "It is not to be seen. Nor can you even begin to search for the ideal I have in mind unless you can discard your gloves, and the attitude of mind they symbolize."

But Caroline at least had the sympathy and the wit to put questions to me that were more personal—and perhaps, in consequence, more pertinent.

"Do you still have nightmares, Dessie?" she asked me more than once, almost as if she cared.

"Occasionally," I had to confess. "No more than once a month, now, and they grow rarer as time passes. They do not trouble me overmuch, for they always evaporate when Sanya brings me the gifts I brought from the island. One day, I hope, my own works will do as well. Then I shall know that I have the art as well as the craft of carving."

"And what does your blind girl think of your efforts?" she asked. "Are they good enough to make her homesick?"

"She is patient," I said. "She knows my inadequacy—but she also understands my hope."

"I wish she were not the only one who does, Dessie," she said. "I wish you could recover the knack of dreaming as other people dream."

Perhaps I should have agreed with her. Perhaps I should have wished that I could.

* * * * * * *

When the nightmares did come, I faced the primitive gods with courage and fortitude, certain now that they could not destroy me. Familiarity allowed me to look into their ravenous faces, and the knowledge that escape was always ready to hand increased my courage. I even began to address them, although I knew full well that they were inarticulate, incapable of inspiring scripture. Perhaps I was vain enough to think that I had something useful to teach them.

"You have lost your dominion over me, as you have lost your dominion over all men," I told them. "Even the tribesmen my fellows call savages have culture enough to have won their freedom from your reign of terror. Once, you were the hunters who made men your prey, but man is now the hunter wherever he lives upon the face of the earth, and the tamer of all wild things. In the remotest depths of the sea and upon the heights of the forested hills you retain the power to kill, but even there you are fugitives, for men have homes to which they may return and you have none. However vast and strange the ocean is, the sailor will return triumphant to the shore, and however remote and high the forest may be, the hunter will descend full-laden into the vale. I am free now, no matter what visions may plague me, for I have hands and a voice."

I knew, though, that there was more hope and bravery in such speeches than real achievement. I worked hard, knowing as I did that naught but practice can make perfect, but still the figures that I made had not the virtue of those that I had brought with me from the island.

Every day I labored in my studio, with my chisels and my knives, and every day I passed my produce to my blind keeper, but as she rolled my figures through her delicate fingers she would shake her head. Her eyes of jet would look mournfully into the infinite, and tears would run from their surrounds.

Whenever she touched me it was with tenderness, and there was nothing in her touch but sorrow and sympathy, but I knew that my progress was slower than she had expected, more painful than she had dared to hope.

When she ran her fingertips over my face she felt my failure, my anxiety, and my disappointment.

I had thought of my task as learning a new skill, but I came to realize that it was more than that. In order to learn, I had first to unlearn. I could keep my sight and my ability to read, and I could keep my voice and my understanding of language, but I had to unlearn the habits that my hands had acquired, in order that they might discover new ones. I had to learn to feel everything anew, and I could not do that by concentrating obsessively on my carving. I began to go out more, so that I could touch all the things that I had learned to know by sight, re-educating myself to think first and foremost of texture, and never to judge by mere appearances.

It was a hard habit to acquire, but I made progress, and I felt the progress I was making in the figures that I made. Slowly but surely, I felt the life and the virtue entering into them. Sanya felt it too, and the anguish ebbed way from her sympathetic touch.

I had always felt the life and virtue of the blind girl's flesh, but I began to feel more as my skill increased. I began to feel the love and the sanctity, the aim of the hunter and the force of the tamer, the softness of her womb and the keenness of her mind, the kindness of her heart and the strength of mind that vanquished nightmares.

There was talk, of course, but there is always talk in a city. Cities are breeding-grounds for prying eyes and Gods Almighty. Mrs Hopkinson knew the truth, and she defended me as best she could.

"If you will not mend your ways," my dutiful brother told me, "We shall have no alternative but to commit you to an asylum. You are bad for business."

"If you will not think of yourself," my little sister said, "please think of me. Would you condemn me as an old maid by your fearsome example?"

"When I have learned the art," I told them, "I shall be vindicated. I shall have a gift that the world will learn to cherish."

"Have you sold a single piece?" William demanded. "Have you earned a single penny?"

"If you would only make prettier things," Caroline lamented. "If you would only devote yourself to the cause of beauty and propriety."

"I have reasons of my own," I told them both. "When I succeed, I shall deliver what I have made to its proper marketplace, where its quality will be fully appreciated.

* * * * * * *

I soldiered on, in spite of all opposition. I unlearned that which had spoiled my hands and I learned to forge as well as to feel, to put into the wood and the stone that which I had only been able to take out before. I began to make fetishes—if that is what they were—in earnest. I submitted every one to the wise judgment of Sanya's fingers, even when I had sensitivity enough of my own to know what they were, and was never wholly satisfied until she declared them good.

In my dreams, I submitted them to the appraisal of another jury, but I never felt that I was doing so in order to appease the primitive gods, or win their fickle favor. I did what I did because they were the peers which had the right to judge me. I committed my soul to the statues I made because that was where my soul had always belonged, no matter what my father or my brother might think.

I discarded my failures, and learned from them.

I never sold a single piece, of course, or earned a single penny. I never made a pretty thing, according to any commonsensical notion of beauty or propriety. But I did work of which I could be proud, and work with which my blind seeress could be satisfied. I made a hundred pieces, and then I made a hundred more, and I made the only fortune I could in paying the debt that I owed.

Little by little I paid out my creditors, in the only currency their coinless world could tolerate. And in due course, I took my patient guardian home again.

I sailed eastwards for a second time, on a better ship than the *Sandoway Star*. I found far better weather in the Andamans that I had found before. I returned Sanya to her own folk, with a treasure-chest as full as they could ever have imagined.

There were half a hundred species of tree on the slopes of the island's hills, and half a hundred kinds of stone and shell to be gathered about its shores, but an island is only an island and I had crossed a world. I brought my former saviors fetishes of Sheffield steel and Stafford pottery, of English oak and Norwegian spruce, of Welsh slate and Devonian granite. I even showed them forms which they had never seen before, although they were indeed the forms of veritable gods, glimpsed and understood in Egypt and Dahomey, Australia and Yucatán. I brought them wealth beyond their dreams of avarice, and gave it to them gladly, for they were the only people on earth deserving of my generosity.

I kept but one image for myself, for I knew that one was all I would ever need, now that I was whole and hale again.

And when the celebration was concluded, I came home.

I came home sane, and fit, and happy. I came home ready to live as men had always been meant to live when they had made their peace with the primitive gods—but I came home to the Great War, which liars called the war to end war or the war to save civilization. I obeyed the call to arms and became a soldier.

My brother William became a captain in the Lifeguards, and was killed on the Somme, but I survived that awful day.

My sister Caroline became a nurse in Brittany, and died of dysentery, but I survived that rite of passage too.

But now I have been blown, if not to Kingdom Come, at least to smithereens. I have been killed on a slope of slippery mud to which no man can put a name. But I am not afraid. I have faced the primitive gods and I have tamed them. They have no power to hurt me even if they had the desire. There are some who would say, even now, that I labor under a curse that was laid upon me many years ago, on an island

141

that has vanished from the map, but I would rather say that I have lived in purgatory and lived in Hell, and that there is nowhere now for me to return but home. I do not go gladly, but I go calmly, and I go well prepared.

A fool I may be, Tom Stackpole, but when I look about me nowadays, I know one thing beyond the shadow of a doubt. 'Tis worse than folly to be wise, when wisdom's whelp is war.

Do you hear me, Tom, my comrade and my friend?

Do you understand the tale that I have told, and will you tell it in your turn?

* * * * * *

The RAMC stretcher-bearers arrived soon after dawn, moving forward with the Staffs and Shrops when they were sent to occupy the ground that the Boche had surrendered, if ground it could be reckoned now the rain had turned it into a gently-flowing quagmire. They found the two unconscious men in a shell-hole that was already half-full of liquid mud.

"This one's dead meat," one man said of the captain, as he carefully folded the officer's empty hands across his breast, so that his pose might better reflect the peace that had descended upon his features. "We can leave him for the burial detail. How's the boy fusilier?"

"Alive," his fellow confirmed, as he parted the mud to expose the wounds on Tom Stackpole's right leg. "Asleep and dreaming, so it seems. He'll likely not walk again without a crutch, but he'll live if the gangrene doesn't eat him away. He's got his ticket home, if home has any place for such as he."

"What's that black thing clutched in his hand?" the first man said, as they pulled the unconscious man clear and laid him carefully upon the stretcher.

"Can't tell," the second replied, as the two men set themselves to trudge across the sea of slime with their burden between them. "He's working it between his fingers still, although it seems half worn away. Never seen the like of it before. Its body might be the body of an ape or a shaggy man, but its forepart's more like the head of a dragon, or a shark. Very queer."

"I wonder where he got it," said the front man, looking back over his shoulder with a puzzled frown, "and why a simpleton like him should cling to such a thing, even in his dreams."

THE RIDDLE OF THE SPHINX

I don't believe in destiny. I don't even believe in luck. Nothing is mapped out for us, and there's no mysterious force outside of us, which touches us with fortune or blights our lives according to its whim. Life isn't a riddle that has to be solved—life just *is*. It doesn't even have to make sense.

Other people called me lucky, of course—and sounded like they were spitting acid when they did it. I was just nineteen years old when I won the National Lottery. I'd only been out of council care for eighteen months, and I'd never had a job. Sure, I bought the lottery ticket with the proceeds of a crime—but it was still my ticket, my numbers. It was my seven million pounds.

I think it was the first time somebody homeless had won the jackpot. I was the first instant millionaire who'd been sleeping in a cardboard box the night before and watched the draw through the window of a TV showroom. That's why the media took such an interest in me, in my story. From friendless orphan to toast of the town; from nothing to everything. I don't think there'd been any transformation quite as dramatic as that since the days when fairy tales were true.

I was utterly and absolutely helpless. It sounds crazy, doesn't it, to say that I had no idea at all how to spend money, but I hadn't. I'd never had a bank account, never owned any significant possession. I had no idea at all what to do with my money, or with myself. There was no shortage of people wanting to take me in hand, of course—but how was I to choose between them? It wasn't that I wanted to find one who wasn't after my money—I just wanted to find one who would do what I needed them to do. Belinda wasn't the first I latched on to; she was the just the one who seemed to be the best. The fact that she had millions herself only mattered because she knew what to do with money: how to use it, how to live with it. Maybe I didn't have to marry her, but I wanted to. The age difference didn't matter to me at all. In this day and age, a woman can look as good at thirty-eight as she did at twenty, if she has enough money.

It wasn't me who started digging into my background. I didn't give a damn about that. It was the *Sun* and the *Mirror*. They were just looking for one more story about the rags-to-riches wonder-boy. I didn't encourage them at all. They got into a kind of race with one another, and they wouldn't give up. The winners must have thought they'd hit a bigger jackpot than I had. Belinda had no idea, of course—never an atom of suspicion. I think she'd blanked out the memory that she'd ever had a child. All that stuff about her subconsciously seeking the offspring she'd given up for adoption and me subconsciously seeking the mother who'd given me up, and the fatal attraction that sprang out of our mutual subconscious recognition, is just so much psychoanalytic garbage. Anyway, this is the twentieth century. So I accidentally married my mother—so what? What do you want me to do—pluck my eyes out?

Personally, I think the digging should stop now. Incest is one thing, but I think the hints they're dropping now are plumbing new depths of malevolence. It was as much a surprise to Belinda as to everyone else when she found out that my father had been murdered the day before I won the prize—she hadn't seen or heard from him in nearly twenty years. And maybe I don't have what you'd call an alibi, given that I was sleeping rough—but nor do half the population of London. I didn't murder a man to get the money to buy that ticket—it was a different crime entirely. It's all just coincidence, and it's quite bizarre enough already, without trying to add anything more to the pattern. The mystery of how that bastard got stabbed, and who did it, is just one of those riddles that never will be solved. Why on earth should anyone think that I might know the answer? I don't.

I truly don't.

And I've got seven million pounds that says no one will ever prove otherwise.

MY MOTHER, THE HAG

As my mother reluctantly submitted to the ravages of old age her memories of the past became increasingly vague. She even had trouble remembering me, although I had always been a very dutiful son. I suppose I was too insignificant to be well-remembered, because I was the least talented of all our kind. That has always been the curse of the *vargr-*folk; as each generation spent its magic, wantonly or not, there was so much less to pass on to the next. Had I been born a mere hundred years later I'd have been no more than human.

By the time she died even my mother was only a *little* more than human, but old age is more than the creeping assault of wrinkles and brittle bones; it transforms the mind as well as the body. As her memories of the past faded by degrees into the mists of might-have-been, her knowledge of the future became increasingly distinct. Not that this provided any great or enduring advantage to either of us, alas. Had her powers of anticipation become more complete and far-ranging she might have assembled a worthwhile legacy to hand down to me, but as they became more specific they became ever more narrowly focused on the manner of her death and the motives of her murderer—and that only served to trouble us both.

She had known the exact moment of her death for centuries, of course, and she had always known the name of her killer, but it was only in the last few decades of her life that the whole history of her destroyer became clear to her. Fate has a tendency to insult as well as to injure those who rebel against its dictates—as the *vargr-*folk did, it seems, by the mere fact of their existence.

146

When I was very young, my mother was still capable of talking about her destiny with a measure of philosophical indifference. "A violent death is the best way to go," she used to say, cheerfully. "It's quick, and it means you don't have to start rotting until you're actually dead. And if you have to die by the sword, it might as well be the sword of a hero. Fergus of Galloway will be a hero among heroes, a paragon of all the virtues, conspicuous even in such an august company as the knights of the round table!"

I heard a good deal about Fergus in those days. I heard about his vanquishing of the Black Knight and the nasty dwarf that was the Black Knight's companion. I heard about his mighty exploits at the siege of Roxburgh—which he could not have contrived, of course, without the glorious shield which he stole from my mother—and his punishment of Sir Kay in the great tourney at Camelot.

I protested, as I was bound to do. "How can you sing the praises of the man who will kill you?" I demanded. "And how can you rejoice that the shining shield which ought to be my inheritance will be he means of his winning fame, fortune and the hand of the lady Galiene?"

"Even *vargr*-folk must die," she told me, "and it is useless to blame the instrument for the necessity. As for your inheritance, the shield is not mine to dispose of as I wish. It is Fate's, and its disposition is Written."

I came to hate the words Written and Fate, pronounced as if they were somehow finer than all others. What I am doing now is, of course, not Writing but only writing.

* * * * * * *

The first note of doubt didn't creep into my mother's tales of her forthcoming demise until I was half-grown, and it was a tentative anxiety at first.

"Of course," she would add to her description of Fergus's triumphs in Arthur's great tourney, pensively, "Arthur won't be Charlemagne, let alone Alexander the Great. He'll only be a local king—but he'll be very well thought of, for all that. There will always be some who'll think of him as *the* king. A few will yearn for his return—and that of his glorious company of knights—long after he's faded into the mists of might-have-been. Nor will Fergus be the most famous of Arthur's knights, in spite of the best efforts of his biographer Guillaume le Clerc. Lancelot will outshine him in memory, and Gawain, and Perceval too. Even the name of the blackguard Kay will be better-known."

My mother's infection with doubt served to redouble my complaints and protests. "It's *not right*," I was wont to wail. "Whatever Arthur is or is not, this liege-man of his must be reckoned a perfect monster. What kind of knight is it that slays a mother and makes an orphan of her loving child? How can that possibly be reckoned *chivalrous*?"

"In actual fact," she would reply, with scrupulous fairness, "the ten commandments of chivalry will not contain any specific injunction against doing injury to members of the female sex, although maidens and mothers of the meek variety will obtain protection under commandment three, which instructs a knight to serve as the defender of the weak. Unfortunately, the *vargr*-folk are dealt with—*en masse* as it were—by commandment six, which exhorts knights to make war against the Infidel *without cessation and without mercy*. You and I, sweet child, are not to be numbered among the people of the book, and we thus constitute fair game, even in our breeding season."

Those were relatively quiet days, although my mother could still be reckoned a seductress. However quiet she consented to become, though, she was *never* meek. When there was no one to love but a man she condescended to love men, but she always did so fervently. It always seemed to me that they loved her all the more in consequence, and ought on that account to have prized her—and all others of her vivid kind—far above their own insipid kin. That, alas, was not their way.

There is something in the strongest of mere men which cannot abide strength in others, although that does not stop them thinking very highly of themselves and naming themselves heroes. Their unreasoning hatred of the *vargr*-folk—and, for that matter, of all things exotic—is but a reflection of their pride in themselves; because they have no magic of their own they are hell-bent on destroying those who have. If

I have outlived all others of my kind it is not because my death was never Written, but because my magic is so slight and unobtrusive.

By the time I was on the threshold of puberty I knew from my mother's accounts of him that Fergus of Galloway would think even more highly of himself than most men, even in an age of vanity rampant. How I hated him! I had fervor of my own, you see, although it was never the equal of my mother's. These days, I'm more tolerant of the company of men than I was then, but I've always preferred the company of honest vipers.

The ability to enjoy the company of vipers was then and still remains my only magic. It was a mean inheritance from one so talented as my mother, but I never blamed her for it, nor felt the lack of any greater sorcery. The one inheritance whose Fated loss distressed me was that fabulous shining shield whose glow was every promise, every glamour, every glory.

* * * * * * *

I was very glad when my mother began to speak of her future murderer less tolerantly. I stopped being glad when I realized that growing doubts and anxieties about the eventual configuration of her legend had begun to cast a shadow over her life and make her permanently sad. It was a shadow that grew and deepened with her increasing decrepitude. The more she remembered about what was Written and what was yet to be written, the more she found to regret—and the more she found to regret, the faster her beauty and her power faded.

"In terms of his actions and ambitions," she told me, the day after I brought home the baby dragon that was doomed to die with her while hardly more than an infant, "Fergus of Galloway will be a knight without compare. Unfortunately, his posthumous reputation will be clouded by the carelessness or mischievousness of his biographer, Guillaume le Clerc."

"In what way clouded?" I asked, more out of politeness than concern. I was momentarily distracted by the lovely dragon, whose misfortunate future had not yet been revealed to me.

"Many readers will think the tale of Fergus mere imitation of Chrétien de Troyes' much better-known account of the life of Perceval," she told me. "Some will deem the imitation tongue-in-cheek and suspect it of irony."

I didn't understand the notion of irony then, although I understand it well enough now. I couldn't see that it mattered overmuch how distant future generations of men would judge the reputation of her nemesis; the real tragedy, it seemed to me, was that there would be none of the *vargr-*folk left in the world to know the truth and curse the name of Fergus of Galloway.

"I don't mind dying," my mother said, repeating it as if it were a ritual spell. "Everyone must die, although I confess that I can't understand the alacrity with which humans rush to their deaths, slaying others as they go. A thousand years and one isn't a long life, by sensible standards, but it's perfectly adequate. I don't even object to the fact that men will rejoice at my passing, for I freely admit that we are of a different kind, whose mere existence stands in the way of their determined progress. What I do object to is the thought that the record of my demise—my only epitaph, in their tradition—will come to be considered a kind of jest, an item of parody. Whatever else I am, and whatever else I may be deemed when I am lost in the mists of might-have-been, I am not an item of parody. If I must be reckoned as a mythical monster or a figment of a fever-dream, so be it—but I'd far rather be a nightmare than a nonsense."

"You'll never be either, Mother dear," I told her, trying to soothe her with gallantry. "For as long as your name is known, you'll have the reputation of a *femme fatale.*"

She was sufficiently fond of me then to ruffle my hair by way of thanks, albeit in a slightly rueful fashion.

"My name will not be known," she told me, plaintively. "I shall be known on as the hag of Dunnottar."

I had never thought to ask her before—perhaps subconscious fear had made me avoid the question—but I asked her then, for the first time, what Fate had in store for me.

"Not everything is Written," she told me, "and not everything that is Written can be known. All I know of your future is that it will be long in extent—but your name will never be recorded, unless you can record it for yourself."

"But what will your accursed Guillaume le Clerc say about me?" I demanded. "How will Fergus of Galloway prevent me from saving you when he comes to steal the shield?"

She looked at me tenderly while I cradled the tiny dragon. "Guillaume will say not a word," she told me, sorrowfully. "When Fergus comes you will not be here, and he will never suspect your existence. Your lovely pet will challenge him, but all serpents are easy meat for men like him, who will drive dragons and a dozen other kinds to dark extinction."

What a deadly phrase! To the likes of Fergus of Galloway my friends, my companions in magic and my brothers in blood were *easy meat*! The insult so offended me that it seemed hardly worth the bother to notice that my very existence would go unrecorded by those who would make legends of the appalling Fergus and his master Arthur.

* * * * * * *

When disappointment had finally driven out the last trace of her cheerful equanimity, my mother lost the ability to accept the compliments I gave her and insisted on construing them as ironic taunts. Had I schooled my tongue more cleverly she might have liked me a little better and remembered me a little longer, but I couldn't help voicing my own opinions as to the manner in which she ought to have been remembered.

I was, after all, a dutiful son.

On the last occasion when I tried to flatter my mother with the assertion that it was her beauty and her charm that ought to be recorded in history she scolded me for a fool.

"What will be, will be," she informed me bitterly, "and they will call me hag! *Hideous* and *shaggy* are the words that vile clerk will use to record the knight's impressions as he gallops towards the causeway where he will slay me. I will have long, plaited whiskers and my misshapen teeth will be discolored. *Fiend* I will be called, and *demon*. I will be charged with lunatic self-confidence in delivering the first stroke of my scythe, and idiotic recklessness in embedding its point so deeply in a marble pillar that I cannot pull it out again. Thus will my ugliness become a kind of comedy, and poor Fergus a petty prefiguration of Quixote, the greatest of all buffoons!"

"Poor Fergus!" I retorted, unwisely. "*Poor* Fergus, is it, who will cut off your hands at the wrists before driving the long blade of his sword into your belly and up through your vital organs? Poor Fergus, is it, who will carry away our fabulous shining shield, so that he may use its glamour to liberate his Galiene and to unhorse Lancelot himself in the joust? *Accursed* Fergus I will call him—thrice-damned Fergus if there is any justice in the world beyond the world."

"There is no world beyond the world," she told me, with dire contempt. "For all the patience of Fate and all the work she has invested in her Writing, the mists of might-yet-be are as infinite and as inescapable as the mists of might-have-been."

She would not condescend to hate her killer! She was perfectly ready to loathe and despise the imbecile cleric charged by fashion to record his exploits for a world over-hungry for mirages of gallantry, but she would not curse the man himself.

I know now that I ought to have let the matter rest. Indeed, I ought to have done my utmost to lay it to rest. I ought to have distracted my beloved mother from her growing pre-occupation with the legend of her passing.

I did try, but she became so obsessed that the only way to distract her from the subject of Fergus of Galloway and the literary treachery of Guillaume le Clerc was to ask her about other writings to come.

"They will be many," she assured me, "but vague. Fancy will be piled upon fancy, until gaudy confusion covers the last fugitive remnants of actual memory. Even the fate of Arthur is unclear, although I cannot tell whether it is as yet un-Written or merely doomed to be unwritten. He will fall out with his bastard Mordred, that much is clear. They will meet on a field of battle but Arthur, being Arthur, will try to make

152

peace. Then the mist will descend—both an actual mist and a mist of uncertainty, for the literal and the metaphorical are very confused in the writings of men. The battle will be fought, it seems, although there is a blur on the future page that prevents my seeing precisely how or why. After-wards...well, even men will call that *afterwards* a Dark Age."

"And will Fergus of Galloway fall in that battle?" I wanted to know. "How will he meet *his* death?"

"I cannot tell," she said, the words weighing heavily upon her. "For all my antiquity and all my sorcery, I cannot tell."

* * * * * * *

It seems to me now that I might have done more to save my mother's memories from the void of oblivion had I only spoken to her of happier times with the same insistence and precision that she employed in speaking of times to come. I dare say that, had I only known how and taken trouble to cultivate the art, I might even have helped her to think better of me. It is true that I had only the one magical talent, and that a rather vulgar one—there has always been something slightly suspect about kinship with serpents—but I had other virtues. At the end of the day, I was a dutiful son, in spite of all my errors.

If I had only had the gift of lightening her spirits, I might have helped my mother to think more about my future than her own. I have now reached the point in my life at which I know nothing at all about what lies before me, ex-cept for the moment and manner of my death, because I have run to the end of the little that my mother was able to tell me. Sometimes, I wonder whether that is because she really could not remember me well enough to look any further into my future, or whether she simply could not bear to tell me what she foresaw. On balance, I would rather it were the lat-ter; I think I could bear to face a future full of horrors more easily than I can live with the apprehension that my mother did not love me at all.

For whatever reason, there came a time when I could not divert my mother from contemplation of her doom, and how it would be weighed in the fraudulent scales of human estimation. I should not have become angry with her, but I did. I even taunted her myself, when it all became too much to bear

"If your future offends you, Mother dearest," I howled at her, as if I might secure my place in her memory simply by raising my voice, "then have the courage to defy it! Given that foresight has revealed to you every mocking detail of the rubbishy record that Guillaume le Clerc will make of your presence on this earth, you ought to be able to use what you know! If you know where and when this Fergus of Galloway will be born, slay him in his cradle. If you know the names of his enemies and when they will strike at him, go to them in advance and give them better weapons. If you know that he must have your precious shield no matter what, refuse to defend it. Are we not *vargr*-folk, when all is said and done— and are not the *vargr*-folk rebels, even against God Almighty?"

"You do not understand, my darling fool of the family," she informed me. "Fate is Fate, and has the means to cheat all those who rebel against it. What will be written truthfully is Written already, and the best that any creature of fate can ever obtain is to obscure a part of the lesser writing with the mists of might-have-been. There is little consolation in that, I assure you. If the ultimate result of all our rebellions is to relegate our best achievements to the realm of misremembered fantasy, we will become less than nothing in the thrust of history. It is better to be an item of parody than that."

"Perhaps I should be glad that I don't understand," I said. "Perhaps, because I don't understand, I can go to Galloway and strangle the infant Fergus in his cradle. Perhaps, because I don't understand, I can stand with you on the causeway when you meet him, and cut him in two before he severs your wrists. Perhaps...."

"No," she said, with a softness infinitely more powerful than wrath, "you cannot. Lack of understanding always weakens; it never empowers. Better to understand, and accept, that you cannot alter any of these things. You cannot alter that which is already Written. Whatever work you do, it must be done in the margins of Fate's pages; only there can creatures of our kind hope to have an effect on the great tide of the world's becoming. We are *vargr*-folk, you see: vampires and shapeshifters, giants and dwarfs, keepers of dragons and makers of wonders, miraculous children of the eternal she-wolf. There have been those among us who spoke all the tongues that birds and beasts know, and even knew the languages of stones, but only humans *write*. That is why, in spite of all their imperfections, they are the darlings of Fate."

"One day, Mother dearest," I told her, still the rebel even while I wept, "I will write. If I must become human to do it, I will write. And before then, however I may and however I might, I shall avenge you. If it is not Written how and where and when Fergus of Galloway will die, I will be there to carve his blood-stained hands from his arms, and laugh at his helplessness."

I think that was the last time she ever reached out to touch my head. She did not ruffle my hair, as she had done when I was smaller, but she touched my brow with tenderness.

Perhaps she was saying goodbye to my fading memory, although she must have known that I would be with her for years to come, and had centuries still to live.

"That would be no vengeance," she said to me. "Poor Fergus is as much a slave of history as any other man. To take an eye for an eye or a hand for a hand is a human way of counting, of which even they will become ashamed in time. Our kind is not adapted to take vengeance; we know too much of what will be, and the only plans that we may make are those that will help to precipitate the Written actuality from the mists of might-yet-be. What satisfaction can there be in serving as a jealous instrument of Fate? In any case, poor Fergus is nothing but a symptom and a symbol of a phase in moral progress; you might as well strike out against the round table, against chivalry itself."

* * * * * * *

I know, now, that my mother was telling me—as best she could, in the near-delirium of her decrepitude—to desist. What she wanted me to do was to become a little wiser, a little more understanding. What she wanted me to do was to cease to think of such ignoble matters as vengeance. Perhaps she had forgotten that I was the fool of the family, or mistaken the magnitude of my foolishness.

I misconstrued her words. Perhaps I did so deliberately; I honestly cannot tell. I too am plagued by the mists of might-have-been, and I am not what I once was. I write, but in order to do that I have had to give up even the meager portion of magic that I once had.

I took my mother at her word. I left Fergus of Galloway alone. I did not attempt to strangle him in his cradle, and I never tried to strike his hands from his body as he struck my mother's from hers.

Instead, I struck out at the round table itself, and against chivalry itself. *You might as well*, my mother said, and so I did.

I did it in the only way I could, according to her account. I struck from the margins of Fate's forewritten page, unsuspected even by those who can read between the lines of the tale that Fate is busy writing. I can say, with a confidence born of experience, that there is satisfaction in serving as a jealous instrument of fate; what came to pass was already Written, but nowhere was it Written that I should be the one to do it, nor was it ever recorded by human hand that I was the one who did—but it is written *now*.

You have never heard my name. Even those of you who have read the tale of my mother's death in that vile mock-romance by Guillaume le Clerc, learning thereby to love and laugh at poor Fergus of Galloway, will not have suspected my existence, until now. You will have read, of course, in your beloved Malory, how Arthur's army met Mordred's on that dismal field of battle, and how they agreed between themselves that they would not fight, and that both companies would withdraw—so long as no man on either side should draw a sword.

You will have read, too, that it was a striking viper which caused a single knight to draw his weapon, precipitating the conflict that brought about the death of Arthur, the end of chivalry and the last deep fall of Darkness.

Was that a tragedy, do you think? Was it a terrible accident of Fate?

No, it was not. It was payment, for what Fergus of Galloway did to my mother, the so-called hag of Dunnottar. It was payment for all that was done by every knight that ever slew a dragon, or ever made war on the precious *vargr*-folk.

I shall not write my name here, for I would rather remain the nothing that your writings have made of me; by that means I add insult to injury and am glad to do it. Know, though, that the *vargr*-folk were possessed of power as well as glory, and that even the last and least of their line had magic enough to carve nightmares from the mists of might-have-been.

Arthur might have been more than a local king, had he been given freer rein; chivalry might have been more than a farcical fraud, if it had only found more fertile soil in which to flourish. Such hopes as those evaporated into the mists that rose as Arthur's final battle began: the battle which my mother—*my mother, the hag*—had foreseen but dimly as an event that never would be written or explained in full.

By the time my mother died, she was, I will admit, a hag of sorts—but she had been a true temptress and worthy daughter of Lilith for centuries before that, and I would have that fact known. She should not be reckoned any less because she spent her own legacy so fully that her son had but a single magical talent, and that a meager one.

As you now know, a great deal may be accomplished by a dutiful son who knows the language of vipers, if only he picks his moment carefully enough.

* * * * * * *

[Note: The story of Fergus of Galloway's encounter with the "hairy hag" of Dunnottar is recorded in lines 4093-4203 of the Frescoln manuscript of Guillaume le Clerc's *Fergus*, rendered into English in pp.66-68 of D. D. R. Owen's Everyman translation of 1991. The ten commandments of chivalry to which the notional author refers were formulated and numbered by Léon Gautier in Chapter II of *Chivalry* (1884; translated into English 1891). The most notable not-quite-full account of Arthur's last battle, to which the notional author also refers, is described in Chapter IV of Book XXI of Malory's *Morte d'Arthur*. The notion of the *vargr*-folk, which here refers collectively to all the supernatural beings of legend, owes its origin to a double meaning pointed out by Sabine Baring-Gould in Chapter IV of *The Book of Werewolves* (1865), which equates *vargr* with "restless" as well as with "wolf".]

THE DEVIL'S COMEDY

Monsignor,

Nothing is more sacred than the secrecy of the confessional, but every priest of the church, however humble his status, also has a responsibility to report to his superiors every unique and potentially insightful incident of earthly happenstance that bears upon the historical mission of the Church, which is to defeat the Devil's snares and prepare mankind for salvation. There is, in consequence, an obligation upon me to make this record, just as there is an obligation upon me to exclude the name of the penitent sinner, and as there is, upon anyone whose duty it may be to read it, never to reveal the contents of this manuscript to anyone who has no right or need to know them.

The man who told me this tale made his confession at the commencement of Lent in the year of our Lord 1790. He is an Englishman, who had recently returned to his homeland from what is nowadays called the Grand Tour, which had taken him about the Continent for two years. Given that the event which it is my duty to record took place a full twelvemonth before, it might be thought that he had been remiss in his observances, but he assured me that he had been very punctilious in attending mass, whether he found himself in Paris, Rome or Florence. He refrained from taking communion only because he had been reluctant to render his confessions in languages of which his mastery was uncertain, lest he be misunderstood. For this reason, he had hoarded the statement of his sins while repenting of them fully in his heart.

The tedious register of the gentleman's stored sins was of no interest or consequence, save for one—which might not even qualify as a sin at all, though he felt compelled to tell me every detail of it. The incident in question took place on the eve of Ash Wednesday in 1789, in Venice. Of the gentleman himself I will say nothing, save for one relevant particular: that although he comes from a good enough family, and does not lack means, he is something of a playwright. I have never seen any of his works performed, but hearsay allows me to testify with confidence that his reputation—which is small, even in his own country—is for a kind of comedy generally called farcical. This knowledge will help to explain—if not to excuse—his dubious conduct in the affair I now transcribe, in words as close to his own as memory and grammar will permit.

Benedict, Order of St Dominic

* * * * * * *

On the last day of the carnival I had already been seven days in Venice, and had never been so utterly sated by ceaseless festivity. In every other European city, save for those that have fallen victim to the curse of Protestantism, Shrove Tuesday is a day unparalleled and a fête unrivalled, but Venice is Venice, where extravagance in pleasure-seeking is almost a matter of course.

In Venice, the most important festival of the year is the fortnight after Ascension Day, when the golden ship *Bucentaur* carries the doge from his palace to cast the betrothal-ring of the Republic into the sea, to seal the sacred bargain that has maintained the city's wealth and power for a thousand years. Second in importance, in those years where the election of a new doge does not license a special fête, is St Mark's Day. Shrove Tuesday remains, I suppose, no less significant than Christmas, but it is more elaborately anticipated because the weather is milder and the twilight later, so it comes at the end of a riot of pleasure that would exhaust the strongest mind and stomach in the continent.

A mere seven days had exhausted me; the residents of the city, inured by long experience, had taken twice as long to reach the same state of surfeit, but reach it they had. Called upon for one last effort of extravagance, they responded with a will—but the will was feverish, as if haunted by a strange kind of panic. Never was *ennui* resisted so forcefully, nor with such desperation.

You have doubtless heard of Venice as a city of canals, where gondolas play the part of carriages on liquid highways, but when the carnival is in full flow the water almost disappears among a motley dress of barges and feluccas, galleys and skiffs. All are decorated with paint and colored cloth, as if they were costumed and masked in the same manner as the people and the booths crowding the Square of St Mark's. The crowds in the Piazza, the Piazzetta and the Mole extend like the coils of a snake around the multitudinous stalls and booths set up there, where goods of every kind are sold, fortunes told by every method known to superstition, all manner of freaks, prodigies and exotic animals displayed, and performances mounted by musicians, acrobats and clowns.

I had two reasons for being in Venice, over and above the natural desire to see one of Christendom's finest cities and only great republic. The first was to see the Carnival of Venice in all its gaudy glory; the second was to see performances of works by Carlo Goldoni and Carlo Gozzi, the two contrasted masters of the new Venetian comedy that has replaced the obsolete *Commedia dell'arte*. Perhaps I should

161

say "transformed" rather than "replaced", for all the characters of the Commedia are still there, not merely in the theatres where Gozzi's plays are performed, but on the water and
the land alike. They have broken free from their former ser-
vitude in becoming models for three in every five of the fanciful costumes that the low-ranking Venetians put on in order to enjoy their festival. Such copies and pastiches have
become the common uniform of barkers and street-
performers—but they are everpresent in the crowds too, no
matter where one looks. Venice is full of new and eminently
fashionable theatres, but on carnival days the whole city is a
theatre of phantoms, relics of times long lost. Every action is
dramatic, and no one can say where the audience ends and
the players begin.

A friar like you, Father, might look upon the Carnival of
Venice and see Sodom and Gomorrah—but a playmaker like
me sees only comedy. We are both right, for Venice now is
what Rome must have been in the days of the Syrian princes,
which some call the Decadence and others a time of madness. The city's morality leaves much to be desired—but if
you had been there on that day, Father, you would not have
seen a city in the grip of the seven deadly sins, but a city in
the grip of fatigue and accidie: a city tired of wickedness and
crying out for release.

And that, Father, is why I was not at all surprised, when
I passed between the booth of a painless dentist and a stall
where the elixir of life could be purchased at a very reasonable price, to be accosted by an exceedingly weary and
seemingly footsore Devil.

His cloven hooves must have been exceedingly uncomfortable as the fitting of a human foot, and he was limping
badly. The material forming the core of his tail had been broken, so that the pointed tip hung limply down. His ill-belted
stomach had broken through the red cloth of his midriff, his
horsehair beard was askew, and beads of sweat had carried
streaks of pigment from the widow's peak ineptly painted on
his forehead, through the barricades of the furry eyebrows
that served him instead of a mask, to stain his eyelids brown.

He hardly looked up as he offered me a playbill, advertising the final performance of a comedy by Gozzi at a tiny

theatre in one of the mazy alleys beyond the Ponte San Rocco.

I had only to take it, put it away and forget all about it, but I was slightly puzzled. The performance was advertised for ten o'clock, but in Venice, as everywhere, the Lenten fast begins at the stroke of midnight, and all festivity must end on that instant. So careful are the Venetians of this deadline that all the Shrove Tuesday fireworks are discharged at noon.

"It must be a short play," I said to the man dressed as the devil. I spoke in Italian, but my accent is dreadful and I usually make three mistakes even in so short a sentence, so I was not unduly surprised when he replied in English.

"It will be exactly as long as it needs to be," he said. I would have passed on with a smile had he not added: "As you will readily appreciate, my lord, as a practitioner of the dramatic art."

Had he said "connoisseur" it would have been mere random flattery, like the "my lord", but he said "practitioner"—and would hardly have done so by accident.

"Do you know me, then?" I asked, pausing to look him in the face. It is a rare privilege to look anyone in the face during the Carnival of Venice, but this man wore no mask to shield his eyes, even though he had a red hood with fake horns to cover his hair and ears, and absurdly-contrived fakes for eyebrows and a beard. Only his bloodshot eyes seemed real, but they seemed very real indeed, and they met my own gaze frankly.

"Yes, my lord," he said. "You have visited six theatres in six nights, Sunday included, and you have watched three dozen street-performances by day. The news of your presence has run right through the city; look for the Englishman, the rumor says, for he has come to honor us by stealing our ideas. As you know, my lord, ours has always been a comedy of improvisation; our greatest triumphs are matters of the moment, lost as soon as they are displayed. All but a handful of our players are illiterate, and it is rare that anyone comes to see us who might deign to remember, let alone to record, our spontaneous jests. I have been hoping for days, and waiting for hours, for the opportunity to give you this advertisement. You will not be disappointed, my lord."

163

Until I heard that speech I had been determined to return to my bed without bothering to wait for midnight to strike. I had had my fill of comedy. As the man costumed as the Devil had observed, all but a few of the great players of Venice utilize scripts only as roughest of guides; most of the dialogue and the acrobatic action in their new versions of familiar plays is improvised for the occasion, in order that the audience might be pleasantly surprised by unfamiliar diversions and topical references. Alas, the usual results of such tampering are far from ingenious, and what tries to pass itself off as innovation is usually uninspired, repetitive and conspicuously dull. There was something about the man in the Devil's guise, however, that made me hesitate. I did not believe for an instant that he had been waiting here for hours in the hope that I would walk by at last, but it was a nice compliment.

"I cannot believe that you will have a large audience," I said, while I hesitated.

"I am glad that you have raised the matter, my lord," the devil replied, "else I could not have done so politely. But as it happens, you might render us both a service in that regard."

"I fear that I am traveling alone," I told him.

"That is not what I meant, my lord. There is someone who ought to be present at the performance, who will come at your bidding if you will condescend to ask him for me. You need only walk a hundred paces, and you would be doing us both a service."

This seemed exceedingly peculiar, but also intriguing. "You want me to invite a particular companion?" I said, skeptically.

"Not exactly, my lord," the Devil replied. "What I would like you to do, if you are agreeable, is to deliver a message. Go, if you will, to the booth of the fortune-teller who advertises himself as Mercutio the Cheiromancer, and tell him that, if he cares to come to the theatre tonight, he will be in the presence of the man who now has the eyes which the father of Caterina di Mastropiero made in Murano for Bartolomeo Collatino, nine-and-thirty years ago."

Murano is the island where the glass-makers of Venice have their workshops. There was a time when Venice was the sole master of all the great secrets of the glass-making art, and not all those secrets were lost when the treasonous *Arte Vitraria* was published two hundred years ago, so I knew at once that the man costumed as the Devil was talking about a pair of glass eyes made for a man who had lost his sight—most probably as a consequence of disease, but perhaps as a matter of judicial torture, or even in a duel.

I had not heard of either of the people he named, but that did not seem surprising.

"Why can you not deliver the message yourself?" I asked, bluntly.

"Because Mercutio has recently hired an assistant and guardian who is something of a ruffian, presently costumed as Arlequino. He would not let me into the tent without paying a fee, and might not let me walk away unmolested if I were to tell him what I have just told you. There are certain messages, my lord, which need to be passed along a chain in order to avoid endangering their deliverers—and it is as well if the final link in the chain is both a gentleman and foreigner, who obviously knows no more than he has been told to say and is safe from any ill-treatment by unruly servants."

You might think, Father, that this was a commission fit for a fool, but I thought at the time that it was equally fit for a maker of plays. At any rate, I was intrigued, and I agreed to do as I was bid.

* * * * * * *

Although several hours of the fete remained, the appetite of the crowd in the Piazza for further amusement had dwindled, and most of the stallholders were quite exhausted. The jugglers had put away their clubs and the fire-eaters had extinguished their brands. All but a few of the mountebanks had grown weary of their own deceptions, but there was not one among them who could not raise himself to one last effort if there were a coin at stake.

There was more than one barker costumed as Arlequino—indeed, there were a baker's dozen—but the one touting for the cheiromancer was still on his feet, maintaining his patter even though his voice had faded to a croak. When I offered him silver he bowed expansively, and lifted the flap of the tent whose door he was guarding.

It was dark inside, all natural light being excluded, but a single candle had been lit for the convenience of paying customers. The chair set before the little table was easy enough to see, but the fortune-teller was shrouded in shadow. It was not until I took my place and he leaned forward to take my hand that I could discern any of his features, but in the split second before he lowered his head, his eyes—or what he had instead of eyes—caught the light.

Perhaps I should not have been surprised to find that he was blind, but no matter how fully prepared I might have been I should still have felt a shock as I beheld that sightless stare. Even English glass-makers can produce false eyes that simulate the real thing, and the Venetians are so artful that they can make a perfect match to an eye that survives, but Mercutio's false eyes must have been made of jet, for they were as black and glossy as a scarab's carapace.

He reached out with his left hand and I placed my right hand within it, palm upwards. He began to run the fingertips of his own right hand over mine, very gently. Not content to track the lines inscribed on the palm, he touched my fingers and wrist.

"A gentleman," he murmured, in Italian, "and a man well-used to plying a pen," he said, obviously having taken note of the general condition of my hands and the callus on the joint of my middle finger.

I confirmed his unremarkable deductions, speaking Italian although I knew that my origins would be clear enough.

He addressed me in my own language as easily and fluently as his dubious friend the Devil. "How do you like the carnival, my lord? It is the experience of a lifetime, is it not? You will remember it fondly when you are eighty years old, I think—all the more so because your children and your children's children will not have the opportunity to see its like."

"Are they fated never to leave home, then?" I asked.

"No, my lord," he replied. "They will be great travelers—but Venice will not be the same. The Republic will be gone, the city looted by a dwarfish conqueror from the west. There will be carnivals here, as everywhere, but they will not be the carnival that you have seen. Make the most of your opportunity, my lord—you are a fortunate man to be here this day. You may never be as fortunate again, although you will live long and prosper."

"I am glad to hear that," I said, agreeably, "and deeply sorry to learn that the fate of this great city will be worse than mine. Where will you make your living then?"

"There will be no necessity, my lord," he said, in a voice so gentle as to belie the bleakness of the sentiment. "Are there any particular matters you would like me to address?"

"Yes," I said. "Tell me about the eyes which the father of Caterina di Mastropiero made in Murano for Bartolomeo Collatino, nine-and-thirty years ago."

I was trying to shock him. There is always a particular amusement to be derived from startling those who claim to have privileged knowledge of the future. In this instance, I failed. There was not the slightest convulsion in the hand that held mine, and the other did not pause in its exploration of my palm.

"Ah," he said. "I am sorry, my lord. I had heard rumors, and suspected that the summons might come, but I had not expected it from you. A jest, I think. Where will the man be found who has the true eyes?"

"You have not answered my question," I pointed out. "I paid Arlequino his fee, did I not?"

Had he had the power of sight, I might be able to say that he looked up. At any rate, he raised his face so that the candlelight caught the polished jet again. It was as if there were two tiny flames deep within his inner being—not so much in the eyes themselves as the interior of his skull, or the profundity of his soul.

"Are you sure that you want to know, my lord?" he asked.

"I am a playwright in search of inspiration," I told him. "I know my Goldoni and my Gozzi, and am eager to hear what Venice can offer in the way of tragedy."

"Tragedy?" he echoed, his voice like velvet. "There is no tragedy in Venice, my lord. There is only comedy. There is Goldoni's comedy, which is all mistakes and misfortunes; there is Gozzi's comedy, which is all fantasy and fabulation; and there is the Devil's comedy."

"Which is?" I prompted.

"All lust," he said, and hesitated for a moment before adding: "and bargains." I could not tell whether he hesitated because he had cast about for an alliterative term and failed to find one, or because did not want to pronounce the word *lies*.

"Will you tell me where I am to go, my lord?" he asked, politely.

"Most certainly," I said. "When I have my explanation."

Perhaps he sighed. "You say that you know your Goldoni," he said. "Do you know *Il Cavaliere e la Dama*?"

"Yes," I said. "It is a play about cicisbei—martyrs to gallantry, he calls them, and slaves to feminine caprice. Was Bartolomeo Collatino a cicisbeo, and Caterina di Mastropiero his mistress?"

* * * * * * *

I ought to explain at this point, Father, that the follies of courtly and chivalric romance came late to Venice, long after the death of the last troubadour. As recently as a hundred years ago, the wives of Venetian patricians were treated in much the same way as those of their great enemies the Turks, locked away in secret apartments—but as the city gradually gave itself over to the year-round riot of festivals, the sternness of solid walls and the guardianship of eunuchs gave way to the delicacy of the carnival mask and the gallantry of cavaliers.

Because the regular society of the Venetian patricians had no place for wives, the wives who began to go abroad made their own, excluding their husbands. It became fashionable for every wife to adopt a *cavalier servente*, or cicisbeo, ostensibly as a protector, and to drag him everywhere— to the theatre, to the houses of her friends, even to mass. Doubtless he waits patiently without while the lady makes her confession, but it is probable that he hears those same confessions in his turn. Many, I hasten to add, are old and

wise rather than young and pretty, and a few are the displaced aristocrats they all claim to be—but it has to be admitted that there are some who serve their idols more as
Lancelot served Guinevere than as Don Quixote served his
Dulcinea; and it has to be admitted, too, that some are *bravi*
in disguise.

I should explain the term "bravo" too, to save the need
for further digression. In Venice, there is a guild for every
craft, and every guild claims great antiquity and total control
over its trade. Each has its own livery, which is worn with
pride—and so deeply entrenched is the system that even rob-
bers and assassins dared to form a guild three hundred years
ago, and adopted a uniform of their own. They were the
bravi: killers for hire. Because all guildsmen are sworn to
defend and avenge one another, it became exceedingly difficult for any agent of the law to take action against any individual bravo without placing himself in extraordinary danger. The Republic even passed a law guaranteeing a free
pardon to any bravo who assassinated another, but the ruse
failed and sterner measures had to be taken. In theory, the
bravi were suppressed more than a century ago, but they
never died out, no matter how fiercely they were persecuted
and punished. Nowadays, the old uniform of the bravi is a
carnival costume like any other, but at least some pretended
bravi are bravi in truth, and the cleverest are treachery per-
sonified.

Keep this in mind, Father, as you listen to the story that
Mercutio the Cheiromancer told me, and the remainder of
my own....

* * * * * * *

The blind man with the velvet voice told me that Bartolomeo Collatino was indeed a cicisbeo, and that Caterina di
Mastropiero was his Dama—he warned me to beware of
words like "mistress", which are so easily mistranslated and
misunderstood.

Caterina was the daughter of Pietro Beroviero of Murano, and therefore felt entitled to consider herself an aristocrat of sorts. The Beroviero family is one of the most power-

ful in Murano, which has its own Great Council and Golden Book, because the glass-blowers are so vital to the wealth of Venice that their microcosm mirrors the greater unity of which it is a part. The Mastropiero family, on the other hand, is one of the most august in the Republic, so from their point of view the marriage between Leandro di Mastropiero and Caterina was seen as reckless condescension at best, and at worst an entrapment, secured by the lure of uncommon beauty.

Leandro was a handsome young man, and very vain. He saw no cause to be jealous of his wife's cicisbeo on the grounds that she might prefer Bartolomeo to him, because Bartolomeo was seven years older than he and a great deal plainer—but that did not prevent him from resenting the fact that Caterina should want a cicisbeo at all. According to the blind man, Leandro would far rather have lived a hundred years earlier, when a wife could be safely prisoned from any sight but her husband's.

"What of the Collatino family?" I asked, at this point. "What was Bartolomeo, apart from being a cicisbeo?" I admit that I was being provocative, for I had already formed the obvious hypothesis that Mercutio the Blind Cheiromancer was none other than Bartolomeo Collatino grown old.

"That is not important," the man with eyes of jet assured me. "Whatever he was before he was a cicisbeo was forgotten, at least by him, as soon as he became one. He played the part to the full, as energetically as any of his peers. As a servant he seemed excessively assiduous, as a guide excessively reliable, as a listener excessively attentive, as a guardian excessively dutiful...and as a friend, impossibly loyal. Everyone said that he had no eyes for anyone but his Dama: a comic figure indeed. He might easily have been a player in a skit by Goldoni, who had forgotten that he was merely acting a part and had continued to improvise...indefinitely, incessantly, absurdly."

The cheiromancer's voice had almost faded away, but he collected himself.

He told me that whispers had been put about—as seemingly sourceless as such whispers ever are—to the effect that Leandro di Mastropiero had been played for a fool twice over, once in marrying beneath him and once in being persuaded to place his wife in the care of a masquerader. This rumor was borne to Leandro's ear by his oldest and dearest friend, Maurizio Scamozzi, who also happened to serve as cicisbeo to Leandro's sister Zulietta, who was married to Andrea Zellini. Zulietta was no friend to Caterina, to whom she always referred as *the bead princess*, because the branch of the Beroviero to which she belonged was the backbone of the bead-makers guild.

The rumors blackening his wife's name were just as effective in blackening Leandro's mood, and he grew morose—but he was vain enough that the mere fact that the rumors were circulating troubled him more deeply than the possibility that they might be true. He wanted them stamped out, and he asked his friend to help him put a stop to them. Alas, denial is to rumor what oil is to a conflagration and Leandro became aware soon enough that people were laughing behind their hands as they watched him pass by. Perhaps unwisely, he swore that he would fight anyone who was heard by a witness to make any slighting remark about his wife or her cavalier.

He was forced to take up his sword twice within the week; he wounded both his opponents, and was fortunate not to attract the attention of the law.

"Perhaps Leandro became desperate then," the blind man went on, "or perhaps his friend, urged on by Zulietta, took it upon himself to save the situation. I do know, though, that a villain was hired: a man who called himself Tondino, after the gambling game tondina. He *was* a gambler, this Tondino, who delighted in ensnaring his victims in crooked games and wagering for pounds of flesh, all bloodshed included. Some say that the game he played with Leandro di Mastropiero one fateful night was a fake from beginning to end, cooked up in conspiracy between the two of them, while others claim that Leandro was the dupe of his sister or his friend, or both...but only the Devil knows the truth. Perhaps the first plan was to inveigle Bartolomeo into the game, and when that failed improvisation took over...but however the masquerade was worked, and whoever was pulling the strings, a situation was produced in which Leandro, with his wife and her cicisbeo looking on, was provoked into a bet that was extremely unwise."

"He pledged his eyes?" I asked, racing to get ahead of the plot.

"No," said Mercutio the Cheiromancer. "He was goaded into betting a ring that had been given to him by the father of his bride as an element of her dowry. It was gold, with a roseate stone shaped like a heart to which no man could put a name."

"But it was only a trinket," I said, disappointed.

"It would have been, had Leandro not grown a little since the day of his betrothal—but he had already let it slip to his friends that the ring was now so tight on his finger that he did not think it could possibly be removed without cutting through the joint. Tondino knew that—as did Bartolomeo."

"But how do we progress from there to Bartolomeo's eyes?" I demanded. "The wager was lost, of course, and Leandro was asked for the forfeit—and Caterina intervened, I suppose, because the ring meant as much to her as to him even if the finger did not. But...."

"She intervened in the only way she could," the blind man said, his voice a mere whisper. "She asked for time, so that all possible ingenuity might be employed to dislodge the ring that was lost from the finger to which it was clinging so stubbornly.

"Tondino offered her twenty-four hours.

"Doctors were summoned, and magicians, and even Pietro Beroviero...but the ring could not be budged.

"So, in the end, Bartolomeo went to meet Tondino, with instructions to buy him off...or to do whatever else might be required to save the situation. What happened afterwards remains a mystery. Bartolomeo was found two days later, unconscious in a skiff drifting on the Grand Canal. His eyes had been put out. Nothing more was ever heard of Tondino. So far as anyone knows, Leandro di Mastropiero wore his ring to the grave, where he was put ten years ago. At any rate, his finger was still intact."

"But Caterina's father was a bead-maker, and she asked him to make a pair of glass eyes for her wounded cicisbeo," I said, still hastening towards an end I thought I could see clearly enough.

"A blind cicisbeo is no cicisbeo at all," the cheiromancer told me. "He must perforce seek other employment—but yes, Bartolomeo was owed a debt that was more than any Venetian noblewoman could easily pay. Her father was privy to the darkest secrets of his guild, and enough of a guildsman to refuse to say who had brought him into the affair, or when, or why. All that anyone knows for sure is that Bartolomeo did acquire a new pair of eyes, without any appreciable delay. Alas, they proved to be too precious for their humble purpose. Bartolomeo had them for barely a year before they were stolen. It is, alas, all too easy to steal from a man who is blind—even the eyes from his face."

"You had no Arlequino then, to keep watch for you?" I said.

"Why should you say *you*?" he retorted, too softly for me to judge whether or not he was speaking ironically. "What have I to do with this, except to understand how precious a good pair of false eyes might be? I know a dozen blind men who would pay very dearly for those eyes, my friend—so dearly that if I thought you knew where they were, I might have you kidnapped and beaten in the hope that I could steal them before my rivals had a chance. You are just a go-between, I know—but you ought not to be vain enough to believe yourself the only one. Now tell me, please, where the auction is to be held?"

"Auction?" I repeated, letting my disappointment show. "I was invited to a comedy by Gozzi, at a theatre in a by-street beyond the Ponte San Rocco." I took the playbill out as I spoke, forgetting that he could not see to read it.

The cheiromancer laughed softly. "Oh yes," he said. "It will be a comedy, I have no doubt. All fantasy and fabulation, all lust and diabolical bargaining. Give the bill to my hireling—he reads no better than he touts for business, but he seems to know the names of theatres well enough. Do come, my lord. It will complete your experience of the carnival of Venice, and give you a fine tale to tell your children's children...or your confessor."

"Why my confessor?" I asked.

"Sometimes," said the man with eyes of jet, "a pretended bravo is a bravo in truth—and a pretended Devil, a Devil in truth."

I could not take him seriously at the time, Father, but that was a mistake. It is a thought that has preoccupied my mind ever since, whose careful phrasing echoes there still. If you have followed the convolutions of my tale with sufficient attention, you will recall that I never once mentioned to the blind charlatan that the message had been given to me by a man costumed as the Devil—and that fact, I am certain, was in no way evidenced by the condition of my hand.

* * * * * * *

I gave the playbill to the bedraggled Arlequino, but I had not gone thirty paces before I realized that he was dogging my footsteps. I turned to challenge him, but he only told me, in Italian, that a Venetian servant had a perfect right to follow an Englishman through the alleyways of Venice—and even to follow his course upon the water if the need arose.

"I am going to my hotel," I told him, in bad Italian. "I intend to dine before I go to the theatre. I shall not be meeting the man who gave me the message."

"I believe you, my lord," he replied, with an exaggerated bow, "but I shall follow you anyway." I could not be absolutely certain, but his accent gave the impression that he was no more native to the city than I was. There was something in it of Madrid, or perhaps of Lisbon.

"What is your name?" I asked, stung by annoyance. "And do not tell me that it is Arlequino."

"Today is Mardi Gras," he told me. "We have all set our names aside, and may not take them up again till midnight strikes."

I was determined that he should not have the last word—for I am, after all, a man whose vocation it is to put my words in other men's mouths.

"What became of Bartolomeo Collatino when his eyes were stolen?" I asked him. "And what was so precious about the eyes that Pietro Beroviero made for him?" At least, that is what I intended to ask—but my Italian may not have been comprehensible to one who was not himself a native speaker of that tongue. He shook his head and bowed again, as if to invite me to proceed on my way.

I did, but I could not put aside the questions that I ought to have asked Mercutio the blind seer, when I had been in too much of a hurry. What had become of Bartolomeo? For that matter, what had become of the now-widowed Caterina? What, exactly, had happened between Bartolomeo and Tondino? Save for being unable to set aside my conviction that Mercutio was indeed Bartolomeo, I had no ready answer to any of these questions—but the other I had flung at Arlequino was of a different sort. If Mercutio really did know of a dozen blind men avid to possess those eyes, surely they must offer some power of sight—but if they did, how was it that their first owner had been an easy target for the unscrupulous thief who had taken them from him?

I looked back when I reached the door of my hotel, but there was not an Arlequino in sight—a fact that would have been rather remarkable even if I had not known that one had been following me.

I ate in my room, and had barely finished my meal when there was a knock on the door. It was a servant, delivering a costume that I had not hired.

It occurs to me now that I have not said a word as to whether I, like almost everyone else, was in costume that evening. The truth is that I was and was not, at one and the same time. I was dressed like an English gentleman, powdered and bewigged—but in Venice on Shrove Tuesday, such an outfit could only be perceived as a pastiche, if not an outright parody. I had worn clothing of exactly that kind for the last six days, and had never felt so perfectly in keeping in a London drawing-room or a civic function in the county. I had not hired a costume because I had not needed one, but someone obviously believed that I might need one tonight— and when I gave the matter some consideration, it seemed to me that it might indeed be wise to travel incognito.

The costume that had been sent up to my room was by no means one that I would have chosen for myself, but the mood I was in made its very unlikelihood seem perfect.

The principal garment was a vast and luxurious satin robe with an equally capacious hood, colored brilliantly yellow. There was a shirt too, and a sturdy cummerbund, and neatly-woven hose, all in the same brilliant yellow, even though they would hardly show beneath the robe. The accompanying mask was neither a mere eyepiece nor a porcelain mould of a face, although those were the kinds of masks that almost everyone in the city was wearing. It was shaped to cover the forehead, the eyes and the bridge of the nose—save for two unusually discreet eye-holes—but the opaque fabric then gave way to a fringe such as one sees at the bottom of an ornamental curtain, whose silken threads hung down over the mouth and chin.

My first thought was that whoever had sent it must intend me to be very conspicuous, for I had not seen another costume like it in seven days—but that he must, at the same time, want me to be quite unrecognisable to anyone but him, at least until I spoke.

It was not until I had put the costume on that I saw that there was a wand too, lurking at the bottom of the bundle. I picked it up and studied it carefully. The shaft was yellow, but the head was painted as well as shaped to resemble the flames of a torch. The weight of the device seemed all wrong until I pulled the head experimentally, at which point a gleaming blade came free from its sheath.

The wand was a swordstick.

I am no fencer, but the blade was not long enough to qualify as a foil; it was more like an assassin's dagger. It gave me pause, I will admit, but I was already caught up in the drama, fiercely curious to know what might happen at the theatre. Perhaps I was a fool—but it was the last day of the Carnival of Venice, when a whole decaying empire was licensed to become a vast flock of fools, and I could not resist the invitation.

I took the wand in my hand and went out into the gathering night, headed for the Ponte San Rocco.

* * * * * * *

The theatre was a little larger than I had expected, and a good deal more ornate. The new theatres of Venice have adopted all the modern conventions, so the stage was raised, surrounded in front by a proscenium arch and cloaked by a huge curtain, but here, as in many others, there was no gallery. There was only space for two boxes on either side, the chairs and sofas between being arranged in seven rows with a distinctly crooked aisle in the middle.

I arrived punctually, as an Englishman should. I expected the place to be three-quarters empty, because Venetians are as habitually late as the Portuguese, but as soon as I was let into my box I saw that I had mistaken the audience. Every seat was taken, save for those in the two boxes opposite and perhaps those in the one beside my own.

The crowd was as brightly-clad as any I had seen on my previous excursions, but it was much quieter. I thought that I had grown used to the irony of seeing more costumes in the audience than on stage—the players had gone to such great pains to make the most of it that their asides had become distinctly tedious—but as soon as I set eyes on this crowd I realized that there were depths of comedic confusion that had yet to be tapped.

I promised you no further digressions, Father, but one more is essential, given that you know so little about Italian comedy. The English stage has borrowed characters from the Commedia dell'arte, but in an overly disciplined fashion. We have standardized the roles and relationships along with the costumes—but in the authentic comedies of old, as in the extravagant fancies of Carlo Gozzi, everything was much more fluid. White-clad Pierrot was not always lost to love of Columbine, who was not invariably fascinated by Arlequino, who was not always contriving pitfalls for clumsy Brighella. The two miserly masters, Pantaloon and the Doctor of Bologna, were frozen in the ignominy of their wretched dotage, as masters tend to be, but their servants were free and every one of them could be as ingenious and mercurial as black-clad Scaramouche, or as full of wrath and bombast as Captain Spaventa.

One lingering result of this fluidity is that people who don the traditional costumes, whether as players on a stage

177

or patrons of the carnival, have considerable opportunity to stamp their own personalities upon their impostures. Thus, one might see three Pierrots sitting in a row, or two Scaramouches engaged in earnest conversation, and know that they were distinctly different as well as vaguely similar: acting, as it were, in different plays, or at least in different versions of the same play. Improvisation was everywhere, carefully paraded for the knowing eye.

And that, Father, was exactly what was missing from the crowd assembled in the theatre to which I went as a fantasy in yellow. I counted four patchwork Arlequinos in the audience, two crow-like Scaramouches and two voluminously-caped Spaventas—and each one was indistinguishable from the others of his type. The fact was, Father, that they were not parading themselves for knowing eyes, because at least one in three of them—perhaps as many as one in two—were sightless. There were thirty men on the theatre floor, and at least ten of them were blind. I could not see the eyes—or lack of eyes—behind the masks they wore, but I could see by the manner of their conversation and their lack of visual curiosity that the people around them might as well have been clad in monkish robes or workmen's blouses.

Was there ever such an audience as that in any theatre in the world? I think not. In fact, I am certain of it. I tried to identify the particular Arlequino who had followed me from the piazza, but if he was still costumed in the same fashion he had exchanged dirty and rumpled silks for dazzling fresh ones. Nor could I make out Mercutio the Cheiromancer, for he too had donned a new costume and a secretive mask.

When I first sat down, the boxes opposite were empty, but they did not long remain so. Two figures moved into the one nearer to the stage; the chair was taken by a woman, whose gaudy gown was sown with a thousand glass beads, while her companion—a man costumed as Scaramouche—stood behind her. A lone man occupied the other; his costume was black as a Scaramouche, save for white shirt-sleeves, but it was cut in a very severe fashion, fashioned from leather and linen rather than silks.

I heard someone enter the box on my right—it was further away from the stage than my own—but I could see nothing of him until the moment came when the curtain began to rise, at which point he placed his left wrist negligently upon the rail, allowing the hand to dangle over.

I was startled to see that hand: firstly, because of the color and cloth of the sleeve from which it extended, which was exactly the same shade of yellow as my own costume; secondly, because of the gold ring, which seemed a little too tight for the finger that bore it, set with a roseate stone shaped like a heart; and thirdly, because the skin on the back of the hand was discolored, like parchment.

Even though the curtain was going up I would have craned my neck to see more, save for the fact that the door of my own box eased open again, and a burly figure came in. There was hardly room for the narrow space to contain us both, even when I had shifted my chair to one side, but the other placed a confidential hand on my shoulder and whispered in my ear, saying: "I am glad that you have come, my lord, and that you accepted my gift."

He was not costumed as the Devil now—indeed, I could not tell how he was costumed, even though I was so very close to him—but I recognized his voice readily enough, I understood, of course, that he must have sent me the outrageously conspicuous costume, and I had begun to understand the reason. Although I had seen no more than the edge of a sleeve, I did not doubt that the man in the box next to mine was wearing an identical costume and carrying an identical wand.

I began to stammer a question, but the fingers resting on my shoulder tightened a little, and the whispering voice asked me, very politely, to be patient.

"Watch the comedy," the voice advised. "You might understand more when you have seen it. If not, and if there is time, I shall be happy to explain."

* * * * * * *

Perhaps, if my Italian had been better, I would have understood far more. Colloquial speech is difficult to follow, though, and witty wordplay even more so. The audience was laughing from the start—everyone there could hear, even though some could not see—but I had to concentrate far too hard to leave myself room for laughter, and even then I had difficulty in following the twists and turns of the overly complicated plot.

Carlo Goldoni had replaced the old Italian comedy with something much more satirical and true to life, but Carlo Gozzi had augmented Goldoni with something far more fanciful and sometimes outrightly phantasmagorical. Although I doubt that what I had come to watch really was a play by Gozzi, it was certainly similar to his work in its fantastic elements. I had half-expected a travesty of the play by Goldoni that Mercutio the Cheiromancer had mentioned to me, *Il Cavaliere e la Dama*, but it was certainly not that, even though it did contain a Dama of sorts—a fairy rather than a Venetian noblewoman—and a cicisbeo of sorts in her guardian ogre. They did not, however, seem to be the leading characters.

The fairy's husband was a human prince, who was delighted to have a fairy for his bride, but he too seemed to be a minor character by comparison with his envious half-sister, who was—presumably in consequence of a fatherly indiscretion—half-Moorish. I gathered that the reason why this bastard offspring was resident in the prince's palace had something to do with a bargain made with the Devil, but its exact terms remained mysterious. I was left in no doubt, though, that this dark witch was exceedingly jealous of the fairy, and loud in her proclamations that her brother had been bewitched by means of a magic ring that he now wore on his finger.

This Moorish witch had neither a husband nor a servant of her own, but she was passionately loved by two typical comic villains, who must have met her long before the play began, under circumstances that were unclear to me. They, too, seemed to be far more important to the play than the prince or the ogre. One was a pirate, the other a brigand, and before the introductory act was done they had conducted an absurd competition in which they tried to out-do one another in complimenting the virtues of the absent witch. It degenerated into a knockabout brawl, but ended with them swearing an alliance, declaring that they would co-operate in every

180

way to make the Mooress captive and then play a game of chance to determine which one would have her, with the loser forfeiting his eyes.

That was the most obvious joke of all, but it was the first that was met with silence from the crowd.

The second act began more promisingly, for one in search of parallels with the story I had heard from the cheiromancer, with the villainess spreading slanders against the fairy that seemed to cause the ogre a great deal of pain. It was difficult for me, as a sighted man, to feel much sympathy for the ogre, whose appearance was bestial and coarsely hairy. The player representing him wore a mask like a gorilla, save only for the horn projecting from its forehead. It occurred to me, however, that the blind men in the audience could only hear his voice, which was plaintive without being hoarse. There was no implication that the ogre was anything more than a faithful servant set to guard the fairy by her mother, who was a queen among her own folk.

The play careered along at a very hectic pace—as it had to do if it were to close before midnight—and I am not sure that I kept up with its finer intricacies, but when the pirate and the brigand contrived to carry off the villainess she immediately volunteered to fall in with their scheme if they would agree to steal the ring from the prince's finger. She let them into the palace in order to do it, but when they fell upon the prince they could not prise the ring from his finger, and his cries for help brought the ogre rushing to save him. There ensued another comic battle, involving several men-at-arms as well as the four main protagonists. At the end of it, the ogre lay dead—a fact announced very loudly for the benefit of anyone in the crowd who had not seem him fall—and the prince's ring-finger had been severed from his hand, ring and all.

The climax of the play was the settlement of affairs between the pirate, the brigand and the villainess. The Mooress took possession of the ring and established the rules for the game of chance that would determine which of her two suitors would marry her, and which would lose his eyes. At this point, however, the fairy queen put in an appearance, exacting a magical vengeance for her ogre by taking back the ring

181

and striking both men blind. When she had made her exit, though, the defiant Mooress called upon the Devil to avenge the insult, and swore that she would still wed the better of the two blind men, if only the Devil would provide new eyes for both of them.

Now the devil came on stage, wearing a costume identical to the one I had seen earlier, but in far better repair. He told the witch that he would do as she asked, and more, by obtaining from a craftsman of Murano two pairs of seemingly-identical false eyes—one of which, and one only, would give their wearer the power to see the one thing in the world that he most desired to see, while the other...but I did not get the chance to hear exactly what the other would do, because it was at this point that the play ceased to be a play, and Gozzi's comedy gave way to the Devil's.

* * * * * * *

The two players who had taken the parts of the pirate and the brigand were only acting the part of blind men, but as soon as the player taking the Devil's part reached into the folds of his red costume to bring forth four glass orbs the size of eyeballs, no less than fourteen real blind men stood up in the audience, howling like wolves and bellowing like bulls as they demanded to take part in the game of chance that the Mooress had defined. The players, with one exception, seemed quite confounded by this turn of events—but the exception was the man costumed as the Devil, who came to the front of the stage and called for silence.

He did not win silence, but the hubbub quieted sufficiently for him to make his voice heard without shouting.

What he said was: "This is a comedy, my friends. I do not have either of the pairs of eyes which Pietro Beroviero made nine-and-thirty years ago." And to demonstrate that he was serious, he dropped the four glass spheres upon the stage, where they shattered.

That brought forth howls of anguish—but then the actor costumed as the Devil raised his arm and pointed a long, taloned finger at one of the audience-members costumed as

Captain Spaventa. "There," the play-devil said, "is the man who has one of them."

The blind men could not see where he was pointing, but their sighted companions could—and they could see, too, that the Spaventa in question was one of their own kind, for he was quick to draw his sword and move its point around him in an very purposeful fashion.

"Very clever," he said, in English. "I see that a trap has been set, and that I have fallen into it. But the eyes that I have are not the ones you want. I cannot use them myself, but I have certainly tried their effect, as at least one Scaramouche and two Arlequinos present here can attest—and every thief who had them before me has doubtless done likewise, including the man who plucked them out of Bartolomeo Collatino's face." He paused for a moment, and voices were indeed raised to testify that they had tried eyes shown to them by an English pirate, and found them useless.

"Tondino must have won the eyes that bore the Devil's gift when Zulietta Zentilli made good what she had cost him," Spaventa opined. "But Tondino must surely be here too, must he not?" He looked around ostentatiously before adding: "Come, Tondino, surely a man like you could not resist a comedy like this?"

That won silence, even though more than half the crowd must have understood less than half of what he said—and every man who had eyes looked about him, wondering whether to look for Tondino among the sighted or the blind.

For a minute and more, no one moved—and then a white-clad Pierrot whose face was completely masked and whose dunce's cap seemed to weigh too heavily upon his head, said in Italian: "Yes, I am here—but I do not have the eyes—and not only because, like Bartolomeo, I too fell victim to a brother thief. I never had them. If the ones you had are useless, then the Devil cheated Bartolomeo as well as me."

All eyes turned again, then, but in the wrong direction. The player costumed as the Devil shrugged his shoulders very eloquently, and raised his eyes to heaven. "I am but an actor," he said. "My lines are spoken, and I have no improvisation to serve this occasion."

A ripple of annoyance ran around the room then, but one voice cut through the rest: a female voice, which came from the box opposite to mine.

"The Devil did not cheat!" she cried. I knew in that instant that she was not Caterina di Mastropiero, as I had assumed—as, presumably, we had all been meant to assume—by virtue of her beaded dress. She must, I deduced, be Zulietta Zellini: no Mooress, but most definitely a villainess. "If Tondino does not have the eyes," she cried, "another has! Make yourself known, or there'll be Hell to pay!"

At that point, I heard the first chime of midnight sound, rung by all the bells in Venice to signal that Lent would begin in eleven seconds' time—or would have done, if time had not...*congealed.*

Nothing stopped, but everything—or *almost* everything—slowed. It seemed to me that I had been gripped by a tremendous force, which made the least action improbably difficult. A reflex had been raising my hand to my mouth, but my arm seemed all of a sudden to be moving through treacle rather than air. My thoughts, on the other hand, raced ahead without the least impedance...and my thoughts were not the only free agency.

"You were right, after all," whispered a voice in my ear. "The play should have been shorter. It was too complicated, and there was far too much improvisation in it. Even I am lost now—and I have but the space of eleven chimes to recover my ground."

I would have turned my head to look at him if I could, but I am glad now that I could not. The kind of curiosity that would make a man look the Devil in the face is a curse. But I could hear him—and it seemed that he could hear my unspoken words, although my lips were turned to stone.

You must know who has the eyes! I thought.

"Alas, no," the whisper went on. "The permission under which I work is hedged around with all manner of inconvenient limitations. I can set traps, but I never know exactly who will fall into them. I can penetrate their superficial disguises, but not their inmost hearts. And my time is severely rationed."

The second chime of midnight sounded then, extended over twelve or thirteen seconds.

"Now let me, see," the Devil said. "Zulietta obviously does not have the eyes, and if Zulietta does not have them, Maurizio Scamozzi cannot have them either, for he has been faithful to her throughout these nine-and-thirty years, despite the pact she made with Bartolomeo."

Bartolomeo! I echoed, silently.

"Of course. Did you think Tondino was telling you the truth? What a fine bad man he is! I owe you an apology, my friend—I was certain that I had hoarded the best errand of all for *you*. I might have guessed, I suppose, when he chose to come as Pierrot and not as Spaventa or Scaramouche—perhaps I should have guessed long ago, when he first became Mercutio the Cheiromancer. But I was so certain that he had switched the eyes when Bartolomeo won the game....ah!"

Even in my thoughts I was speechless. The third chime seemed to last for nearly half a minute.

"What has comedy become?" the Devil whispered in my ear. "Of course he switched them—but they had already been switched. By Bartolomeo, do you think? I doubt it. Perhaps by Zulietta, if she knew that Tondino would try the trick, but far more likely that....do you see the man in the box next to Zulietta's, my friend? Not Scamozzi, who stands behind her, but the one whose Scaramouche is all leather and honest linen? That, my friend, is Giovanni Beroviero, son of Pietro: Pietro the fox, the keeper of secrets unknown even to me. I looked into those pairs of eyes before I bought them, playmaker, and knew exactly which was which...but he played me false, for Caterina's sake. He knew it all, was determined to cheat the treacherous Bartolomeo, and did not trust me to cheat him myself. Does he have the eyes, do you think?

The fourth chime sounded, drawn out into a long whine. It required only the slightest movement of my eye to direct my gaze at Giovanni Beroviero's face, but it was a long-drawn-out agony nevertheless.

It would have needed an equal effort for the son of Pietro Beroviero to lock eyes with me, but he showed no sign of so doing. He was staring, but not at me—and not at the Devil. He was staring at the man in the box next to mine: the *other* man costumed in lurid yellow.

The fifth chime sounded, and the Devil waited for the sound to fade before saying: "Oh, he doesn't have them. I only brought Leandro back from the grave today, for one night only. He is only here to murder Zulietta for his widow's sake...or rather, for his own, since Caterina—unbeknown to him—has long since found a cicisbeo far more loyal to her charms than Bartolomeo Collatino ever was.

"But who does that leave, playmaker?"

No one, I would have said, had I had a voice. *Everyone is accounted for.*

The sixth chime sounded, and the Devil said: "It seems, my friend, that the trap is sprung. I admit defeat. The hell with it."

And the wings of time began to beat full force again, with six strokes still to go till midnight. Perhaps they beat a little more forcefully than before, to make up a little of their loss, but it might have been that matters moved with astonishing rapidity.

What followed, I fear, was complete chaos. Sighted men fell upon blind men to wrench away their masks, convinced that one or more of them must be hiding the eyes that Pietro Beroviero had made for the Devil, to stand as stakes in a contest between Bartolomeo Collatino and the bravo Tondino, to determine which of them would win the affection of Zulietta Zellini. Two Pierrots fell slain, a third held a bloody dagger high above his head. Two Captain Spaventas were fighting a fierce duel, with their great cloaks flapping like the wings of giant eagles. The reanimated corpse of Leandro di Mastropiero bounced from the box, tearing the naked blade from his wand and carving this way and that as he tried to make his way through the confusion on the floor—but by the time he arrived at the brink of Zulietta's box, Maurizio Scamozzi had come forward to protect his Dama. Scamozzi engaged my double in a fencing contest that was far too fast and furious for a dead man to win. I was grateful at the time, for the thought occurred to me that if Leandro had succeeded in winning his misguided vengeance before returning to his grave on the stroke of midnight, the finger of suspicion would have fallen on me—as, perhaps, the Devil had intended when he made me his gift.

It was, I presume, by way of completing that particular misfired jest that the Devil vanished too, a mere instant before one of the Captain Spaventas—perhaps the English bandit and perhaps the other one—vaulted the rail of my box and tipped my chair precipitately backwards.

I think I heard the final chime of midnight sound as my head hit the wooden floor, but I might have been a little confused.

* * * * * * *

I cannot have been unconscious for more than ten or fifteen minutes, but when I came around terror struck into my heart, for the man that I saw standing over me, in the half-light left by the extinction of most of the theatre's candles, was all wrapped around in livid yellow, with a mask like a theatre curtain. He was holding aloft a wand shaped like a torch.

What could I think, except that it was the reanimated Leandro, intent on taking his anger out on his duplicate?

Then I realized that I was clad in nothing but a yellow shirt and hose, and realized that my cloak, mask and sword-stick had been stolen. I could not have had the slightest inkling as to the identity of the thief had he had time to do away with his own cape, but it still lay draped across the fallen chair. It was the cloak of a Captain Spaventa.

The yellow-shrouded figure helped me to my feet, and I looked out into the auditorium. Like the stage, it was empty of living men—but I counted seven dead. They included three Pierrots, one Scaramouche, and a Captain Spaventa, but no remortified corpse in yellow.

"Are you the pirate?" I asked tremulously—hoping that he was, on the grounds that an English robber might be more kindly disposed towards me than any other kind.

"No, my lord," he said. "I'm the other. That was a close run thing, was it not?" His English was far less perfect than his double's, spoken with an accent that might have been Spanish, or perhaps Portuguese.

"Arlequino?" I said, uncertainly.

"But of course. I hired myself to Tondino knowing that the invitation would come, although I was as surprised as he was when you turned out to be the man who had it. Was it not extraordinarily ingenious of me to dress in exactly the same fashion as the English pirate who had asked the actor to point him out, so that he might deny that he had the true eyes and deflect attention to the cheiromancer? I was one step ahead of him, of course, for I knew well enough that Tondino had never had the true eyes."

It was all too much, and far too difficult to follow. I could only shake my head in disbelief.

"I guessed what use the Devil intended to make of you when I saw the costume delivered to your hotel," the yellow-clad nightmare continued. "There was not another like it in Venice, so there had to be two of them and a confusion to be created—or is that a paradox? I had the advantage of having thought of a similar trick myself, of course. You really ought to be more careful, Englishman. Not many men consent to run an errand for the Devil and come away unscathed. You'll be safe for a while, because his permission to be here ran out at midnight—be sure to mention it to your confessor, though; it's a taint not easily escaped, and he has a long memory. He'll certainly be back, and you'll probably run into him again in a subtler disguise. You might have to work a great deal harder for your salvation then."

I sat up, rubbing my head. I wanted desperately to ask him who he really was, but I no longer expected the answer to be meaningful and there was another question more important than that one: a question that had confounded the Devil himself.

"Do you have the eyes that everyone wants?" I asked. "The eyes that will allow a man to see the one thing in the world that he most desires to see?"

"I have them both now," he admitted. From a pocket hidden in the right-hand corner of the cloak he had discarded he took two globes of glass, not quite as black as the ones Tondino had worn when I had consulted him in his guise as

Mercutio. Then, from a similar pocket hidden in the left-hand corner, he took another two. He threw the cloak aside then, and righted the chair. He set the two pairs of eyes down on the cushion—and then, very ostentatiously, he took one eye from one pair and exchanged it with one from the other.

"It still might not be the right arrangement," he said, "and even if it is, I'll need a blind man to tell me which is which—one who is not Tondino, who was almost as dangerous blind as he was sighted, until he met his little accident just now. After that, I'll need to be discreet in arranging a sale, but I'm more than half way there, I've cheated the Devil on the way, and for all that anyone knows for sure, I'm lying dead over there."

"The two pairs of eyes were mixed up," I said, wonderingly. "Tondino must have made a mistake when he switched them."

"No mistake was made," the thief assured me. "Unless you count the Devil's. Pietro Beroviero mixed them up, knowing it was perfectly safe to do so. Giovanni was here tonight to make sure that they hadn't been unmixed in the meantime—he seemed happy enough when he left."

I realized then what the words must have been whose meaning I had not been able to make out. The Devil had commissioned one pair of eyes that would give a blind man the power to see, at least in his mind's eye, that which he most desired to see in all the world—and had commissioned a second that would make it impossible for their wearer to see, even in his mind's eye, that which he most desired to see in all the world. A man with one from each pair—or two men, each with one from each pair—would see...nothing at all. So Bartolomeo Collatino and Tondino had each spent the rest of their lives believing that the other had been given the pair worth owning.

"I should go now, my lord," the man who had been Arlequino and the second Spaventa said, replacing the stolen eyes in their secret place. "We shan't meet again, I hope—but if we do, you won't know me. You may have the other cloak if you wish, but you might do better to leave it behind, given that it's stained with the blood of murdered men."

So saying, he turned on his heel and left, leaving me to trudge back to my hotel alone, in my yellow shirt and hose, like a slender flame flickering in the Venetian night.

* * * * * * *

When I thought about it afterwards, though—and as I have told you, Father, it has been very much in my thoughts, from that day to this—I began to wonder whether either of those pairs of eyes, even in the correct combination, was really worth having. After all, if the version of the story that Mercutio the Cheiromancer had told to me had been the truth, what would Bartolomeo have been able to see had he received the magical eyes? Caterina di Mastropiero. And what would the Bartolomeo of the other version have been able to see, in the same situation? Zulietta Zellini. In either case, how long would it have taken him to be disappointed in his vision?

The one thing that those devilish eyes could not have shown anyone is Heaven; of that, Father, I am certain.

I began to wonder, too, whether I had really been drawn into the affair for the reason that the Devil and the brigand had indicated—which is to say, to be implicated, by virtue of my costume, in a murder committed by a reanimated corpse. I think not; such a narrative move is too simple, too hackneyed, for a modern Venetian comedy, by Gozzi or the Devil. Having consulted my conscience most carefully, I believe that the Devil lured me into his trap for quite another reason: to write an account of what I saw, and what I falsely understood. I am convinced that he wanted me to make a play of it, and still does: an absurdly convoluted comedy, with a ridiculous climactic twist.

To tell the truth, I have tried, but I cannot quite make it work. At the end of the day, my Italian was not good enough to get every detail of the affair in place. Anyway, it has become clear to me that it is not proper meat for a comedy at all, but only for a confession—and the only thing I seek now is absolution.

As far as my plays are concerned, I have decided to be a perfect Goldoni in future, content to mock the very ordinary foibles of very ordinary men and women.

As a good Catholic, I have no wish to deal with the Devil again, even in the relative safety of a farce.

THE POWER OF PRAYER

When the great plague arrived in the lush farmlands and market towns of Central Aquitania, forty years before its conquest by Charles the Great, panic swept downstream through the valley of the Dordogne even more rapidly than the disease itself.

Aquitania had then been a Catholic country for more than two centuries, although the descendants of Clovis were well enough aware of the fact that their ancestor's conversion of his kingdom had been made for political reasons, in imitation of a stratagem once successfully employed by the Roman emperor Constantine. There were some among the Aquitanians, even at eight generations removed, who thought it unbecoming of conquerors to be so slavish in their imitation of the manners and pretensions of those they had conquered, and were therefore careful to maintain older beliefs and rituals alongside those of the Roman church.

"It was, after all, the Goths who triumphed over Constantine's descendants," the secret heretics argued. "Should the descendants of Clovis not be proud of their Gothic heritage?"

These proud men understood well enough that history was securely in the custody of the churchmen, but they were also prepared to be proud of their refusal to learn to write. For this reason, no matter what the churchmen recorded for the benefit of posterity, the great upsurge of religious sentiment and devotion provoked by the panic that came rushing down the Dordogne was by no means confined to the established churches.

This is not to say, of course, that the churches were not full, or that the convents did not enjoy a sudden influx of pious novices. Monasteries and nunneries alike doubled their personnel overnight, and their superiors were very glad to be so richly deluged with gifts and bequests. Alas, when the plague arrived, hot on the heels of the panic, the newly-repopulated convents and recently-swollen congregations of the riverside towns were as comprehensively decimated as the remote villages and hamlets where the habits of confession and communion had never becoming deeply entrenched.

Far upriver, in the foothills of what is nowadays called the Massif Central, there was then a small market town named Coramdram, which has long since vanished from the map. The people of Coramdram and its environs were sharply reminded, by more than a score of exceedingly ugly deaths, of the duties which they owed to all the gods who might protect them. Prayer was a duty that Coramdram's Christians and pagans alike had been rather apt to neglect, but the Christians, at least, resumed it without suffering too many pangs of conscience; human vanity is ever-ready to assume that a good God will always be on hand, patiently awaiting the attention of His followers during those intervals when other occupations seem far more important.

Perhaps the Christians were correct in this assumption, and the streets of Coramdram would have been profusely littered with rotting corpses had the Lord not extended His mercy to a reasonable extent—but people rarely count their misfortunes accurately, nor do they often agree on the final sum. Those who consider that they have endured far more than their fair share of disaster are outnumbered only by those who think that their neighbors have had far more than a just allotment of good luck. The moral arithmetic of human existence is always inclined to overestimate an individual's own immediate aches and pains, while refusing to acknowledge all but the most fatal afflictions of others. Perhaps it is this imperfection in the artistry of calculation that is responsible for the continued popularity of deities whom Christians deem far less worthy of worship than their own jealous God.

At any rate, there were some in Coramdram—as there invariably were in those days, whenever the Visitor of Plague and Pestilence set his footprint upon a recently-Christianized region—who preferred to address their placatory prayers to the gods that had been theirs for hundreds of generations rather than a mere eight.

In the opinion of the church's historians, these heretics were addressing the plague-demon's immediate superior, Satan, instead of the Lord who had cast that fallen angel into the depths—but that was not the way the unrepentant followers of Gothic tradition saw their own situation. In their eyes, the author of the disaster was merely one god among a company of equals, none of whom was any better or worse disposed towards humanity than the rest.

Why should one pray to a good God for protection, the pagans' reasoning went, when even a blind man could clearly see that evil was a more powerful force than good in the world of men? What good could it do to beg Jesus Christ and the martyred saints to provide a shield against disease, given that not one of them had been able to defend himself or herself against the direst misfortune? Was it not more sensible to cut out all mediators and go straight to the source of the trouble? Was it not more reasonable, instead of asking that an entire street, or a whole town, or even a region should be spared, to pray instead that the disease would strike down everyone except for one's own immediate family? Surely, the pagans thought, the god of plague and pestilence must be grateful for such prayers, given that they offered a welcome endorsement to his overall strategy—which was always to spare a few while killing the many, in order that he might find each of his old haunts deliciously repopulated whenever he chanced to pass that way again.

One of the careful folk who assessed the situation in these terms was Ophiria, wife of the ruddy-faced harness-maker Remy Brousse, Indeed, Ophiria went even further than others whose philosophy ran along the same lines, because she did not trouble to accommodate Remy in her prayers for salvation. Quite the reverse: the advent of the plague seemed to her to offer a welcome chance of deliverance from a marriage which had come to seem unbearably tedious. When she offered up her secret prayers to the god of pestilence, therefore, she took care to include Remy in the list of names of those she would most like to see breaking out in horrible spots, seething with fever, streaming mucus from every orifice and writhing in hideous agony.

Ophiria's list was quite long, because Coramdram was the kind of town in which everybody—even those who were scornfully excluded from the best gossiping-circles—knew everybody else's name. Because she was a scrupulous person, she never allowed herself the luxury of any casual omission or forgetful abbreviation. On the other hand, by way of ameliorating what some of her neighbors might think unwarranted malice, she never specifically mentioned buboes among the afflictions she wished upon her more distant acquaintances.

Even Ophiria's closest acquaintances—none of whom was sufficiently close as to think of her as a friend—would have been surprised to discover the extent of her disaffection from her husband. Remy Brousse was not cruel or quarrelsome, nor was he given to adulterous liaisons. By the standards of the region at the head of the Dordogne valley, that was sufficient to make him an unusually good and devoted husband. His only marital crime, if crime it could be reckoned, was to have allowed himself to become extremely fat and rather indolent.

There were corpulent wives in Coramdram who would not have reckoned the former item as an unforgivable sin, but Ophiria had remained as slender throughout their marriage as the day she was wed, when her late mother-in-law had been unkind enough to judge her unpromisingly thin. An indolent husband is always reckoned undesirable even by an indolent wife, but Ophiria was far more energetic than the average—perhaps surprisingly so, for one of her meager dimensions. Had she borne her husband any children she might have lost her energy as well as her trim figure, but the marriage was barren.

Remy Brousse was a popular man in the district in spite of his indolence, because he was very ingenious with his hands. Although he did not like to work hard he did take considerable delight in working cleverly; he took as much pride in the ease with which he accomplished a task as in the perfection of the result.

"It is the glory and privilege of mindful beings," Remy often told his clients, "that we may accomplish our ends without breaking our backs or sweating away our bodily mass." This saying was repeated far and wide along the Dordogne—perhaps even as far as Bordeaux—in a relatively good-humored manner.

Remy had another saying too, which had an equal bearing on his popularity, which was: "Necessity is the mother of improvisation." He said this because he was not a man to walk far in search of conventional materials when there was something close to hand that could be pressed into service. In a region where leather was reckoned expensive, he was always able—and perfectly willing—to make harnesses for poorer folk from rope, or cord, or anything else which came conveniently to hand.

Alas, this virtue, like his others, went unappreciated by Remy Brousse's bitter spouse, who had an instinctive dislike of any object or instrument that had not been formed from its proper material, according to its proper pattern.

At the time when the great plague came to Coramdram the Brousses had been married for nineteen years. Ophiria, having recently passed her thirty-fourth birthday, felt that old age had not yet marked her irredeemably, but knew that cruel time would not leave her unmolested for many years longer. She knew, too, that if she were to obtain a second husband more to her taste, she would need better bait than her narrow face. Given that her husband's shop would make a very attractive marriage-portion for an ambitious leather-worker, she felt that her own necessity required a certain amount of improvisation. This factor also entered into the equation whose solution was expressed in her devout prayers to the god of plague and pestilence, causing her not merely to mention Remy's name in her prayers but to give special prominence to it.

"Please, please, *please* take my husband Remy, even if you take no one else I have identified as a suitable sacrifice," Ophiria would say, whenever she reached the end of her exhaustive list. "He has become useless and burdensome to me, but he would make a fine and fleshy morsel for one such as you—and it is surely the glory and privilege of divinity that

196

a god such as yourself may accomplish your ends without bending your back or shedding a single bead of sweat."

The church's historians would dispute the identity of the being which responded to this prayer, but whether it was a member in good standing of a pantheon of peers or merely one of Satan's imps, it did as it was asked. Remy Brousse fell dreadfully ill with the plague.

First the unfortunate harness-maker broke out in horrible spots, which turned into hot sores that drove him mad with their unquenchable itching. Then he developed a seething fever, which exported acrid moisture from his shriveling flesh by the gallon. His every orifice began to drip mucus—most of it grey-green in color, except when it was mingled with blood, when it became blue-black. All the while he writhed in hideous agony. The only mercy was that his arm-pits and groin remained free of buboes—but even that, in the end, only served to prolong his suffering for a day or two longer than was strictly necessary.

While she watched the corpulent body of her husband fade gradually away, as if the flesh were melting from his bones—which observation she was careful to make from a safe distance—Ophiria took some trouble to pose as a de-voted Christian widow-to-be. There were several reasons for this precaution, of which the first and foremost was that wor-shippers of a god of pestilence need to be even more secre-tive than usual in a time of plague. Ophiria had always been suspected by her neighbors of being the sort of person who might pray to a dubious god, and there was not a man or woman in Coramdram who would not have been glad of a scapegoat upon whom they could vent their righteous anger against the ravages of the disease. Supplementary to that fundamental caution, however, was Ophiria's knowledge that if she hoped to obtain a new and better husband, she had to advertise herself—much more carefully than she had con-trived to do heretofore—as a devoted and loyal wife. For these reasons, she set herself to outdo her neighbors in her public displays of grief, although this was not an easy thing to do when there was not a family in the district that had not suffered its own grievous losses.

Perhaps, in addition to these practical considerations, Ophiria actually began to feel slight stings of guilt and remorse while her husband came nearer and nearer to his end. It is, after all, never pleasant to observe—even from a respectful distance—the many ways in which disease and decay can maltreat a man. If so, her improvisations of grief might have contained at least a tiny measure of necessity.

When the death-cart paused outside the door of Remy Brousse's harness-shop, so that his body might be collected and ferried to the hastily-dug and abruptly-consecrated pit that was to serve as a collective grave for all Coramdram's plague-victims, Ophiria commenced to make loud protestations against the unkindness of the cruel demon who had robbed her of all that she held dear in the world. When the cart pulled away again she followed it through the streets, weeping and wailing in a prodigious manner.

Because the pit had been dug on the far side of the town, and because the route that the death-cart followed through the streets was so circuitous, Ophiria had to walk for miles, but she never faltered in her keening. She was joined in due course by other wives, and by mothers and grandmothers too, but the competition they provided only spurred her on to greater efforts.

Hundreds of people—almost every one of whom was named on her secret list—saw Ophiria following Remy Brousse's body. If they were surprised by the fact that a woman as thin as she could cry so effusively, they only had to remind themselves that she had always been an uncommonly energetic woman. Even the most snobbish and scornful among them must have felt a pang of sympathy as they saw how badly she had reacted to her loss.

"Perhaps, after all," a few good Christians whispered to their neighbors, "Ophiria Brousse was not as unloving as she sometimes seemed. Perhaps she was one of those unhappy souls who are incapable of giving voice to their true feelings until the worst comes to the worst, and then must endure in a few desperate hours the irresistible flood of emotions pent up for years."

Ophiria heard more than one such comment, and was greatly gratified to discover that her performance was appre-

ciated. Never one to proceed by half-measures, she decided
to carry the masquerade through to its limit. When the cart
reached the pit and Remy Brousse's body was thrown in on
top of a hundred others, she cast herself upon the ground and
beat the turf with her fists. When the priest of the parish and
the town's mayor decided that the pit could hold no more
and would have to be filled in, she hurried to the rim for one
last lingering look at her beloved—and when the spade-men
began to seal the grave, every clod that fell wrung a moan
from her emaciated lips.

Nor was that enough for her; unlike her late husband,
Ophiria believed that if a job was worth doing it was worth
doing properly. On the next day, the widow went to the
church on the hill above the place where her late husband
and a hundred others lay, to join the throng of mourners.
Like the wives of other men, and the mothers and grandmothers who had lost children, she was clad entirely in
black, with no shoes on her feet. Like these others, she went
after hearing mass to kneel upon the freshly-turned earth,
directly atop the place where she had seen her husband's
dead body set upon the terrible heap. Like all the other wid-
ows, she cried and cried and cried.

Even Ophiria's energy began to flag in the end, but she
carried on regardless, forcing more tears to come in floods
by surreptitiously pinching her tenderest flesh between her
sharp fingernails. Her voice was very conspicuous in lament-
ing the vile injustice of the world, and the awful cruelty of
the demon which had sent the plague—but within her secret
thoughts, she made her apologies and gave abundant thanks
to the Visitor of Decay, who had taken such care in answering the most fervent of all her prayers.

On the first and second days after Remy Brousse's
death, this performance proceeded exactly as his widow had
planned, and won more than a few admiring and sympathetic
glances from those fortunate enough to witness it. On the
night that followed the second day, Ophiria paused to wonder whether she might now have done enough, not merely to
allay suspicion but also to establish her worth as a potential
wife for some unlucky widower—but she liked to do things
properly, and she decided that a person as completely lack-

ing in indolence as herself owed it to her audience to continue the pantomime for one more day.

The following morning, Ophiria got up bright and early and put on her black dress. Leaving her shoes beside the hearth, she walked yet again to the church, where she heard another morning mass sung by a sadly-depleted choir. Afterwards, she went to the grave which Remy Brousse shared with so many of his erstwhile clients and friends. She knelt down on the darkened earth, exactly as she had done twice before, at the very spot where Remy Brousse's buried body lay. When the tears did not begin to flow spontaneously, she carefully mustered her resources, and pinched herself bruisingly, sobbing in a heart-ending manner.

The other mourners who had taken up their stations immediately after hearing mass looked sideways at the sound of Ophiria's sobbing, but they paid her little enough heed. They had seen and heard it all before, and they had their own aching grief to nurse. No sooner had Ophiria begun to moisten the earth with her false tears, however, than the earth sealing the mass grave was disturbed by a horrid churning and wriggling.

Ophiria recoiled in dire alarm, but she was too late to regain her feet. She turned heads readily enough when she screamed—and this time, once the eyes of the other mourners were fixed upon her, they could not easily be torn away.

It seemed to the dizzied Ophiria that a monstrous earthworm had coiled itself around each of her wrists, holding her tightly and making certain that she remained on her knees. Another graveworm appeared, and then another, each one longer by far than any she had ever seen before—and then the worms began to crawl upon her body, climbing up her prisoned arms to her shoulders, neck and face.

The sensation of having such creatures crawling on her flesh filled Ophiria with the purest horror, and she tried to scream even louder, but she could not do it. She discovered that she was already screaming as loud as she possibly could; there was no further margin to be exploited or explored when the worms began to extend themselves over her terror-stricken face, around her skinny neck, and into her thin blonde hair.

Had she been less confused, Ophiria might have been able to feel, if not to see, that the worms that had arranged themselves about her head and shoulders were combining their bodies like the threads in a cord or a rope. The resultant amalgamation was further entwined into the shape of a bridle and rein. More worms—many, many more—were winding themselves about her waist to form a girth-strap, while a huge mass of them was accumulating on her bent back to form a kind of living saddle.

It did not matter that Ophiria could not feel or see any of this, for she could not possibly have given further expression to the horror of it. She had exhausted her capacity for screaming now—and also her capacity for weeping, moaning, crying and groaning.

While the looping graveworms bound her hands to the moist brown earth Ophiria could not even stand up, let alone run away—but that was a temporary inconvenience. The worms that held her down were quick to release their grip as soon as their multitudinous kin had crowded a sufficient wormy mass on to the makeshift saddle to depict the form of a small but conspicuously well-rounded rider.

By this time, it did not matter that Ophiria Brousse was no longer able to scream, because the other mourners at the mass grave had seen and understood what was happening. Even those who had been grieving the longest had plenty of screams still in reserve.

Where Ophiria's peculiar rider took her, when it began lambasting her with its whip of worms, no one ever discovered—but she was never seen in Coramdram again.

Her neighbors shook their heads, and speculated as to the reasons for the Widow Brousse's fate. What judgment the church's historians might have delivered must remain forever unknown, because none of the scribes in the troubled convents of Aquitania ever found the time to write it down, so we are free to speculate that they would probably have proffered the incident as evidence of Satan's continuing war against the devout. Ophiria's illiterate neighbors, however, were inclined to whisper different interpretations, confident that the opinions would vanish on the wind and never return to haunt them.

Some of these whispers suggested that Ophiria Brousse must have been driven mad by grief, and brought by her extremity to curse the god of pestilence far too loudly for his liking, with the result that he had taken a cruel revenge. Others, equally numerous, hazarded the guess that she had simply cried a little too loudly and too long, and that some other member of the pantheon of peers who was less fond of the sounds of grief than the god of pestilence had become so irritated that he had improvised a means to shut her up. Whichever side of the argument the doubters favored, however, the great majority were prepared to agree that, although it is a perfectly understandable error for a widow to grieve too much for the husband she has lost, it is an error nevertheless.

Once the plague had passed on and the death-rate in Coramdram reverted to its normal pedestrian pace, the affairs of the town soon reverted to their ordinary course. Although the strange flight of Ophiria Brousse was not forgotten, it became a thing that people did not care to discuss, and her name was never mentioned again by anyone in the neighborhood. Remy Brousse's name, on the other hand, was often heard on the lips of those who remembered him regretfully— of which there were many, for he was sorely missed, not only in the town but in the surrounding districts.

Remy Brousse's favorite maxims were often quoted in the course of such remembrance, and they continued to be quoted long afterwards, although—like all the most precious elements of oral tradition—they were gradually detached from any attribution to their source. His name was not entirely lost, however; it was separately preserved as the core of a self-contained item of folklore.

Long after all those people who had ever seen him alive had gone to their separate graves, there were men in Coramdram who did not hesitate to express the firm opinion that there never was an artisan in all of Aquitania who was cleverer with his fingers than Remy Brousse, nor any man in the entire world who could weave useful harnesses out of such unpromising materials.

ABOUT THE AUTHOR

BRIAN STABLEFORD was born in Yorkshire in 1948. He taught at the University of Reading for several years, but is now a full-time writer. He has written many science fiction and fantasy novels, including: *The Empire of Fear, The Werewolves of London, Year Zero, The Curse of the Coral Bride*, and *The Stones of Camelot*. Collections of his short stories include: *Sexual Chemistry: Sardonic Tales of the Genetic Revolution, Designer Genes: Tales of the Biotech Revolution*, and *Sheena and Other Gothic Tales*. He has written numerous nonfiction books, including *Scientific Romance in Britain, 1890-1950, Glorious Perversity: The Decline and Fall of Literary Decadence*, and *Science Fact and Science Fiction: An Encyclopedia*. He has contributed hundreds of biographical and critical entries to reference books, including both editions of *The Encyclopedia of Science Fiction* and several editions of the library guide, *Anatomy of Wonder*. He has also translated numerous novels from the French language, including several by the feuilletonist Paul Féval.

www.ingramcontent.com/pod-product-compliance
Lightning Source LLC
Chambersburg PA
CBHW030524020726
47494CB00004B/1218